Angelina's Secret

Spencer Hill Press

Contact: Spencer Hill Press, PO Box 247, Contoocook, NH 03229, USA

Please visit our website at spencerhillpress.com

First Edition: February 2012.

Rogers, Lisa Maynard. 1965
Angelina's Secret : a novel / by Lisa Maynard Rogers – 1st ed.
p. cm.
Summary:
A high school cheerleader starts communicating with ghosts again and must find a way to keep from being locked up in a mental ward while still being true to herself and her gift.

The author acknowledges the copyrighted or trademarked status and trademark owners of the following wordmarks mentioned in this fiction: Band-Aid, Dr. Pepper & Diet Dr. Pepper, Kleenex, Google, National Builders Supplement, Charlie's Angels, P!nk, Sears and Roebuck, and Michael Jackson's Thriller

Cover design by K. Kaynak

ISBN 978-0-9831572-8-1 (paperback)
ISBN 978-0-9831572-9-8 (e-book)

Printed in the United States of America

Angelina's Secret

A Novel by

Lisa Rogers

SPENCER HILL PRESS

Also By Lisa Rogers:

On Haunted Ground:
The Green Ghost & Other Spirits of Cemetery Road
(Llewellyn, May 2012, ISBN: 9780738732367)

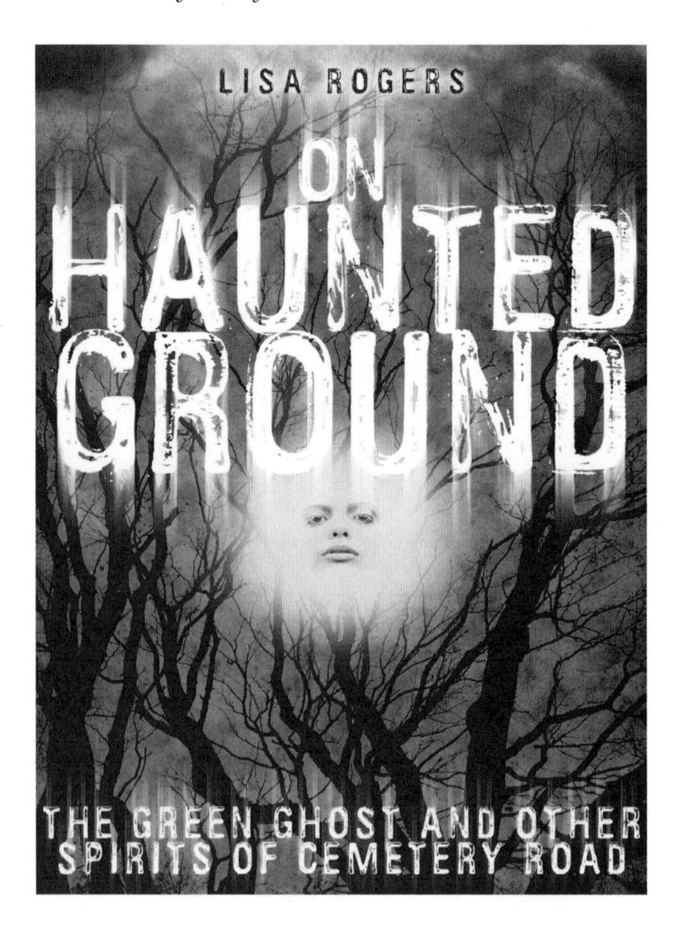

Some families are so tightly intertwined you can't mention one person without the others. I am fortunate enough to have such a family and I'd like to dedicate this book to them.

To my parents and many, many, siblings I thank you for teaching me the true meaning of the word family.

To my husband Wes, who is and will always be, my best friend— I thank you for being my rock and for keeping me sane.

To my children, Keshia and Troy: the two of you have been my greatest accomplishments in life and I love you more each day.

To my son-in-law, Stephen, and my daughter-in-law Meagan: I couldn't love you anymore if you were my own children, which you now are.

Last but definitely not least, to my grandchildren, the joys of my life, Jacy, Joey, Jagger: stay true to your raising and remember Whose you are.

Chapter 1

The premonitions always made her feel this way—weak, disoriented, scared. Angelina clutched a nearby branch to keep from falling as she watched the water shimmer under the morning sun. She closed her eyes, hoping the sound of the ripples would calm her. She jolted. *Something isn't right.* A sense of dread washed over her as her eyes shot open and darted around the park. Nothing had changed.

But still...

Bits of her latest premonition—or nightmare, as her mother liked to call them—flashed through her mind. She could see a police car, the driver's door hanging open as the lights whirled an array of dizzying colors across the road. There was an ambulance; people were running around everywhere. She covered her ears to drown out the noise as sirens wailed through her head. She blinked, willing the scene to go away. Instead, the vision became even clearer.

In disbelief, she looked into her own crystal blue eyes. She watched herself standing by the playground on the other side of the park, watched mascara stream down her own face.

Is this what it's like to go crazy? Why is this happening to me? I can't do this anymore. Breathe. That's it—slowly. In and out.

She turned to take a different route to school. She hated the visions; they were like huge jigsaw puzzles with half the pieces missing. This time, all she could be sure of was that something bad was going to happen in the park. She didn't know when it was going to take place or even to whom, but she knew she wasn't going to like it.

The further she got from the park, the more things returned to normal. Somehow, seeing Mr. Putman watering his lush lawn helped her heartbeat return to its usual rhythm. Wearing his everyday attire of Bermuda shorts, he waved and smiled a toothless grin. His bony knees struggled to support him as he wobbled on across the yard.

"Angel! Hey, Angel. Wait up!" It didn't register that someone was calling out to her until Daphne put a hand on her shoulder. "Hey, what's going on? Are you lost?"

"Lost?" Standing under the oak tree, Angelina pulled her gaze from Mr. Putman's yard. "No, I'm not lost. I'm… uh, I'm…"

"I was kidding, you goofball. I didn't really think you were lost a block from your own house. I've just never seen you walk to school this way before. Come to think of it, I've never seen you walk to school at all." Daphne's short brown hair bounced as she squealed and jumped up and down. "Oh, wait a minute! This is way too funny. Don't tell me Little Miss Perfect is grounded! Because that's why *I'm* walking *again*. Surprise, surprise. Two weeks this time. Two weeks without my car; two weeks without my cell phone—and all for being thirty little minutes late coming home Friday night. It's *so* not fair." Her foot slipped off the curb. Never missing a beat in the conversation, she continued. "So, what'd you do to get in trouble? Did you, like, get an A minus or something?"

Angelina walked without saying a word.

"Okay, I give up. What'd you do?"

"Do?"

"Hello? Earth to Angel. Why did you lose your car?"

"Oh, my car. I didn't lose my car; it's in the shop. The starter or something went out."

"Of course you didn't. What was I thinking? I mean, the mere possibility of you getting into trouble is kind of… out there." Daphne lowered her voice. "Hey, speaking of out there, put your head down and keep walking. Here comes Kobi."

"Who?"

"Kobi. You know, the newest freak to be added to our illustrious school system. I swear, that girl gives me the creeps. I think she's a witch or something. All she needs is a pointy black hat to go with her black hair and all of those black clothes. I mean seriously, even her lipstick is black. What's up with that?"

As Daphne continued to ramble on about potions and hexes,

Angelina's mind went back to the vision. If she didn't go back to the park for a while, would that keep her premonition from coming true?

Cutting through her thoughts, Daphne said, "Did you already buy tickets to the dance after the game on Friday? Because, thanks to my mom, I guess I won't be going. You know that whole 'being grounded' thing and the 'You have to come home immediately after the game' thing."

"No, I—"

"Cool. You can buy mine off of me then."

"I don't think I'm going to the dance. Isn't it supposed to be an early game this week?"

"Uh, yeah. Because of the dance." Daphne rolled her contact-enhanced, "evergreen" eyes skyward. "The game is supposed to be over by, like, eight o'clock, or something."

"That's what I thought. I already told Sarah I'd watch Tommy after the game."

"What? You're kidding, right?"

"No, I—"

"Just because you're not going out with Jason anymore doesn't mean you need to sit at home, or even worse, babysit on a Friday night." Daphne jockeyed an acorn back and forth with the toe of her shoe as they continued down the sidewalk. "Besides, going to the dance would give you the chance to, you know, dress up for once."

"I already told Sarah I'd babysit." Angelina watched the acorn roll off the curb and fall through the drain. "Besides, what's wrong with the way I dress?"

"Oh, come on! Seriously?"

"What?"

"All you ever wear is jeans. I won't even go into how all of your shirts are, like, three sizes too big. If it weren't for seeing you in your cheerleading uniform, no one would even know you had boobs."

"So? I like being comfortable. Sue me."

"You could be comfortable in a slinky little dress, too. C'mon, buy my ticket and I'll do your hair and make-up. We'll make Jason sorry he ever broke up with you."

"Thanks, but I already promised Sarah."

Daphne puckered her lips into a "Pretty in Pink" pout. "You could get out of it if you wanted to."

"That's just it—I don't want to. Believe it or not, I like babysitting Tommy. He's a great kid."

"I know you like watching him. But seriously, you'd rather babysit than go to the dance?"

"Yeah, well… sometimes." Angelina stopped to untangle a section of her blonde, curly hair that had gotten wrapped around the strap of her backpack. "I'm not like you." She winced, freeing her long hair. "I don't have cute little brothers running around."

"Lucky you. I'd be glad to trade my little brothers for your big brother, especially since he's away at college and wouldn't be able to drive me crazy."

"You know I wouldn't trade Sam for anything, but I'd still like to have a little brother." Angelina looked at her watch and picked up the pace.

"Believe me, you'd change your mind."

"I don't think so. You're lucky and you know it."

"Lucky? Yeah, right. Tell you what. I'll let you borrow my little brothers any time you want. They say absence makes the heart grow fonder, so let's give it a try."

Angelina laughed. "Whatever. You'd miss them."

"If you say so." Daphne kicked her newest acorn soccer ball onto the school's freshly cut grass. "I'd better get to class. I wouldn't want to be late and give my mom a reason to lengthen my grounding. See you later."

"Later." Angelina watched her take off across the campus. Daphne wove around the flowerbeds, which had been installed to "instill school pride." She jumped across one of the smaller gardens and missed her mark. Her size five shoe stomped the pride out of several of the brightly colored marigolds. Daphne reminded Angelina of a Chihuahua. She was tiny, spunky, and more than a little irritating at times.

Starting the day out knowing something awful was going to happen was bad enough, but Angelina was pretty sure she'd bombed a pop quiz, too. This day just kept getting better and better. Now she was going to have to see about retaking the quiz or doing extra credit. She knew it wasn't like one bad grade was going to mess up her GPA, but not doing everything she could to fix it wasn't an option.

Having an overwhelming desire to succeed really blew at times.

Loaded down with books, she stood at her locker and mentally checked off what she needed to take home. She had to study for another test, do a huge math assignment and, of course, there were the never-ending science worksheets. Staring into her locker, she felt Jason's breath on the back of her neck as he brushed past her.

"Hey, Angel." His voice was way too sexy for anyone's good and it made her heart do this little flippy thing in her chest.

She turned and watched him walk down the hall with his broad shoulders and his soft, thick dark hair and his—

"You're drooling." Daphne walked up behind her and poked her in the ribs.

"Am not." Angelina unconsciously wiped the corner of her mouth. She slammed her locker. "I was just wondering why his locker has to be so close to mine. Shouldn't there be some kind of rule about these things? Rule #1: hot guys who break up with their girlfriends without giving them reasons have to change lockers, preferably to another school."

Daphne stuffed her books into the locker. "Come on. We're going to be late for practice."

Adjusting her earpiece, Patty frowned at the chip in her newly manicured nail. She pulled up next to the practice field as she talked to her husband on the phone. "I'm telling you, Ken, it's time to put a stop to this nonsense. I could tell by the way Angel was acting this morning she'd had another one of those dreams."

"I think you should just let it go. Why does everything have to be such a big deal with you?"

"Ken, our daughter thinks she can see into the future." She paused. "Call me crazy, but I think that's cause for concern."

"Concern? Maybe. I'm just saying to tread carefully. If you have to bring it up, do so casually. It seems more natural."

Hearing his sigh, Patty imagined him rubbing the bridge of his nose as he always did during stressful situations.

He continued. "I don't want you blowing this into a huge ordeal."

"I'm not blowing anything into a huge ordeal. I'm just going to try talking to her, that's all."

"Just remember: whatever *is* going on, it was just a dream."

"I know that and you know that. I just need to convince Angel of that. Speaking of which, I see her coming. I'll talk to you later." Patty rolled down her window and waved. "Yoohoo! Over here!"

Angelina sprinted toward the car. *Great. I wonder if she could try a little harder to embarrass me?* She pulled open the door. "Hey, Mom. What are you doing here?"

"I was on my way home from the salon and thought you might want a ride." Patty waited for Angelina to get in and put her seat belt on. "How were school and practice?"

"Not too bad, actually. School was… well, you know… school. But practice was great."

"Really? What made practice so great?" Patty eased away from the curb.

"Well, Mrs. Cooper said she thinks we have a good chance of competing in the state cheerleading competition this year. She also said we have more talent on our team than she's seen in a long time, and then she said if we practiced really hard…"

Sirens cut through the air and the world seemed to restart in slow motion. Angelina had intended to stay away from the park, but in her excitement over the competition, she'd forgotten. Now something terrible had happened.

Angelina stared out the windshield as she watched her vision unfold. But this time was different; this time it was real. When she turned, she saw the flashing lights of the emergency vehicles splash across her mother's face. Red, blue, red, blue. "Mom." She almost choked on the word. "This is exactly what I dreamt last night." A sob escaped her throat. "And then this morning… in the park…"

"Stop it, Angelina! Don't start with that again." Patty's hand flew to her mouth. She drew in a pained breath and lowered her voice. "Shhh, Angel. I'm sorry, but please, be quiet. These dreams of yours are nothing more than dreams." She rolled up the car window. "They don't mean anything. They're only coincidences, and you simply can't go around saying things like that."

Angelina jerked her head up when she heard Sarah scream. "No. No! Tommy, no!"

"Tommy!" Angelina shrieked as she threw open her door and bolted from the car.

"Angelina! Stop!"

As she sprinted toward the commotion, Angelina saw old Mr. Eddelson standing in a crowd of people, frantically waving something in the air. The police officers ushered Sarah across the park to where a limp, wet pile lay motionless on the ground. "Oh, please, please don't let it be Tommy," Angelina cried as Sarah's wails echoed through her head.

As Angelina tried to push through the crowd, an overweight police officer wearing half his lunch on his tie shoved his pudgy hand in her face to stop her. "That's as far as you go, kid." He spun her around to face the opposite direction.

"No, wait! Is it Tommy? Is he okay?"

He wiped grease dribbles from his chin onto his shirtsleeve. "Kid, don't make me do something we're both going to regret."

"Sorry, Officer." Patty grabbed Angelina's arm and directed her to the car. "She's just upset. I promise she won't bother you again."

Angelina tried to act rationally, but she couldn't make herself get back into the car. She had to know if Tommy was okay. She struggled against her mother's grip. "Mom, stop it!"

Patty relented and led her to the far edge of the park, away from Officer McNasty. This way, they would at least be out of the way while they tried to figure out what was going on.

Trying to slow the thoughts racing through her head, Angelina leaned against the monkey bars and realized she was standing exactly where she'd seen herself in the vision.

Chapter 2

Patty stopped at the door of hospital room 202 and gave Angelina a kiss on the cheek. She looked into her sparkling blue eyes that were much like her own. "He's going to be fine, you know." Giving her a reassuring smile, she winked and pushed open the door. "Five-year-olds are like cats; they have nine lives."

Tommy squealed when Angelina walked in holding a large bouquet of helium-filled balloons and a big, brown teddy bear dressed in overalls. "Angel, guess what?"

"What?" Angelina asked with equal enthusiasm.

"I'm in the hospital."

"You sure are." She put the teddy bear beside Tommy and tied the balloons to the metal railing at the foot of his bed.

Tommy proudly pointed to the big, blue goose egg on his forehead. "Did you see this?"

"I see it. I also see your black eye. What happened today?"

Before Tommy could answer, Mr. Eddelson shuffled through the doorway, leaning heavily on his cane.

Sarah jumped up from her seat beside Tommy's bed and helped the old man to a chair. "Mr. Eddelson, you didn't need to come all this way. You've already done so much for us."

Pride lit up the old man's face. "I'm just glad I was there to help. Besides, it wasn't anything anyone else wouldn't have done."

"But you're the one who did it." Tommy's dad, Jack, extended his hand to shake Mr. Eddelson's. "And we'll forever be in your debt."

Mr. Eddelson tried to wave away the praise. "There ain't no sense in all this fuss."

Angelina looked from Tommy to Sarah to Jack to Mr. Eddelson and back to Sarah again. "I'm a little confused. What happened today?"

Sarah was the first to answer. "Well, Tommy noticed that you've been walking home from school lately. He wanted to surprise you today, so we were out in the yard waiting for you to come by." She sat back down beside Tommy. "I heard the phone ring and, like an idiot, I went inside for just a minute and..." She paused as she wiped at a stray tear. "I'm sorry. I know I'm being silly, but I keep thinking of what could've happened."

Jack put his hand on her shoulder. "He's going to be fine, dear."

"I know he will, thanks to Mr. Eddelson." She reached over and squeezed the old man's hand. "Why don't you explain it from here?"

Mr. Eddelson stood his cane up in front of him and propped both of his gnarled hands on it. "I was sitting on my bench feeding the ducks when I noticed young Tommy, here, crossing the road. I knew he shouldn't be coming to the park by himself, so I decided I'd better keep an eye on him. It's a good thing I did, too, because before I knew it, he was wading at the water's edge. So's I yelled out to him, 'Get out of that water!' Well I guess I scared the little tyke a bit because that's when he tripped and hit his head on a rock." Mr. Eddelson looked over at Tommy and grinned. "I suspect that's where that shiner came from."

Tommy was sitting straight up in bed—wide-eyed—bobbing his little blond head up and down.

"Well he just lay there right at the water's edge and he wasn't moving a'tall. By the time I got over to him, he was starting to slip further down into the water and—let me tell you—he was out cold. I tried to pull on him, but this old leg just wasn't cooperating." Mr. Eddelson stopped talking just long enough to give his left leg a firm pat. "I looked around for some help and seen that we were the only two in the park. I knew something had to be done—and fast."

Mr. Eddelson reached into his shirt pocket and pulled out a cell phone. "That's when I dialed 9-1-1. I never wanted one of these cellular phones. I just never saw the point in 'em. The dang buttons are so tiny you can't even use the blasted things most of the time." He held the phone up close to his eyes and shook his head. "Anyway, my son insists I carry it with me at all times and, boy, let me tell you, I sure was glad I had it today. Within minutes of makin' the call, that park was crawlin' with people."

"Hey, Angel. Guess what else?"

"What?" Angelina ruffled Tommy's fine hair.

"I got to ride in an ambulance!"

"You did? Wow! I've never ridden in an ambulance before. Was it fun?"

"Yep. Maybe next time you come over and take care of me we could ride in one."

Angelina laughed. "No, Tommy. No more ambulances, okay?"

"Okay." Tommy lowered his head, disappointed. "That's what Josie said, too." Tommy pointed and shook his finger as he imitated the voice of an old woman. "Now, no more ambulances for you, young man."

Did he just say "Josie?" No way. That would be too weird.

Angelina glanced in her mother's direction and saw her smile fade into a pinched look of concern. The room grew hot. Angelina fanned herself by waving a card in front of her face. Despite her effort, beads of sweat broke out on her forehead. "Tommy, who—who's Josie?"

Sarah winked. "Josie is Tommy's imaginary friend."

No one else seemed to notice the mist swirling at the foot of Tommy's bed. Angelina watched as it formed into the shape of Josie. Josie had also been her childhood "imaginary friend." The room started to spin and the walls closed in around her. Angelina's knees buckled and she hit the floor.

She could hear voices, but she couldn't comprehend what they were saying. Her eyelids fluttered. When they finally opened, she was lying flat on her back, looking up into a circle of worried faces. The nurse waved smelling salts under her nose again and Angelina heard Mr. Eddelson say, "Well if you're going to faint, I guess the hospital is the best place to do it."

"What… what happened?"

"Well, darling, you passed out." The nurse squeezed her hand. "How are you feeling now?"

"I'm, um… I'm fine, I think."

Patty reached down to take her other hand. "Here, honey. Let me help you up."

"That was cool." Tommy's eyes glistened with excitement.

"Cool, huh?" Angelina rubbed the back of her head. "Now I've got a big bump, too, and I didn't even get to ride in an ambulance."

"That's because mine is worser than yours."

"Oh, I'm sure it is. And look, this isn't fair—your bump is right out front so everyone can see it." Angelina turned around to show Tommy the back of her head. "But mine is hiding under all this hair. I won't get any sympathy at all."

Tommy grinned from ear to ear.

Patty tried to hide her trembling hands as she inspected the knot on the back of Angelina's head. "Are you sure you're okay?"

"Yeah, I'm fine."

"Well, if you're sure, I think we've all had enough excitement for one day. We should probably get going and let Tommy get some rest." Patty gave Angelina a look that made it clear that they *were* leaving, whether she liked it or not.

Angelina bent over to give Tommy a kiss on the top of his head. "I guess we'd better go for now. I'll see you tomorrow, okay?"

"Okay. Are you going to bring me more presents tomorrow?"

"Tommy!" Sarah scolded.

Tommy cast his eyes toward Angelina and grinned. "Sorry."

"I'll see what I can do about those presents." Turning to leave, Angelina again watched Josie materialize. Josie smiled and put her finger to her lips as if to say, "Shhh."

Back in the car, neither Patty nor Angelina spoke. With no noise but the hum of the motor, Angelina tried to make sense of what had happened. *Was Josie really there? Of course, she was. No, of course, she wasn't! It must have been the heat, or the bump on the head—I was imagining things.*

Patty reached over and squeezed her hand. "Are you feeling better?"

"Yeah, I'm fine." The silence resumed. She wasn't quite sure how to approach the subject of Josie with her mother. After a few more minutes, she said, "Mom, don't you think it's a little strange that Tommy's imaginary friend's name is Josie?"

Patty took a deep breath and held it for a minute. She slowly let it out with a sigh. "Is that what all of this is about? Is that why you fainted at the hospital? Because if it is, you're just being silly, Angelina. I barely even remembered the name, myself." She took another deep breath. "We put this behind us a long time ago, so let's just leave Josie in the past where she belongs. Are we in agreement?"

Angelina looked down at the floorboard. "Agreed." The two drove on in silence.

Barely remembered her name? Yeah, right. How could you barely remember her name? I spent three years in counseling over that name. Whatever. You remember her and, more importantly, so do I.

Angelina went into the house and raced up the narrow Victorian staircase. Pacing the length of her bedroom, she reminded herself what the years of counseling had taught her. *Josie's not real.* She repeated this over and over in her head. *Sure, I can see her. She's sitting in the rocking chair beside the window. But still, that doesn't mean she's real.* She averted her eyes from the chair, sat down at the vanity table and brushed her hair.

"You've always had such long, beautiful hair." Josie's soft voice hung in the air. "I'm happy you didn't follow the trend and cut it off."

Angelina ignored her. She hummed a song that was stuck in her head as she continued to brush her hair.

"I know you can see me. You might as well acknowledge me because I'm not going anywhere."

Angelina stopped, turned around, and looked deep into Josie's pale green eyes. She looked real enough, but she couldn't be.

Josie. Wasn't. Real.

She turned back around and continued to hum.

"Well, at least I'm glad to know you haven't forgotten everything I taught you. We used to sing that tune when you were just a little thing."

Angelina remembered. She remembered many things about Josie. She remembered her green dress with the delicate lace collar. She remembered how the dark green apron over the dress had two big pockets. She remembered Josie's white hair and how her smile always lit up her eyes. But most of all, she remembered the fun they used to have. She wiped at the tears that rolled down her cheeks. "Okay," she whispered. "If you're real—and I'm not saying you are—but if you are, why did you leave me?"

"Leave you?" Josie's voice went up an octave in surprise. "Honey, I never left you. I've been here all along."

Angelina moved to the corner of her bed. She touched Josie's weathered hand, and then quickly pulled away. The realization that she couldn't feel Josie's hand in hers made her spine tingle. "Th—then why couldn't I see you?"

Sadness clouded Josie's face. "I reckon, for the most part, it was because you didn't want to."

"I did, Josie, but I thought you'd left, or maybe that you were never here at all. They told me..." She sniffed. " They told me..."

Josie wiped at her own tears. "I know what they told you. I was there in those awful counseling sessions when they told you not to talk to me anymore."

"You were?"

"Of course, I was. I've never been too far from you. I was there at your first dance recital. I was there when you broke your arm. I was even there, not long ago, when you cried yourself to sleep over that blue-eyed boy, Jason."

"Sometimes I thought you were still here, but..." Angelina shook her head in disbelief. "I thought I was going crazy—again."

"You're not crazy, Angel," Josie scoffed, "and you never were. You have a gift."

"A gift? What do you mean?"

"You can see ghosts."

"Ghosts!" Angelina back peddled across her bed and stared at Josie. "No, no, no. This can't be happening. I really am crazy!"

Josie sat quietly and watched Angelina hunker on the far corner of her bed. She finally asked, "Are you done? Are you ready to talk?"

"I'm seriously freaking here." Angelina stared at her for a long while. Finally, she crawled back across the bed and reclaimed her spot closer to Josie. "A ghost? Seriously? Is that what you are?"

"Well, I prefer the term 'spirit.'" Josie's eyes twinkled. "But yes, I'm a ghost."

"A ghost. I always thought you were… I don't know what I thought you were. You were always just… Josie."

Josie chuckled then waved her arms in the air. She drew out the words. "Boooo. Boooo. You're not scared, are you? Because I don't think I could pick you up off the floor if you decided to faint again."

Angelina put her face in her hands. "That was so embarrassing." She looked up. "Wait a minute. If you really are a ghost, aren't you supposed to be see-through or something?"

"It depends. Some people see me that way, while others may see a shadow, or a vapor, or—most likely—nothing at all." Josie smiled. "But your gift is strong. You see me as I used to be."

Weighing the fact that either Josie was real or she had definitely gone bonkers sent a shudder through her. "This 'gift' you're talking about, does Tommy have it, too?"

Josie's pale eyes drifted to a distant place. "No, honey. Tommy can only see me because he's a child."

"A child? What do you mean?"

"Most children can see past their world, but once they reach a certain age—usually about six or seven years old—my world closes to them." She brightened and clasped her hands. "But every once in a while, someone special—like you—comes along."

There was a knock on the door. "Angel, may I come in?"

Angelina's heart thumped wildly as her mother pushed the door open.

Josie winked. "It's okay. She can't see me."

"I wanted to check on you before I went to bed. Have you had any more… dizzy spells?"

"No."

"All right. You seem a little tense. Are you sure you're okay?"

"No… I mean, yeah. I'm fine."

"Stay calm." Josie's voice was quiet.

Angelina jumped.

Josie chuckled. "She can't hear me, either." She scrunched her wrinkled face in thought. "Just play it cold."

Angelina cocked an inquisitive brow toward Josie.

"Oh, shucks. I must've said it wrong. What's the word I'm looking for?" She tapped her forehead. "Cool! Yeah, that's it. Just play it cool."

Angelina smiled.

"Honey, are you sure you're okay?" Patty asked as she sat down on the bed and patted the spot next to her.

Angelina sat down. "Yeah, I'm fine. Um… Mom? I was wondering… where'd that rocking chair come from?" Angelina asked, drawing Patty's attention to the chair where Josie was sitting.

"Oh, I can't say where, exactly. It was one of the pieces left in the house when we bought it. I don't think it's quite as old as the house, but I can certainly try to find out."

"Older," Josie said as she rubbed her hands down the arm of the rocking chair. "I've always been fond of this old chair. It's been around for a long, long time."

Patty walked over to the rocking chair and rubbed the intricate leaf carvings—right through Josie's arm.

"That kind of tickles."

"Hmm, I may have been wrong about the age. It may be older than the house. Now that I look at it, if I had to guess, I'd probably say late Victorian—probably about 1895 to 1900. I might be mistaken, but I think this is made of mahogany."

"Not bad," Josie said. "It was made in 1886 and the wood was stained to look like mahogany, but it's actually ash."

Angelina watched as her mother continued to inspect the chair.

This can't be happening. This just isn't right.

Patty turned to see Angelina's expression. "What? Did I wow you with my vast knowledge of antique furnishings?"

"Um, yeah. I mean… you do seem to know a lot about it."

"Well, good. It's nice to know all those countless hours I spent in the library researching the history of our house and learning all I could about these antiques wasn't for nothing."

"When was our house built again?"

"1908," Josie and Patty said in unison.

This is just too weird. Angelina watched her mom place her hand through Josie's arm again. *Way too weird.*

"I'm so glad to see your new interest in all of this. I've almost finished researching the history on this place if you'd like to see it sometime."

"Yeah, that'd be great, Mom." *Now, what have I gotten myself into? House history?*

"This could be fun. We could even go antique shopping. Oh, would you look at me rambling on? You'd better get in bed. It's getting late and you have school tomorrow."

"Yeah, I…uh…I guess I'd better." Angelina hugged her mom and watched her walk out the door.

She turned to Josie. "She really couldn't see you."

"I know."

"Josie, I—I… You really are real, and you've been real all along." She turned to look at her. "It's no wonder everyone thought I was crazy when I was a kid. They couldn't see you—but I could."

"Yes." Josie clicked her tongue. "It was an unfortunate mess."

"An unfortunate... It was more than a mess, Josie. My own parents thought I was crazy."

"For that, I will always be sorry. But now that you're older, you understand the need to be more careful. And that's exactly what we're going to do." She paused. "That is, if you want me to stay."

"Of course, I want you to stay! You were like a Grandma to me."

Josie smiled. "This will be so much better than me trying to communicate with you in your dreams."

Angelina whirled around. "My dreams? That was you? Why would you do that to me?"

Josie lowered her head. "I'm sorry. I only did it when I felt I had no other choice."

"But... but, why?"

"Since you'd chosen to not see me anymore, it was the only way I could talk to you." She met Angelina's eyes. "I only did it when it was really important—like me trying to warn you about Tommy, for instance."

"Tommy? Josie, how did you even know something was going to happen to Tommy?"

"That's a pretty good question, Angel, and one I'm not sure I can answer. All I can say is my whole life—and after, as it turns out—things sometimes just come to me. I know what's going to happen."

"You mean, like, you can see into the future?"

Josie nodded. "Something like that."

"That's pretty cool." Fascination sparked in her eyes. "So, can you tell me where I'm going to go to college? Or how about who I'm going to marry?"

A smile tugged the corner of Josie's mouth. "Let's see, you won't be attending college, but you will marry and have seven children before you turn twenty-five."

She gasped. "Seven children! Are you— You got me."

Josie smiled. "I'm not a circus act, Angel. My ability is real. I can't do it on a whim. It happens without my control."

"It's still pretty cool, though. Right?"

"Sometimes, but not always. It took me years to trust in myself and my abilities, and even then... Oh, well. That's neither here nor there. I learned a long time ago that there is a lot of hurt in this world. If my ability can help prevent a little of that, then I'm gonna use it." She lowered her head. "That's why I came to you in your dreams. I was trying to get you to help me."

"I understand now, but I hated those dreams. I could only remember little pieces of them, but I knew something bad was going to happen. Now that I can see you again, you don't have to come to me in my dreams. If you ever know about something that's going to happen, just tell me and I'll try to help."

"Deal. We're going to make a great team."

Angelina smiled. "And no more of those awful dreams."

"Unless..." Josie paused. "Angel, how many people do you see in this room?"

"Now?"

"Right now."

"Just the two of us."

Josie hoisted her small frame out of the chair. "I'm so happy to have you back, but I'm going to go now and let you get some sleep."

"No! Josie, wait!" Angelina watched Josie dissipate into tiny green particles. "Josie!"

There was no answer.

Chapter 3

Patty tapped the spoon on the rim of the pitcher and tossed it in the sink. After dumping her husband's leftover coffee, she went to answer the knock at the kitchen door. "Good morning, Daphne. I didn't know you were coming by this morning."

"Yeah, I thought since Angel and I are both on foot, we might as well walk together."

Patty removed the bread from the toaster. "I didn't realize you were having car trouble, too."

"I'm not. Not like you mean, anyway. I'm grounded. *Again*."

"I see." Patty sat a plate of toast on the table. "Help yourself. There's also some freshly squeezed orange juice on the counter. You know, the concentrated kind that comes from a can." She smiled.

"Thanks." Daphne picked up a piece of toast.

Through the doorway, Patty yelled, "Angel! Daphne's here!" She picked up the newspaper and sat down at the table. "I don't know what's keeping her this morning, but she should be down in a minute."

"That's okay." Daphne looked through the jelly choices. "While we're waiting, could I ask you a question?"

"Of course, you can," Patty said as Angelina walked in and joined them at the table.

"Okay, it's like this. I came home just thirty little minutes late and now I'm grounded for two weeks. As a parent, don't you think that's a little harsh? I mean, seriously, two weeks?"

Patty tucked a section of short blonde hair behind her ear and stared across the table. "Well, as a parent, I can tell you that parents have to do what they feel is right in raising their own children. Now, when I was growing up, my parents' rule was, for every minute you came home late, you'd be grounded for one day. So according to that rule, I'd say you got off pretty easy."

"One day for every minute? Now *that's* ridiculous." Daphne waved a piece of toast in the air. "I mean... um... I mean that's kind of strict, don't you think?"

"Oh, I don't know. That was the rule. I never really thought about it." Patty got up and poured herself a glass of juice. "Speaking of rules," she took a sip, "isn't there one pertaining to being late for school or something?"

"Okay, we get it, Mom. You ready, Daphne?"

Heading down the sidewalk, Daphne leaned in close. "I swear they get together when we're at school and make all this stuff up."

"What?"

"Seriously, I think they get together and talk about ways to make us miserable. Then, it's like some kind of code of conduct or something, but they have to agree with each other to make it look like they're not so bad."

After cramming the last bite of toast in her mouth, Angelina laughed. "You may be on to something."

"Oh, I know I am."

As Daphne continued talking about her conspiracy theory, Angelina replayed her reunion with Josie in her mind. *I talked to Josie last night, didn't I?* Angelina nodded now and then to make her think she was listening. *If Josie really was there, where is she now? Maybe I dreamed the whole thing. Crap! Maybe I really am crazy.*

Daphne waved her hand in front of Angelina's face. "Are you listening to me?"

"I'm listening."

Daphne pointed toward the park. "I heard about what happened to Tommy. How is he?" She didn't wait for an answer. "You know, I really don't like kids. Well, it's not that I don't like them, it's just, you know, they're always messy and, well, sticky. Anyway, I hated to hear about what happened to him. I know how much he means to you. As kids go, I guess he's pretty cool. So, is he okay, or what?"

"Did you say 'sticky?'"

"Yeah. You know what I mean."

"Not really, but to answer your question, he's going to be okay. They wanted to keep him overnight for observation, but he should be coming home soon."

Angelina jumped when Josie appeared out of nowhere. "They're preparing to bring him home as we speak."

"You're back."

Josie put her finger to her lips. "Shhh."

"What?"

"I, uh… I said, 'Ouch, my back.' Cramps. You know." She picked up the pace.

"That bites." Struggling to keep up, Daphne pulled on her arm. "Hey, remember me?" She pointed at her legs. "Short legs, here."

Angelina slowed.

"So, where did they find Tommy yesterday?"

"I'll show you when we get there."

"I heard Mr. Eddelson was trying to hide his body when the cops showed up."

"What? Where'd you hear that?"

"My mom's friends were burning up the phone lines last night. Since I no longer have a cell phone, I had to wait half the night to use the house phone. Marjorie told Mom she'd heard Mr. Eddelson had thrown a rock at Tommy. I guess after he knocked him out, he got scared and tried to hide what he'd done because Marjorie said he was trying to cover Tommy with leaves, or something."

Josie followed beside, mimicking Daphne's mouth movements with her hands.

Angelina tried not to laugh. She definitely had missed Josie. "That's ridiculous. If anything, Mr. Eddelson's a hero. He tried to save Tommy, and he's the one who called 9-1-1 for help."

"That's not what I heard. I also heard he had to go to the police station for questioning and Tommy's dad was really mad and he was out looking for him late last night."

"None of that's true. He was at the hospital last night visiting Tommy, and Tommy's dad was very grateful to him."

"Oh. You have to admit, though, it's kind of creepy how he comes to the park every day and sits there all alone. I mean… what's he doing there, anyway?"

"He comes to feed the ducks and I, for one, am glad he was there yesterday."

"You know what your problem is?"

"No, but I'm sure you are going to tell me."

"You're simply too nice. You think everyone's good, and to be honest, they're not. The sooner you learn that, the better."

Ignoring Daphne's comment, Angelina pointed. "See where that girl is standing? That's where Tommy was when the paramedics got here."

"*That girl* happens to be Kobi. What's she doing here? She doesn't live on this block. Oh, wait. I get it. Yuck. I mean, that's totally gross."

"What?"

"She just wanted to see where Tommy almost died. Her type always goes in for the gruesome stuff. That's just sick."

"Tommy didn't 'almost die.' Besides, you wanted to see where it happened, too."

"That's different. I was just curious."

"Hey, Kobi," Angelina said as she and Daphne walked up behind her. "You want to walk the rest of the way with us?"

When Kobi turned around, she looked confused—maybe even scared. "No. I…uh… I've got to go back home. I forgot something." Kobi turned and rushed off.

Daphne turned to Angelina. "What? Are you kidding me? Did you seriously just ask her if she wanted to walk with us?"

"And the problem with that is…?" Angelina watched Josie disappear.

"The problem with that is she's a freak."

"Is that why she looked so scared? Have you been messing around with her?"

"Please. I've never even talked to her. I make it a point to stay away from freakazoids."

"Maybe you should give her a chance." Angelina purposefully picked up the pace again. "She's probably a pretty cool person."

"Yeah, I doubt that. If anything, she'd probably put a hex on me or something."

"You're being ridiculous. Just because she dresses a little differently doesn't mean she's a witch, or whatever it is you think she is. Maybe that was in-style at her last school."

"Yeah, school of the dead maybe. She's such a loser."

"Would it kill you to be nice? Seriously, would you like to be the new kid at this school? Most of us have been together since elementary school and I don't think we always make new people feel very welcome."

"From what I hear, she should be used to being the new kid by now. Marjorie told my mom she's with her third foster family this year."

"Good old Marjorie. She was wrong about Tommy and poor Mr. Eddelson. I'm thinking it's a pretty good bet she's wrong about Kobi, too."

"Well, she's not."

"What makes you so sure?"

"Because Kobi lives with the Turners and the Turners are neighbors with Marjorie, so she knows all about her."

Angelina shook her head. "Marjorie likes running her mouth. I'd hate to know what she says about me, or even you, for that matter."

"Oh, she likes us. She said we're two of the few 'good girls' in this town."

"Well, goody. Now I can sleep better at night knowing I'm on Marjorie's approval list."

"What's this? Is little Miss Perfect being catty? There may be some hope for you yet, girl." Still a half of a block away from the school, they heard the bell ring. "Ah, crap. I'm going to be late for Mrs. Goodman's, which is never a good idea." Daphne took off and called over her shoulder, "If I don't see you before, I'll talk to you at lunch."

Angelina wasn't in any rush. She had Mr. Higgins for the first hour. He was usually late and didn't really care if his students were on time or not. She went into the restroom to check her hair and make-up before going to class. Just as she put her hairbrush back into her purse, Josie popped up in front of the mirror.

"You look wonderful, darling."

"Oh, Josie!" Angelina put her hand over her heart. "You almost scared me to death. Can't you wear a bell or something to give me a little warning?"

Josie's eyes twinkled. "Oh, my. I didn't realize you were so fragile, dear. I'll try to be more careful."

"I can see the headlines now. 'Girl, seventeen, dies of a massive coronary in the high school bathroom.'"

Kobi walked out of one of the stalls. "Oh… uh… Hi, Kobi. I didn't realize anyone else was in here. I was just, well…um…I was..."

"And they say *I'm* the crazy one. At least I don't carry on conversations with myself. What do they call me again? Oh, yeah. Freak, isn't it? Looks to me like maybe they're picking on the wrong one, here." Kobi pulled the bathroom door open then turned around. "Oh, wait a minute. You wear a cheerleading uniform. I guess that makes everything you do seem cool."

"I… uh… uh, Kobi."

Kobi walked out.

"Oh, dear." Josie appeared at her side.

"You know what? Don't even worry about it, Josie. Maybe Daphne's right. Maybe she *is* a loser."

"I wouldn't go that far. I suspect your friend, Daphne, is seldom right about much of anything."

A group of girls walked in and Josie vanished.

Angelina walked into class, with Mr. Higgins right behind her. "Okay, people." He checked his watch. "I've given you plenty of time to get ready for class. Get settled down now."

Angelina took her seat. Turning to hang her backpack on the chair, she noticed Kobi sitting in the corner with her chair cocked back on two legs. Angelina hadn't even realized Kobi was in this class. Feeling a little guilty about that fact, she acknowledged her with a smile. Kobi turned away.

"For those of you who care, there will be a test on Friday." Mr. Higgins picked up his book and strolled around the room. He pushed Kobi's chair down to its proper position. "Out of the goodness of my heart, I've decided to tell you a few things you might want to pay closer attention to."

Taking notes, Angelina could feel Kobi's hot stare on the back of her head. *Whatever. Come Friday, she'll wish she'd spent her time taking notes instead of glaring at me.*

Daphne slammed her locker. "Another fantabulous day almost over. Ready for practice?"

Angelina leaned against the wall. "Do I have a choice?"

"Are you sick? You look terrible."

"Ah, thanks. You look pretty great yourself."

"You know what I mean. Seriously, are you sick or something?"

"No, I'm not sick. It's just been a long day."

"Want me to tell Mrs. Cooper you're sick so you can go home?"

Angelina thought about it for a minute. Kicking off from the wall, she said, "No, let's go. You know, for once, I wish I could be irresponsible and do what I want to do and not what I need to do. But, no. Not me. Not little Miss Perfect and all that crap."

Daphne laughed. "Well, I could try and talk you into skipping practice, but we both know you won't. We'd better get to the field before we're late."

Mrs. Cooper blew the whistle and motioned everyone to circle around. "Girls, I have an announcement to make." She stood with her feet apart and her hands firmly planted on her small hips. She waited until she had everyone's attention. She gave the team captain a piercing, "don't even try me," kind of stare. "First, Kathy, this takes nothing away from you—you're still our team captain."

Kathy broke eye contact and looked at the ground while everyone else shifted uncomfortably. No one wanted to be on Kathy's bad side and this didn't sound too good.

Mrs. Cooper continued. "For the state competition, I feel we should place Angelina in charge of the routine. She's had such good ideas for our halftime shows, I believe she'd be a great help to take home the trophy."

Everyone watched Kathy shift her weight from one tanned leg to the other. Daphne slowly started clapping and the others followed.

Kathy twirled her long dark hair around her finger. "Yeah, I'm okay with it." Her fake smile was less than convincing. "We can work together on this and come up with something awesome."

"That's the team spirit I was looking for. I wish we had time to start on the routine right now, but we have a football game this Friday and we have to do something about our pyramid formation. Last week was an embarrassment." Speaking over the murmurs, she continued. "Angelina, I want you and Kathy to kick some ideas around and we'll talk about it later in the week."

With practice over, Angelina and Daphne headed over to the water table. Before they grabbed their bottles, Kathy sidled up behind them.

"Hey, congratulations."

"Oh. Uh… thanks."

"Just don't let this go to your head. After all, it's only one little routine. It doesn't mean anything. In the end, I'm still the team captain and, well..." Her eyes drifted over Angelina. "You're just...you. What I say goes."

"Except, of course, for the routine. And then what I say goes."

"Don't count on it," Kathy sneered over her shoulder as she stalked off.

"She's such a..." Daphne stopped when Angelina cupped her hands over her ears. "I know, I know... virgin ears."

"You can laugh if you want, but you weren't raised in my house. I swear, if I even hear a four-letter word, bubbles come shooting out of my mouth. When Sam and I were little, my mom kept the soap company in business."

"I know, and I wasn't laughing. It's just... weird. But speaking of moms, I have to get home because mine is carrying this grounded thing way too far." Daphne grabbed her bag.

Josie appeared in front of Angelina. "I think most kids at this school would benefit from a little mouth washing,"

Angelina looked around nervously.

"No one can see me. Act casual. I just wanted to pop in and say congratulations on your position. Of course, I don't have the foggiest notion of what it is, but I know it must be good." With both of her thumbs sticking up in the air, she said, "Is this how you kids do it now?" and disappeared.

Chapter 4

Angelina saw her car sitting in the driveway when she got home. "Mom!" she yelled as she came into the house. "Mom. Is it done? Is my car fixed?"

"Indeed it is." Patty met her at the door with a hug. "This has turned out to be quite a good day for you. First, your car's fixed, and now, you're on your way to leading the squad to a state championship, or so I hear."

Angelina dropped her books onto the antique side table. "What? How'd you know about that?"

"Oh, a mother has her ways."

"Yeah but… but I just found out myself. You couldn't possibly—"

"You found out right before practice, which is precisely when Marjorie found out."

"Marjorie?" She frowned. "How'd she know anything about it?"

"Well, apparently, she was at the football field restocking the concession stand when the news broke and she rushed home to congratulate me. Or," she shrugged, "to be more accurate, she probably wanted to brag she knew something about you that I didn't."

"Does anything go on in this town that woman doesn't know about?"

"Probably not." Patty laughed. "Now then, I've already talked to your dad and we want to take you out to celebrate." She clasped her hands in front of her. "So, where would you like to go for dinner?"

"Dinner? Thanks, Mom, but it's really not that big of a deal."

"Not that big of a deal? Of course it is, honey. It is quite an honor to be picked for something like this and we want to take you out to show you how proud we are. So, where's it going to be?"

"Well..." Angelina smiled. "If you insist. I have been really hungry for Italian."

"Say no more." Patty kissed her fingertips and attempted an Italian accent. "That-a can only mean one-a place." She whispered the name, "Rosalie's," with reverence.

"Is there any place else?"

Patty pushed her toward the stairs. "You'd better hurry and get ready. Your dad will be home in less than an hour."

Forty-five minutes later, they stood in line outside the restaurant. "This is torture." Angelina sighed. "How can they expect us to smell all of these wonderful smells and make us keep waiting?"

"I'm with you." Her dad sniffed the air. "I didn't even realize I was this hungry, but I'm about to go in there and help myself to some poor stranger's plate."

"Cartwright, party of three."

"That's us." Ken followed the host like he hadn't eaten in days.

Angelina hurried to catch up with him and almost ran right into a woman who seemed to have appeared out of nowhere. The woman was trying to squeeze in between her and one of the columns that ran through the center of the restaurant. "Oh, excuse me."

The woman whirled around. "What? You can see me? Oh, my! You can, can't you?"

At the same time, Patty pushed Angelina forward. "I've always tried to teach you good manners, but seriously, honey, you don't need to apologize to a column. Now get going. I'm starving!"

"A—a column? Didn't you see that woman with the big hair and sequined top?" Angelina's eyes scanned the restaurant. Now she couldn't see her either.

"All I see is your dad being seated. You know there won't be a breadstick left if we don't hurry."

"Big hair?" The woman appeared before Angelina again. "Honey, you can't get a do like this without some serious work." She fluffed her hair. "I'll never understand you kids plastering your hair down flat against your heads. It always looks as though you just stepped out of the shower. Whatever happened to style? A little pizzazz?"

This seriously can't be happening.

"Um… Mom? I need to run to the restroom. Save me a breadstick," Angelina called over her shoulder as she and the mystery woman headed toward the back. Angelina closed the bathroom door and checked under each stall to make sure they were alone.

"I have no idea what you're doing, but I'm intrigued." The woman watched Angelina check the stalls. "So, what are you? I mean, are you a psychic, or medium, or what?" She readjusted her short skirt. "Of course, I've heard there were people like you, but I've never seen one in my restaurant before."

"Your restaurant?"

"Yes. Well, technically, I guess it's not anymore." The woman checked her hair and makeup in the mirror. "I mean, if you really want to get specific, I guess it was never actually mine, but I ran the place for years. If it weren't for me hanging around and helping, this place would've closed down right after my untimely demise. I still keep the place going."

"Demise? Does that mean… you're dead?" Angelina cleared her throat. "I mean… uh… are you a—a ghost?"

"A ghost? Hmmm, I never really thought about it like that, but I guess I am." She flashed a dazzling white smile. "But don't you think I'm much prettier than your typical ghost?"

"Uh…. well… yes. I mean, you're very pretty." Angelina held onto the sink for support.

"Hey, are you okay?"

"Yeah. Um… I'm fine… I think." She turned the water on and splashed her face. "It's just that seeing ghosts tends to freak me out a little bit."

"Okay." The woman clicked her bright red nails on the counter. "Now that we've established I'm a ghost—however pretty I might be—the question remains, what are you?"

"Me? I—I don't know. I'm just… me."

"You can obviously see me, so if I'm not mistaken, that makes you a medium, or maybe a psychic. Or is it a mediator?"

"I—I—"

"Well, you *have* seen ghosts before, haven't you?"

"No. Yes. Maybe… I mean, there's Josie."

"Who's Josie?"

"She's a... um... she's my friend. Or... um... my imaginary friend, I guess."

"Imaginary friend? Aren't you a little old to have imaginary friends?"

"Yes. Well... um... no. She's not really imaginary. It's just no one else can see her. No one else except Tommy, that is."

"Tommy? Who's Tommy?" Her heavily made up eyes brightened. "Is he your boyfriend? Oh, how romantic! A couple of psychics who are actually a couple. Isn't that sweet?"

"Uh, no. It isn't like that. Tommy's a little boy I babysit."

"A little boy? Darn! So, no boyfriend, huh?"

"Uh, no. Not really. Not anymore, anyway."

"Ah, this sounds like my kind of story." She perched herself up on the counter and crossed her ankles. "So, tell me about this not-anymore-boyfriend of yours." She swung her feet, which made her sequined top shimmer like a disco ball. "Is he cute?"

"Oh, yeah. Very. And sweet and smart and—"

"So what happened?"

"That's the thing. I don't know! We went out for a while and I thought things were going good, but then he said he thought maybe we should just be friends."

"Friends?" The woman jumped down from her seat on the counter and waved her arms in the air. "Oh, I hate that line! So, in other words, he wanted to go out with someone else."

"That's what I thought, too... at first." Angelina took the vacated seat on the counter. "But I haven't heard about him going out with anyone else and lately... I don't know... he's been acting kind of weird."

"Like how?"

"I see him staring at me in class sometimes, and he has called me a few times, but he just mumbles something about a wrong number then hangs up."

The woman held her hands in front of her face. "And you know it's him because you're psychic, right?"

"No, I know it's him because I have caller ID."

"Caller ID? What's that?"

Patty opened the door to the bathroom and saw Angelina sitting on the counter. She narrowed her eyes. "Angel, what are you doing?"

Angelina had almost forgotten the woman she was talking to was a ghost. Seeing the open door divide her voluptuous figure in half served as a good reminder. Knowing she must look like an idiot sitting there on the counter in a public bathroom, she jumped down. "My… uh… shoe was untied."

"Well come on. The server's ready to take our order."

Angelina followed Patty to the table and took a seat in the booth opposite of her mom and dad.

"Scooch on over a bit, honey." The woman slid in beside her.

Angelina looked up to see her dad peering at her over his menu. He was doing that weird eyebrow twitching thing. "Expecting somebody?"

"No. I—I think the spring on that part of the seat is broken."

The server came to the table, sparing her any more questions. "Is everyone ready to order?"

"I think so," Patty averted her attention from Angelina. "I want the house specialty—spaghetti with meatballs."

"Give me the seven layer lasagna." Ken ran his hand over his upper lip, smoothing his salt and pepper mustache. "And could we get some more breadsticks?"

The server nodded. "I'll have them right out." She looked at Angelina. "And for you, Miss?"

"I think I want the seven layer lasagna, too. That sounds really good."

"Normally, I'd agree with you," the mystery woman said. "But the chef got a little carried away with the garlic tonight, so… unless you like too much garlic, I'd recommend the chicken alfredo."

"Oh, um. Actually, could I change that to the chicken alfredo?"

"Sure. No problem."

"Good choice." The woman stuck out her hand. "By the way, my name's Rosie."

Turning to shake the woman's hand, Angelina noticed her mom watching her. "Angel, what are you doing?"

Angelina looked across the table at her mom's icy stare. "Oh. I… uh… I thought I had a piece of string connected between me and the seat." She brushed an imaginary thread from her shoulder.

"Well, this is awkward." Rosie shrugged. "I take it they don't know about your gift."

Not making eye contact with the woman, Angelina jumped at the loud clang coming from the kitchen.

"That's my cue to run." Rosie slid out of the booth. "No telling what kind of catastrophe that was. I swear, I can't have five minutes to myself. So much for rest in peace and all of that nonsense."

Trying to regain the festive mood, Patty asked, "So, what kind of routine are you going to do?"

"I'm not sure. I haven't had time to think about it."

Thankfully, the server arrived with their salads, distracting everyone from the awkward start to the meal.

"Oh, this looks wonderful," Patty said as the chilled plate was placed in front of her.

Angelina was about to take her first bite when Rosie rushed up to the table and slid in beside her. "I wouldn't do that if I were you. Unless, of course, you like eating food that's been on the floor." She sighed. "That was the noise we heard. The entire salad bowl crashed to the floor and those imbeciles just scooped it back into the bowl and are serving it to my customers."

With her fork poised over the salad bowl, Angelina stared at Rosie for a few seconds then set her fork back down.

Patty looked across the table at her. "What's wrong? Aren't you going to eat your salad?"

Angelina's stomach churned at the thought of her parents eating salad that had been on the floor. "I—I thought I would skip the salad to make more room for the main course."

"That's probably not a bad idea," Patty said between bites. "You should at least taste it, though. It's particularly good tonight."

Angelina put her hand over her stomach as she silently heaved.

"Oh, for goodness sake. It's not *that* bad. It did fall on *my* floor, which is always clean, relatively speaking."

The server came to their table with their food. Angelina looked at Rosie and picked up her fork.

Rosie nodded her approval. "Eat. It's perfect. I promise."

"Oh, this is good." Angelina's stomach rumbled in anticipation of more. "I mean, very, *very* good. How's yours?"

Patty reached for another breadstick. "Wonderful, as always."

"Mine, too. Lots of garlic. Just how I like it," Ken said around a mouth full of food.

"What'd I tell you?" Rosie got up from the table with a big smile. "You enjoy the rest of your meal. I've got to get back into the kitchen."

Back in the car, Angelina leaned her head against the back seat and closed her eyes. When she opened them again, Rosie was sitting beside her. Angelina let out a yelp and covered her mouth.

"Angel, are you okay?" Patty asked.

"Uh, yeah. I just hiccupped."

"Nice save," Rosie said.

"What are you doing here?" Angelina mouthed.

"Not to worry. The restaurant can do without me for a few minutes. I hope, anyway. I just wanted to see where you lived in case I ever need your services."

Angelina's eyebrows shot up. "My services?" She said under her breath.

"You know, in case I ever need you to do something for me."

Angelina gave her a blank stare.

"Sheesh, don't you ever watch television? You know, I might need you to go and talk to someone for me or, or something." She sighed. "Besides, you have to finish telling me about your boyfriend. Who knows, I might be able to help you out in that department. In my day, I was quite the— "

"I do believe that was one of the best meals I've ever eaten," Ken said.

"I'd have to agree with you. It was wonderful. It always is, though. And to think they actually talked about not reopening after the fire."

"Fire?" Angelina's ears perked up. "What fire?"

"Oh," Patty continued. "I sometimes forget how young you really are. Years ago—you were probably just a baby, now that I think about it—there was a terrible fire. Half the restaurant burned to the ground."

Angelina had a sick feeling in the pit of her stomach. "Was anyone hurt?"

"Let me see… the best I can remember, the fire broke out after hours."

"The manager died, remember?" Ken broke in. "She was a beautiful woman. We'd met her a time or two."

"Oh! I remember now. Her name was Rosalie. As a matter

of fact," Patty snapped her fingers and pointed at the dash, "they renamed the restaurant in her memory. Before the fire, it was called Antoine's. Remember?"

"I'd forgotten that, but you're right."

"It was such a tragedy. They said she was in her office doing paperwork. No one even knew she was there. When the fire broke out, everyone else got out, but I guess by the time she realized the place was on fire, it was too late. Part of the structure had fallen and had pinned her, and even though the fire didn't get that far, she died of smoke inhalation."

Angelina watched in horror as Rosie went up in flames. With her hands clawing at her face, she screamed, "I'm melting! I'm melting!" Moments later, Rosie lay charred and motionless beside her in the backseat.

"No!" Angelina screamed.

"Angel, are you okay?" Patty asked.

"Please stop the car, Dad. I think I'm going to be sick."

Ken pulled onto the shoulder. Before the car had even come to a complete stop, Angelina threw open the door and jumped out. She was gulping in the fresh air when Rosalie appeared next to her.

"I'm sorry, hon. That was insensitive of me, but I used to love that movie and I thought it was fitting, given the circumstance."

"But—but, how can you joke about this?"

Rosie sighed. "Memories can be very powerful, at times, and laughing is always better than crying." She re-poofed her hair and wiggled her skirt back down. "At the end of the day, I'm still dead."

"Angel," Patty called as she rolled down her window. "Are you all right?"

"I'm fine." Angelina fought back tears as she and Rosie got back into the car.

"I didn't know you weren't feeling well. Maybe we shouldn't have gone out tonight, honey. I wonder if you have a concussion from that fall you took at the hospital."

"No, Mom. I'm fine."

When they pulled into the driveway, Rosie said, "Nice house. Is this where you live?"

Angelina nodded.

"I'll be seeing you, but for now, I'd better get back to the restaurant." She smiled and disappeared. Angelina bolted from the car and ran into the house.

"What in the world?" Ken shot a look at Patty.

Patty shrugged. "Who knows?"

Chapter 5

Angelina ran up the stairs and threw open her bedroom door.

"Land sakes, child. You almost gave me a heart attack!" Josie clutched her chest and stumbled backward. "That would've been quite an accomplishment, too, considering I'm already dead." She grabbed the post of Angelina's bed to balance herself. "Now, what's the meaning of this? Where's the fire?"

"Fire!" Angelina burst into tears.

"Well, my goodness. What's all of this about?"

"Oh, Josie." Angelina sobbed. "I met this woman and she... she..."

"She what?" Josie balled her frail hands into little fists. "Did she hurt you?" Her eyes sparked. "If she did, I'll make her sorry she ever drew a breath of life!"

"No, Josie." Angelina took deep breaths to slow her racing heart. "It wasn't anything like that. It's just... well... she's a ghost."

"A ghost?" Josie chuckled. "All this fuss over a ghost? My, my. You scared me half out of my wits for nothin'. Here I was thinking something terrible had happened!" She ran her weathered hands down her apron and walked toward her rocking chair. "I guess you finally met Adie. I knew you'd see her eventually, but I had no idea it would upset you so. I know she tends to be a little on the uppity side but..."

"Adie?" Angelina knitted her brow. "I—um, no. Her name's Rosie. Who's Adie?"

Josie scoffed. "Well, that can wait for another time, I suppose." She turned to Angelina. "Now, who's this Rosie that has you so upset?"

"Rosie's the woman—or the ghost—I met at the restaurant tonight. We started talking and—" Angelina's voice cracked. "I really liked her and there was this fire and—"

Josie spun back around. "A fire!" Concern etched her face. "Well, my goodness, honey! No wonder you're so upset." She circled Angelina, checking her for injuries. "Are you all right? How about your parents? Are they okay?"

"No. I mean, yes. We're all fine, Josie. The fire was a long time ago," Angelina sniffed, "but it killed Rosie. She showed me how she died."

"Hhmph. She did, did she?" Josie made her way over to the chair. "It sounds to me like this Rosie character has a flare for the dramatic. She had no right to upset you like this with something from the past." She eased herself down into the chair. "What's wrong with her, showing you all of that gore? I've half a mind to go hunt her down and give her a good tongue lashing."

"No, Josie. It wasn't anything like that. Mom and Dad were talking about the fire and I think the memories caused her to—"

"Angelina? Who are you talking to?"

The question went through her like a bolt of lightning. She turned and saw her mother standing in the doorway. "I… uh… I—"

Patty walked across the room and sat down hard on the bed. "We need to talk."

"Mom, I—"

Patty's blonde bob flounced as she shook her head. "Angel, it's time. We're going to nip this thing before it gets out of hand. We're not going to go through this again."

"Mom, let me explain—"

"Explain?" Patty's voice rose. "Explain what, Angel? That you're seventeen years old and you're in here talking to—to nobody?" Patty put her face down in her hands, and then jerking her head up, she yelled, "No! I don't want you to explain. I want you to stop this nonsense. I thought all of this was behind us."

"Mom, it was, but—"

Patty held her hand up. "It all started again after Tommy said that name, didn't it?"

"Yes, but—"

"There are no buts! Tommy having an imaginary friend with the same name is a coincidence, pure and simple."

"That's what you say about everything, Mom." Angelina's voice rose. "Every time one of my dreams came true, you said it was a coincidence and now—"

"Angel, I want you to listen to yourself." Patty clenched her teeth. "You are a normal, intelligent young woman and I want this to stop." She relaxed her jaw. "You have to know there are no such things as premonitions. Just like you have to know your friend isn't real."

"Mom, that's the thing… I'm not really… uh… normal." *It's now or never.* "See, Josie says I have a gift and—"

"Angel, stop it!" Patty clutched her hands in tight fists as she fought to get control over her emotions. "I'm begging you to stop," she whispered.

From the rocking chair, Josie said, "Careful, Angel. She's not going to be able to understand. You'd do well to leave this alone."

"Okay, Mom. Fine!" Angelina whirled around. "If I'm so normal, then why do these things happen to me?"

"I guess," Patty choked back a sob, "I guess it's because of me."

"You? You!" Angelina flung her arms up in the air. "Why does everything end up being about you?" She glared at her mother. "Maybe you should look at who *I* am," she spat as she thumped her own chest. "Take time to try to believe in me, for a change."

Emotion thickened Patty's voice. "Angel, I do believe in you. I just think you're a little… confused." She swallowed hard as she fought back the tears. "And that is my fault. When you were little and had an imaginary friend, everyone said it was normal—it was just a phase. But I couldn't let it go. It was normal for other children, but not mine. Not you." Her shoulders sagged. "I insisted on all of that counseling. If I'd have left well enough alone, you would've outgrown it like other children."

Angelina sat down beside her. "No, Mom. It's not like that." She put her hand on her shoulder. "Mom, please. I'm sorry. I just wish I could make you understand about Josie."

"That name!" Patty shot up from the bed. "I never want to hear that name again." She turned and dabbed her eyes. "Angel," she sniffed. "I don't want to fight with you."

"I don't want to fight with you either, Mom."

Patty took a deep breath. "I want to try and explain something to you. I'm not making excuses for myself; I just need for you to understand." She picked up a little glass angel that was sitting on the dresser. She wiped her tears with one hand while she held the angel up to her cheek with the other. "Do you know I bought this for you before you were even born?"

Angelina nodded.

"I actually bought this when I was pregnant with Sam. When I found out I was having a boy, I put it up in hopes that someday I'd have a girl." She set the angel back in its place. "You know, I didn't have a good relationship with my mother. So, I thought if I had a daughter of my own, I could do all of those special little mother-daughter things with her. I dreamed of how we'd go shopping and go get our nails done and—"

"Mom, we do all of that."

A tear slid down Patty's face. "I wanted to be the perfect mother, but somehow I ended up pushing you to be the perfect daughter. I've pushed you so hard, it's no wonder you need someone to talk to."

"Mom, that's not it at all. You haven't pushed me."

"Oh, but I have, sweetie. I have. I think it's more than a coincidence that your 'friend' showed back up after all of these years, just when your brother goes off to college. You and Sam were so close and now that he's gone, you feel like you're all alone."

"What? No, Mom. This has nothing to do with Sam."

"You're right. It's not Sam." She shuddered. "Like I said, it's me. Once Sam left, I focused all of my attention on you. I've always been too hard on you, but since he left, I've pushed you even harder."

"Mom, you don't push me. Not any more than any other parent does. You just want what's best for me. I know that."

"What's best for you—what would be best for all of us—would be for you to forget about..." She couldn't even bring herself to say the name.

"Josie."

Patty took a hold of Angelina's hand. "I'm going to ask a favor from you."

"What?"

"I'm going to ask that you not talk to her anymore."

"Mom, I—"

"Angel, I want you to talk to me instead." Patty swallowed hard. "I'm here for you… and I'm real."

"Mom, I wish I could make you understand."

"Angel, I don't want to understand. I want you to stop talking to her. Is that really too much to ask? Won't you please just promise me this one thing?"

Ken rapped on the door and stuck his head in. "Everything okay in here?"

"Sure." Patty dropped Angelina's hand and wiped away her tears. She walked toward the door. "I was on my way out. We're just having a little girl talk."

"Hmm." Ken backed out and closed the door.

Patty smiled. "It still works."

"What works?"

"Those two little magic words: 'girl talk.'" She laughed. "That's all you have to say if you want a man to leave you alone. They'll turn and run every time."

"That's too funny, Mom."

"Yes, it is, but it's also true. Of course, 'I'm cramping' works wonders, too."

Angelina smiled.

Patty hugged her. "Are we good?"

"Yeah, I just want everything to be okay between us."

"Everything *is* okay." Patty tucked a stray section of hair behind Angelina's ear. "We can work through this. Just remember, if you want someone to talk to, I'm here."

"Thanks, Mom." Angelina watched Patty close the door.

As soon as the door had closed, Josie blurted, "Angel, I'm sorry. I'm so sorry."

"What?" Angelina turned and looked at her. "You don't have anything to be sorry about."

"I just don't know how we're going to be able to make this work. We've tried to be careful, but when you came in so upset over that Rosie person, I let my guard down. I didn't even think about someone overhearing us."

"I know." Angelina plopped down on the bed. "I didn't think about it, either. We'll just have to be more careful."

Josie dropped her chin to her chest.

"Josie, it'll be okay."

"I feel like I'm betwixt and between."

"What? That doesn't even make sense."

Meeting Angelina's stare, Josie crinkled her forehead. "How about 'I feel like I'm between a rock and a hard place?' Does that make sense?"

"Yeah, sort of. You mean, you don't know what to do?"

Josie nodded.

"Josie, are you crying? What's wrong?"

Josie threw both hands in the air. "Okay, broken!"

"Broken? I don't understand. What's broken?"

Josie looked confused. "Didn't I say it right? When someone catches you at something, isn't that what you kids say now? Broken?"

"Broken… Oh! Josie, you crack me up. It's busted. You mean busted!"

"Yes, busted. How's an old woman supposed to keep up? Broken, busted, and cracked up—you kids sure are a destructive lot!"

"Okay, Josie, you've been busted." Narrowing her eyes, she continued, "Now, what'd I catch you at? What are you trying to hide from me?"

"You caught me being a selfish old woman."

"You're not selfish. Why would you say that?"

"My being here is causing you so much trouble. Sometimes, I think I should just go and leave you in peace."

"Josie, don't even think about it. You can't leave me!"

"Shhh. Calm down. I won't. I can't. And even if I could, I couldn't." She sighed. "Ah, fiddlesticks! Just look at me. I'm so flustered I can't even make my own words come out right."

"Josie, what are you trying to say?"

"I'm saying I'm no longer the only ghost you can see. If it's not me your mother overhears, it'll be someone else, so I might as well just stay." She slid her hands down the carvings of the chair and sighed. "That's where the selfish part comes in, I reckon." She cast her eyes toward Angelina. "I can't help but wonder if I might just be making excuses to stay."

"You don't need an excuse, Josie. I want you here. I don't ever want you to leave."

Josie smiled. "Thank you, honey. That means more to me than you'll ever know. Besides, now that you can see the others, you might even need my help. Ghosts can be a pesky lot, at times."

"Others? You mean Rosie?"

Josie pursed her thin lips. "I reckon she'd have to be included."

"Josie, how many ghosts are there?"

Josie chuckled. "Honey, that's like asking me to count the stars in the sky."

Lost in their conversation, neither noticed the quiet scrape of Patty's ring as she stifled a sob while she listened to half their conversation from the other side of the door.

Chapter 6

Beep! Beep! Beep!

The sound ricocheted through her brain. Without opening her eyes, Angelina stuck her hand out from under the covers and hit the snooze button. She heard Josie's voice.

"If you're not going to get up when that blasted thing goes off, why do you bother setting it at all?"

She smiled. After all, she was the one who told Josie to never leave—and never could be a long, long time. "Good morning." Angelina stretched. "I'm going to get up. I just wanted a few more minutes."

"A few more minutes?" Josie clicked her tongue. "Then why even get up? You've already slept half the day away."

She grabbed her alarm clock. "Half the day? Josie, it's seven a.m. That's what time I always get up, except for the weekend. Then I sleep a lot later than that."

"Later than seven! My, my. I don't know what this world's a coming to." She wrung her frail hands. "It's laziness—pure and simple laziness, is all I got to say."

Angelina forced herself from the bed. "So, what brings you here so *early* this morning?"

Josie walked over to the window and peered out. "I thought I'd pop in and check on you. I know you had a rough go of it last night, between meeting that Rosie character and having that talk with your mother. I wanted to make sure you're okay."

"I'm fine." Angelina yawned. "I must have been really tired, though, because I slept like a... Wait a minute. Josie, you didn't try to talk to me in my dreams again, did you?"

Josie whirled. "I certainly did not!" Her pale eyes sparked as she folded her arms across her chest. "I don't have to do that anymore, now that you can see me again."

"Okay." Angelina tried to hide her smile. For such a little woman, Josie could sure get an attitude. She wandered over to her vanity. "I was just checking. I had a really weird dream."

"It was no fault of mine." She uncrossed her arms, now intrigued. "What was it about?"

"I'm not sure. I think we'd gotten a new cheerleading coach, or something. I never saw her face, but somebody kept yelling at me during practice. She kept telling me to kick higher and spin faster. I told her I was doing it right, but then she started yelling even louder. She said she'd tell me when I was doing it right." Angelina picked up her brush and raked it through her tangled hair. "I don't know… it was just strange."

"Hmm, is your school looking to replace the coach?" Josie winced in the mirror each time Angelina's brush met a tangle.

"Not that I know of."

"I'm sure it was nothing. You probably dreamt it because of the routine you have to come up with." She turned away. "I think you're putting too much pressure on yourself."

"You're probably right." Angelina's stomach growled as she dug through her closet, looking for something to wear to school. "I must've had a good workout, though, because I'm starving and I don't usually eat breakfast."

Josie's eyes widened. "That noise came from you?" She laughed. "I thought we were in for a thunderstorm with all of that rumbling. You'd better go get something to eat."

"I think I will." Angelina walked to the door. "You coming?"

"Given our predicament last night, that's probably not a good idea. You run along. I'm going to go see Tommy."

Could this day possibly get any worse? Angelina made her way down the crowded hallway. *It's just now lunchtime. I swear, it feels like I've been here for three days straight. First, that crazy dream I can't get out of my head. Then my pen exploded, ruining my homework, not to mention what it did to my backpack, and then…*

"Hey, watch it!" Kobi yelled as Angelina plowed into her, sending her books flying down the hall.

"Oh, Kobi. I'm so sorry." Angelina bent down and picked up Kobi's books. "Here—let me help you."

"Stop it. Don't touch my stuff."

"Sorry." Angelina watched Kobi scramble around, scooping up her things. "I was just trying to help."

"I'd say you've already done enough." Standing, Kobi glared at her. "Just leave me alone."

"I said I was sorry." She met Kobi's stare. "What's your problem? I mean, seriously, why are you so mean?"

"Oh, boo hoo. Are you like in third grade, or what? You'd better toughen up, princess, especially if you're going to walk around talking to yourself." Kobi pushed past her and hurried down the hall.

"Wow." Daphne had come up from behind. "What's that all about?"

"I have no idea." Angelina slumped against the wall. "I am so ready for this day to be over."

"Well, that ain't gonna happen." Daphne cocked her head to the side and whispered, "Don't look now, but Kathy's heading our way."

"Hey, girls." Kathy came up and draped her arm over Angelina's shoulder. "You're just who I wanted to see." Her eyes locked on something above Angelina's head. She smiled sweetly. "So, have you come up with your little routine yet?"

"No, I—"

Her fake smile never wavered. "How about the music?"

Angelina turned to see what Kathy was looking at—the security camera. *You've got to be kidding me.*

Finally making eye contact, Kathy continued. "So… you haven't come up with any songs yet?"

"No, I haven't had time."

"Of course you haven't. Besides, I'm sure you'd want to run it by me first." She flipped her dark hair over one shoulder. "Hey, I know. Why don't we go to the mall after school and check out the music store for some ideas?"

"Uh, yeah. Sure."

Kathy squealed. "This will be fun! Meet me out front right after school." With a final smile she said, "See you later, Ang." As she departed, she flashed another brilliant smile and did the beauty pageant wrist-wave for the camera.

Daphne glanced up. "Was she seriously posing for the security camera?"

"That's what it looked like to me."

"Wow."

"Yep."

"Well, Ang." Daphne imitated Kathy's sickly sweet voice. "Looks like you're going to have fun after school."

"You think?"

"Definitely, as long as you enjoy being stung by scorpions while simultaneously getting stabbed in the back with a long, serrated knife."

"Oh, thanks. That makes me feel better." Trying to stop her headache, Angelina pressed her palm down on the top of her head. "Hey, I have an idea. Why don't you go with us?"

"Um, no." Daphne's short brown hair swayed from side to side. "Not that I don't want to, it's just I have this thing I've got to do."

"'Thing,' huh?"

Daphne smiled.

"Some friend you are."

"You know you love me. I'll see you later and, uh, good luck at the mall."

Having Mr. Higgins once a day should've been enough punishment for anyone, but when Angelina saw him sitting behind the desk as she walked into her last period, she silently cursed her fate. When the bell rang, he rolled his chair back and stood up. "Okay, people. I need your undivided attention." He paused. "Your regular teacher has had, shall we say, some sort of mishap. Since this was supposed to be my planning period, I now get to fill in for her." He looked around the classroom with thinly veiled annoyance before plopping back down into his chair. "I've no idea what her original plans were for you today, nor do I care." He picked up a stack of papers. "You may consider this a study period."

A few students started to whisper.

"I said a study period, people, not a free-for-all." His dark eyes scanned the room. "Most of you are fortunate enough to be in my history class and, as you know, we had a test today.

I'll be grading these tests now and if I'm disturbed, I might get carried away with my little red marker. We wouldn't want that, now would we?"

A guy named Tyler leaned over and pulled his dirty blond hair away from his eyes. "Why should I care? I'm not in one of his stupid classes anyway."

Without raising his head, Mr. Higgins peered over his glasses with the red pen twirling between his fingers. "If anyone feels like visiting, you may do so in the office."

The classroom fell silent except for the clock on the wall. Tick-tock, tick-tock. Angelina put her head on the desk and let it lull her to sleep. At the sound of the bell, she bolted upright and yelled, "Quit screaming at me! And my name isn't Patty!"

"Well, that's good to know," Mr. Higgins said. Angelina felt her face burn as the class exploded with laughter. Laughing himself, Mr. Higgins rose from his chair. "Class dismissed."

She walked to her locker as the expected comments followed her down the hall. "Nice nap, Angelina. Or should I say 'Patty?'" Someone from behind called out.

"Cut it out." Jason's voice rang through the hallway.

Her heart flopped at the sound of his voice. She walked a little faster, wondering why he was defending her. He was, after all, the one who had wanted to call it quits.

When Angelina stepped outside, Kathy came up beside her. "My car's over there." She pointed in the general direction of the student parking lot.

"We can take mine if you want."

"No, that's okay." With no cameras in sight, Kathy scowled. "If it's all the same to you, I prefer to be seen in a little newer vehicle. Besides, *Patty,* while we're on this subject, don't you think we should work a little harder to keep our reputations at a higher standard?"

How did she... Oh, never mind. Angelina climbed into Kathy's car. *Let the fun begin.*

The engine revved to life. "Now, what's this I hear about you falling asleep in class and waking up screaming?"

"How could you have possibly heard about that? It happened less than ten minutes ago. And, for the record, I wasn't screaming. Not really."

"Ang, I don't mean to sound like a snob—I really don't—but we do have a reputation to uphold. To be quite honest, your little nap today was only one of many complaints I've been hearing about you."

Angelina put her head back on the leather seat and closed her eyes. "Who, exactly, has been doing all of this complaining?"

"That's not important. What *is* important is how you're letting your reputation slip into the mud."

"And how am I doing that?"

Kathy checked her makeup in the rearview mirror. "Don't get mad. I'm just trying to help. Some of us are just a little concerned about you."

Angelina sat up and met Kathy's stare. "What, in particular, are you so concerned about?"

"Well, for starters, how about your friend?"

"Daphne? What's wrong with Daphne?"

"It could take hours to answer that question." Kathy waved her hand in the air, along with the diamond ring that was, no doubt, another gift from "Daddy." "Daphne is, however, a cheerleader, so therefore, she's approved. I was referring to that Kobi girl."

"Kobi? You can hardly call her my friend. She can't stand me, for some reason."

"Oh, Ang. Can't you see? That's precisely what I'm talking about. We're the elite group. *They* want to be a part of us, not the other way around. Kobi is the type we shouldn't even associate with, let alone grovel to."

"For the record, I don't associate with her. And I didn't realize we had a list of 'approved people' we could hang out with." After glancing at the speedometer, Angelina double-checked her seatbelt.

"There you go, getting all defensive." Kathy wove the white convertible in and out of traffic. "You know very well it's not like that. We cheerleaders should just have an understanding, that's all."

"You know what? I'm really not in the mood to do this today. Just take me back to my car and I'll pick out the music later."

"Don't be ridiculous. We're almost there." Kathy flashed her beauty queen smile. "Let's just put this conversation on hold and go have some fun."

As Kathy whipped into a parking space, Angelina said, "I have a better idea. Let's end the conversation and go look for some music." Without waiting for a response, she got out of the car and headed into the mall.

Kathy rushed to catch up with her. "Well, while we're here, we might as well do some shopping."

"Let's just get this over with." Angelina continued toward the music store.

"See? I knew you were mad." Kathy's full lips turned into a pout. "Come on, let's go look at shoes."

Angelina walked faster. "I don't need shoes."

"Actually, it wouldn't hurt."

That little... "Soap bubbles, soap bubbles," her conscience screamed.

Angelina took a different approach. "Or I can go pick out the music myself while you go to the salon and try to get something done about your hair."

"My hair? Why? What's wrong with my hair?"

Angelina stopped walking and let her eyes scan Kathy. "Oh," she cocked a brow, "nothing." She walked into the music store with a satisfied smile.

Coming out of the bathroom with hairbrush still in hand, Kathy joined Angelina by the CDs. "This is stupid, anyway. If the school even *tried* to keep up with modern technology, we wouldn't even have to come to the mall. We could just download the music. I can't believe the principal wouldn't let us use a burned disc, either. Making a copy isn't piracy."

Angelina gave her hair another look and shrugged. "This works."

"How about something from P!nk?"

"Um, I don't think so."

"Are you sure? Because that could be awesome." Kathy ran a brush through her long dark hair again. "Oh, wait a minute. How about Rob Thomas?"

"Who?"

"Oh, come on. Rob Thomas. You know, 'Lonely No More?' That'd be perfect for a routine."

"Yeah, maybe." Angelina continued to flip through the selections. "How about this one?" She pointed to a Michael Jackson CD.

Kathy rolled her eyes, "Yeah. Like, what are we going to do, wear poodle skirts or something?" She put the brush back in her purse. "That's as old as my mother."

"That's it! We could do something retro."

"Oh, Ang. You can't be serious!"

"Yes… well… no. Not the poodle skirts, anyway. Poodle skirts were popular in the 50s. This album was popular in the 70s… or maybe the 80s. We could—"

"I don't think so," Kathy snapped. "I still like 'Lonely No More.' Come on. I'll help you work up the routine and everything."

"I don't know… Let's keep looking. What do you think of the Dave Matthews Band?"

"Mmmm, maybe. Or what about Kelly Clarkson?"

"Let me see it." Kathy handed her the case. "I thought you said no to Michael Jackson."

"Uh, I did." Kathy tapped her foot. "That's Kelly Clarkson."

"No, it isn't." Angelina handed the CD back to Kathy. "This is what you gave me."

"Oh, my bad." Kathy put it back and withdrew another. "What're the Js doing in with the Cs, anyway?"

"I don't know." Angelina glanced at the playlist. "I wanted to buy this Kelly Clarkson one anyway. I'll go ahead and get it and we'll see if any of the songs would work for the routine."

"Sounds good to me. If you want, I could come to your house this weekend and we can listen to it and see what we think."

"Um, I'm not sure. We may have plans. You know, family stuff. I think Monday will be soon enough."

"Yeah, okay. Monday's fine. Hey, I know. Maybe if we get our pyramid right at the game tonight, Mrs. Cooper will let you and I work on the routine during practice next week."

"Maybe." Angelina looked at her watch. "Speaking of the game, we'd better get back."

"Are you sure you don't want me to buy it? I mean," her eyes dropped to Angelina's shoes, "if you don't even have enough money to buy a decent pair of..."

"I've got it. Hold on to your money. Maybe you can use it to do something about your hair."

Chapter 7

Angelina woke to the sound of muffled voices coming from the living room. She rolled over and looked at her clock. *You have to be kidding. What could possibly justify anyone talking at six o'clock on a Saturday morning?* She covered her head with pillows and willed whoever it was to go away—or at the very least, to be quiet so she could go back to sleep. No such luck. If anything, they were getting louder. *Wait a minute… was that Sam's voice?* No one had told her Sam was coming home.

She jumped up and ran down the stairs. "Sam!" She threw her arms around him and practically knocked him down. "I didn't know you were coming home."

"Whoa." He gripped the stair rail for support. "Taking up wrestling now, or what?"

She punched him in the arm. "Why didn't you tell me you were coming home?"

"I wanted it to be a surprise."

"I'm sorry if we woke you, Angel." Patty rounded the corner from the kitchen.

"Are you kidding? You should've gotten me up as soon as he got here." She hugged him again. "So, what brings you home? And why didn't anyone tell me you were coming?"

Sam glanced at their mom. "I already told you, I wanted it to be a surprise." Sam's brown eyes flickered again.

What's going on? With a sinking feeling, she looked from one to the other. "Is everything okay?"

"Sure, honey." Patty wrapped her apron around her waist and fiddled with the ties. "You two go ahead and visit for a while.

I'm going to go make us all a big breakfast. Ken, would you come and help me, please?"

Angelina hadn't even noticed her dad sitting in the corner of the room. When he got up, it looked more as if he was heading to the gallows instead of the kitchen.

When both of their parents had left the room, Angelina looked at Sam. "Okay, what's really going on?"

"Nothing." He held his hands up as if he were being arrested. "Can't a poor, starving college boy come home for a little TLC once in a while?"

She pulled his arms down to his sides. She knew she'd eventually figure out why he was home. "Of course, you can."

Sam directed her to the two oversized, wing-backed chairs in front of the bay window. This had been their spot for as long as she could remember. "So… how long are you home for?"

"Just the weekend." He shifted in the chair.

She narrowed her eyes at him. "Uh-huh. So you expect me to believe that nothing's wrong and yet you drove over 150 miles to come home for the weekend?"

He smiled. "Okay, can you keep a secret?"

"Depends. What's the secret?"

He leaned in close. "I'm hungry."

"What?"

"That's right, I'm hungry." He settled his broad shoulders back into the chair. "I didn't think it was possible to get sick of cheeseburgers and pizza, but it's true. I need food. Real food." He lowered his voice. "Besides, all my clothes are dirty."

"Oh, whatever."

His thick brows furrowed in mock seriousness. "You'll see for yourself, one day. College life isn't all it's cracked up to be. Eating out for every meal, having to do my own laundry, and don't even get me started on my roommate."

"And what's wrong with your roommate?"

He ran his fingers through his short, curly hair. "For starters, he keeps a bag of burritos in the bathroom."

"Oh, he does not!"

"Yes, he does."

"No way! Are you serious?"

"Completely serious. And he never sleeps. I mean, like, ever."

"Sam, I'm sorry. I thought you were enjoying college."

He shrugged.

"So what are you going to do? Are you going to switch to a closer school so you can move back home?"

"You wish!" He grinned, showing a row of perfect white teeth. "And give up my freedom? I don't think so."

"So, it's not all bad, then?"

"No, not all of it. For the most part, I really do like being out on my own. But that burrito guy has got to go."

"Sam, that's so gross." She scrunched her forehead. "Why would he keep burritos in the bathroom?"

"Don't know." He shuddered. "Don't even want to know."

"Shouldn't they be kept in the refrigerator or something?"

"One would think. But no, he keeps them in the bathroom right next to the toilet. I don't know. The guy's weird."

They both sat in silence, contemplating his roommate.

Sam pulled the lace curtain to the side and looked out the window. "Now, on to a more pleasant subject, after I get some food, why don't we go to the park and walk the track?" He dropped the curtain and it drifted back into place. "I could use the exercise and the fresh air." He heaved a dramatic sigh and hung his head. "You know, being cooped up all the time… studying."

She laughed and scooted all the way back in the oversized chair. "Yeah, whatever." She let her feet swing back and forth. "I would be surprised if you've even opened a book this semester."

"Then be surprised." He feigned a weary look. "You have no idea, little sister. College is hard. You'd better enjoy what's left of your high school years."

"Okay, old wise one, so now I guess you're going to tell me these are the best years of my life."

"Not a chance." He pummeled the air with his fist. "College rocks!"

Ken poked his head in the doorway. "Time to eat."

Sam literally ran to the table. Angelina watched in amazement as he ate—if it could actually be called eating. It was more like watching a garbage disposal work overtime. Biscuits and gravy—gone. Fried potatoes—gone. Bacon and eggs—gone. Maybe he really *had* come home to eat.

Sam wiped his mouth with a napkin and leaned back in the chair. "Mom, that was great!"

Patty looked at the empty platters. "Did you get enough?"

"Enough?" Ken threw a napkin across the table at Sam. "I'd say he had plenty! I had to keep ducking so I wouldn't get caught in the crossfire."

"Well, he did say he was hungry." Patty picked up a platter. "Want me to make you something else, Sam?"

He patted his stomach. "I couldn't eat another bite."

"I should hope not." Ken looked at Patty. "You should be asking me and Angel if we got enough. I was downright scared to go for seconds."

Patty smiled and rubbed the back of his hand. "You'll be fine, dear. How about you, Angel? Did you get enough to eat?"

Laughing at the expression on her dad's face, she said, "I'm fine."

"Sure, don't worry about me. I can remember a time when you cared if I had enough. But not anymore. Now it's all about the kids."

Sam stretched his arms high above his head and yawned. "Angel, if we're going to take that walk, we'd better get to it before I decide to trade the exercise and fresh air for a comfortable bed."

"Oh no, you don't." She got up from the table. "If you can stay up all night for burrito guy, you can stay up for me."

"Mom, you need any help?" Sam pushed his chair in.

"Thank you, dear, but no. You two run along. Your dad will help."

"Who said?" Ken groaned, already picking up the plates.

Sam used his shoulder to push Angelina off the sidewalk as they strolled to the park. She pushed him back. "Why did you do that?" She laughed.

"Because you looked like you were a million miles away."

"I was thinking how good it is to have you home. I didn't realize how much I'd missed you."

"Oh, gee. Thanks." He pushed her again. "So, what are you saying? Out of sight, out of mind? Am I that easy to forget?"

"You know better. I've just been busy. But now that you're here, I intend to spend every minute with you." She grabbed his arm and swung it back and forth. "It'll be just like when we were kids. I'll be your shadow. I'm not going to let you out of my sight."

"As long as my shadow doesn't mind me taking a nap later, we're good. And food. Let's not forget about the food." Pulling his arm back, he tapped the side of his head. "I wonder what Mom's making for lunch?"

"Lunch?" She pushed him again. "You can't be serious! Is that all you think about?"

"Yeah, pretty much."

The conversation ended when Sam's feet hit the track. He set the pace a little quicker than what she would've done if she had been alone. After counting off two miles, she fell into a park bench, panting. "Okay, I give up. You win."

"Was there ever any doubt?"

"Well, since you've been living on cheeseburgers and pizza, I thought maybe..."

"Think again, little sister." He flipped the sweat from his forehead. "Want to go again?"

"No, you definitely win." She pulled him down on the bench beside her.

They watched the ducks float across the lake, their orange feet paddling through the clear water. Angelina's thoughts drifted until Sam spoke. "So… Mom told me about that little kid you babysit getting hurt. How's he doing?"

She picked up a stick that was lying beside the bench and twirled it in her fingers. "I've only made it to his house once since he came home from the hospital, but he's doing okay. He's still pumped about getting to ride in an ambulance." She laughed. "I guess that's the biggest thing that's ever happened to him."

"I can see that. I bet it was fun for the little guy." Sam picked up his own stick and used it to dig the gravel out of the tread of his shoes. "So, what happened to him, anyway?"

"Tommy and his mom were out in the yard waiting for me to come by after school." Angelina flapped her hands in an attempt to get rid of a duck that had waddled up beside her. "Anyway, I guess Sarah heard the phone ring and ran in to answer it. But, apparently, he got tired of waiting and went to the park. He slipped and hit his head on a rock, or something, and—"

"I get it. That's why you feel so guilty. He was waiting on you when he got hurt, so you feel like it's your fault."

"I didn't until just now, but thanks for that."

Confusion flashed through his eyes. "Mom said something

about you feeling like it was your fault. I assumed you thought it was your fault because he was waiting on you."

She threw her stick down. "So, I guess that's the real reason you came home." She pulled her knees up to her chest and stared straight ahead. "Mom called you and told you I was going off the deep end again." She sighed. "Sam, I'm not crazy."

He put his hand on her chin and turned her face toward him. "Angel, look at me. No one ever said you were crazy. Mom's worried about you and so is Dad. Me? I'm just trying to figure out what's going on."

"There's nothing going on. I'm fine." She turned her head from him as a tear rolled down her cheek.

"Obviously, you're not fine. What are the tears about?"

"I just get so frustrated." She wiped an angry hand across her cheek. "I always feel like I'm being watched."

He shifted around uncomfortably on the bench. "What do you mean, Angel? Who do you think is watching you?"

"You see? That's exactly what I'm talking about! I said I felt like I was being watched so you automatically assume I think someone is lurking around every corner and spying on me!"

Sam rubbed the stubble on his face. "In all fairness, that's what you said. What am I supposed to think?"

"You're supposed to give me the benefit of doubt like you would anyone else. When I said I felt as though I was being watched, I was talking about Mom and Dad." She slid her feet around in the gravel beneath the bench. "Don't you see? Everything I do is analyzed. When you look at anyone that closely, they're bound to look a little quirky, at times."

"I guess you're right." He squeezed her leg. "I, for one, apologize." He let his eyes follow the ducks that were swimming out on the water. "You have to admit, though, there are a few things that," he turned and looked at her, "well… are a little past quirky."

"Like what? Lay it on the table, Sam. What have they told you about me?"

"I didn't want the conversation to go like this." He slowly let out the breath he had been holding. "They're worried, Angel, and I guess I am, too."

Her eyes locked onto his, challenging him to look away. "Let's just get this out in the open. What exactly is everyone so worried about?"

"For starters, why do you feel guilty about what happened to Tommy?"

"I don't. Not really. It's just... sometimes I have these... dreams." She looked away. "I can never remember them completely, but they're usually like a warning of some kind. When I have one, I know something bad is going to happen." She met his eyes again. "I had a dream the night before Tommy got hurt."

"You mean like a premonition or something? Do you... do you think you're psychic?"

"No, Sam. That would mean I was crazy, wouldn't it?"

"Not necessarily. I've heard about people that somehow know things. My roommate watches all this weird stuff on TV and some of it's pretty interesting, once you get past the weirdness of it all." His eyes sparkled. "Some police stations even use psychics to help solve crimes. Is that what we're talking about here?"

"No, it's not like that. I couldn't help anyone solve anything because I can't even remember all of my dreams."

"Angel, you might really have a gift."

You could say that, but it's not what you think.

"I'm telling you, they have shows about this sort of thing. My roommate said his mom is psychic. Last week, he hurt his arm in practice and she called to check on him because 'she knew something was wrong.' It was weird."

"As interesting as Mr. Burrito and his mother are, it's not like that. I'm not psychic. It's just that... well... I can see— Do we really have to talk about this? Why can't I just enjoy having my big brother home? I really have missed you."

"Sure, Angel. We don't have to talk about it if you don't want to. Just don't give up on this psychic thing." He playfully punched her on the shoulder. "It really could come in handy. Maybe you could help me out when it comes time for finals. You know, you could tell me what's going to be on the test."

"Sure, I'll get right on that, as long as you report back to Mom and Dad that I'm not crazy."

"Will do. But speaking of Mom and Dad, I have to ask you about one more thing." He paused, choosing his words carefully. "Promise you won't get mad?"

"What?"

"You have to promise."

"Fine." She crossed her heart. "I promise."

"Mom seems to think you're talking to Josie again."

She closed her eyes, gathering her courage. "I am." She met his stare. "But that still doesn't make me crazy."

"But why? I thought that was all behind you."

"It was." She exhaled. "Tell you what—I'm going to respect you enough to not lie to you, but I'm asking that you respect me enough to give me a little time to figure some things out."

"Okay, but I'm not sure I'm following you. What are you trying to figure out, and what does it have to do with Josie?"

"All I can really say right now is there are some things going on. I can't explain them because I don't understand them myself. I can tell you I'm not crazy and, eventually, I'll get this all figured out. When I do, you'll be the first one I tell. Just trust me and give me a little more time."

"I can do that—if you're sure you're okay—but what am I supposed to tell Mom?"

"I'm sure you can think of something. After all, you're in college now."

"Yeah, but..."

"You'll come up with something." She stood up and rubbed her lower back. "Come on. Let's go home. I'm cramping."

"Oh. Uh… um, okay." Crimson crept down his cheeks onto his neck.

Cool! Thanks, Mom.

Chapter 8

"Angel! Hey, Angel! Wait up!"

Angelina turned as Kathy sprinted across the field toward her. She could hear her ragged breaths as she ran up.

"You could've at least met me half way." She bent over as her gasps began to slow.

"I was on my way to practice. What's up?"

"Don't you remember? I talked to Mrs. Cooper about her letting us go to the gym and start working on the routine."

"Oh, yeah. I forgot." She shrugged. "What'd she say?"

"She said we could." Slinging her hair over her shoulder, she frowned. "And what do you mean you forgot? Does that mean you also forgot the CD?"

Angelina patted her backpack. "It's still in here. My brother came home for the weekend so I didn't even have time to listen to it."

"Oh. Well, good. If you haven't listened to it yet, that saves me the trouble of talking you out of using something lame." She waited for a response. Not getting one, she continued. "Just in case we don't like anything on the Kelly Clarkson CD, I borrowed one of Rob Thomas with 'Lonely No More.' I still think that would make an awesome routine. But *I* haven't decided which one *I* want to use yet."

Soap bubbles. Angelina pulled the door to the gym open. The smell of old popcorn and dirty socks drifted through the air. "I'm sure *we'll* find something." She handed Kathy her backpack. "I need to run to the bathroom. Get the CD out of the front pocket and I'll be right back."

Kathy took the backpack. Breathing in the smell of the gym, she pinched her nose. "That smell is so gross."

Angelina returned from the bathroom and saw Kathy sitting in the middle of the basketball court with the entire contents of her backpack dumped on the floor. "Hey! What are you doing? I told you it was in the front pocket."

"Very funny." Kathy waved a CD in the air. "Where's the one with Kelly Clarkson?"

"You might try looking in your hand."

"Nooo. This is Michael Jackson." She tossed it into the pile. "I thought we agreed to get Kelly Clarkson."

"We did." Angelina picked up the CD. "How did this get in there?"

"Like I said, very funny." She rolled her eyes. "You know, Ang, I had hoped we could work together on this project. But if you're going to pull stunts like this, then..."

"I didn't pull anything. You were with me when I bought it. I have no idea how the Michael Jackson one ended up in my backpack." She picked up a piece of paper from the pile. "Look, here's the receipt." She thrust it at Kathy. "It says Kelly Clarkson."

Not even looking at the receipt, she crumpled it up and tossed it in the air. "Yeah, like you didn't go back to the music store and exchange it. I told you no then, and I'm telling you no now. It's lame."

Angelina picked up the receipt and tried to smooth it out. "I haven't been back to the music store since I was there with you."

"Whatever. I guess the CD just changed itself, then."

"Listen, I don't want to fight with you." Angelina stuffed her things back into her backpack. "I honestly don't know how I ended up with that CD. Let's just listen to the one you brought."

"Fine." Kathy grabbed her backpack and yanked it out. "How did you... When did you...?"

"What?"

"Don't play dumb with me! What'd you do with Rob Thomas?" Kathy shook another Michael Jackson cover in her face.

"What?" Angelina stared at the unopened case. "I—I— Wait a minute. I didn't even know you had brought a CD until just a few minutes ago." She burst out laughing. "Good one! You really had me going for a minute."

"What? I don't know what you're talking about. What do you mean I had you going?"

"You're the one who 'found' both of the CDs, but somehow it was me who exchanged them? Obviously, you agreed with me that a Michael Jackson song might have potential. But since it was my idea, you—"

"I did not! You know what? Just forget it. Let's listen to the stupid thing and then you'll see—it'll never work."

"Whatever you say, Kathy. Go ahead and play it."

"Fine." Kathy grabbed the case and stomped over to the stereo. "But I need that one of Rob Thomas back. It wasn't mine."

"Uh, huh." Angelina snapped a rubber band over her wrist and gathered her hair into a ponytail.

With Michael Jackson's voice blaring, both girls sat on the bleachers, trying to figure out exactly what it was the other one was trying to pull.

When "Thriller" came on, Angelina closed her eyes and swayed to the music. *This is it.* She'd seen this somewhere before. She hadn't only seen it; she knew it. When the song stopped, she got up and set the stereo to play it again. She walked out onto the gym floor.

"Oh, come on, Angel. You can't be serious."

Angelina closed her eyes and let the music fill her body.

"Angel, this is stupid."

The lights flickered, and then went out, leaving the gym shrouded in darkness. The center light—the one directly above Angelina—popped and flared back to life.

Kathy screamed. "What was that?" She fell silent as she squinted against the dim lighting. Her jaw dropped as Angelina landed a perfect handspring. Every movement was precise—flawless.

The song ended and Angelina turned. "Play it again."

Kathy was walking toward the stereo when the rest of the lights popped back on and the music started again. The hairs on her arms stood on end as she felt a cold trickle creep down her spine. She rubbed her arms and watched Angelina execute the routine again.

With the song's end, Mrs. Cooper yelled, "Bravo!" as she clapped from the doorway. "Wow! I thought you were just picking out the music. I had no idea you'd already started working on the routine." She walked the rest of the way in, still clapping. "I must admit, I was worried about the two of you working together, but this…" She smiled. "This is wonderful!"

Kathy met her out on the floor. "You really liked it?"

"Liked it? I loved it!" Her eyes sparkled. "You girls have far exceeded my expectations."

"So, you think doing something retro is okay, then? I mean, it *is* kind of overdone. Don't you think?"

"Typically, I'd agree with you. But not this time. This is perfect."

Angelina had yet to move. She stood in the exact spot where the routine had ended.

"I agree." Kathy glanced over at Angelina. "I mean, we still have to work out a few kinks, but I think..."

"Oh, no you don't." Mrs. Cooper shook her head. "I want to see it performed exactly how I just saw it. No changes." She walked over to where Angelina stood and squeezed her shoulder. "I'm so proud of both of you."

Angelina blinked a couple of times and smiled.

Mrs. Cooper continued. "We're weeks ahead of schedule now. All you have left is to teach it to the others. I'll turn them over to you tomorrow."

"Um, tomorrow?" Kathy twirled her hair around her fingers. "I'm not sure that I'm... I mean, that *we'll* be ready by tomorrow." She cleared her throat. "We'll probably need a few more days to—"

"After what I've just seen, I have complete confidence in the two of you." She patted both of them on the back. "Again, good job, girls."

They watched her leave then Kathy turned and met Angelina's eyes. "I... uh... hope I didn't make you mad." She looked down at her feet. "If it seemed as though I was trying to take partial credit for the routine, it's just... well... we were supposed to work on it together and I... didn't want you to get into trouble."

"No, I'm—I'm not mad." It was hard to focus. She couldn't get her words to come out right. She felt dizzy. "I need to sit down. I—I feel kind of funny." She sank to the floor.

"Ang? Ang! Are you okay?" Kathy knelt down beside her. "Do I need to go get somebody? Are you going to be all right?"

Angelina didn't answer. Her eyes rolled back in her head and her body went limp.

"Help!" Kathy yelled. "Someone help us!"

Angelina's hand gripped Kathy's arm. "Stop it! Stop yelling. She's fine."

Kathy jerked her arm back and jumped up. "What do you mean *she's* fine? Angel, what's wrong with you?"

Angelina's eyes fluttered opened. She rolled over on her side and propped herself up on her elbow. "What'd you think of the routine?"

Kathy backed away. "You sound kind of funny. What's going on?"

Angelina sat up and looked around the gym. "Why am I on the floor?" She stood. "Don't tell me I passed out again."

"Again? You mean this has happened before?"

"No. I mean, I did pass out awhile back, but—but that was different." She met Kathy's stare. "Why are you looking at me so funny?"

"You really scared me, Angel." She shifted on her feet. "If you've been passing out, maybe you should go get checked out."

"I'm fine." Angelina pulled a bottle of water from her bag and downed it.

"Are you sure you're okay?"

"Yeah." She massaged her temples. "I'm getting a really bad headache, though. I think I'm going to go home and rest for a while."

"Um, Angel?" She picked at her cuticles. "I don't mean to be insensitive or anything, but if you're really okay, you need to teach me that routine."

"I was just goofing around. We'll get serious and come up with something tomorrow."

"Are you kidding? Don't you remember what Mrs. Cooper said? She wants us to do the routine exactly how you just did it."

"Mrs. Cooper? Uh, oh, yeah." She rubbed her head. "I don't feel right using that routine. I must have seen it somewhere before."

"You should have thought of that before you showed off to Mrs. Cooper." Kathy tapped her foot. "It doesn't matter, anyway. What *does* matter is that I'm supposed to help you teach it to the rest of the team tomorrow and I need to learn it myself first."

"I see your point." Angelina took a deep breath. "Just give me a few minutes."

"Okay. I need to warm up anyway." Kathy put her arms in the air and bent from side to side, stretching her torso. "I have to say, you surprised me with that routine. It really is good. I just wish you would have told me about it instead of playing these head games with me."

"I haven't been playing head games with you." Angelina joined in the stretching.

"Oh, come on, Ang. Cut the crap. You already had the routine and you switched those CDs and you know it."

"No, I didn't." Hands on her hips, she lunged forward, stretching her leg muscles. "And I haven't been working on it. I told you, I was just goofing around."

"If I can be a big enough person to admit I was wrong about the song choice, then surely you can admit you've had all of this planned for a while."

"You can think whatever you want, but—"

The sounds of "Thriller" boomed through the gym. Kathy jumped. "How are you making it do that?"

Angelina didn't answer. She was already lost in the routine.

Kathy tried to follow. "Wait! Slow down! I can't keep up."

Determination flashed in Angelina's eyes. "You will keep up!"

"Wait a minute. Is this right?"

"I'll tell you when you're doing it right. You need to spin faster! I said faster!"

Each time the song ended, it would start again, and so would Angelina's tirades. The song played over and over until they were both drenched in sweat. When the music finally stopped, Kathy prepared herself for another outburst. Instead, Angelina grabbed a towel and mopped her forehead. "Now that's what I call a practice!" She smiled. "What'd you think?"

"Good. I, uh… I thought it was good." Kathy was barely able to catch her breath.

Angelina threw her a towel.

Still gulping for air, she used the towel to fan her face. "Can I make a suggestion?"

"No! We're not changing anything." Angelina clenched her teeth, the muscles in her jaw bulging with the effort. "We will do it just like I showed you."

"Calm down. I'm not trying to change the routine." Kathy took a few steps back. "Mrs. Cooper already made that perfectly clear."

"Okay. Then what?"

"I would just like to suggest that when we teach the other girls, that you… well… you chill out a little bit. You were like some kind of a crazed drill sergeant. You almost killed me."

Wringing sweat from her hair, she nodded. "Sorry about that." She got another bottle of water and sat down on the bleachers. "When we teach the others, we'll have more than a couple of hours."

Getting her own water, Kathy twisted the top off. "True."

"Do you think you have it down now?"

She swallowed. "For the most part."

"You want to go through it again?"

"No! Are you serious? My legs feel like rubber. I'm not sure how I'm going to make it to my car as it is."

"I'm really sorry I pushed you so hard. I guess I got a little carried away. I just… I want it to be right. No hard feelings?"

"We're good." Kathy gathered up her things. "Hey, Ang. How did this get in here?"

"What?"

Kathy held up the Rob Thomas CD. "This. It was lying right here and I know it wasn't there earlier."

Angelina looked at the artist's face smiling back at her. "I have no idea."

"I know you couldn't have done it. I know I didn't do it." Kathy looked around the gym. "So who did?" The lights flickered, and a chill ran down her arms. "Something very weird's going on around here. You know what? I'm too tired to try to figure it out. I'm sure it somehow makes sense, but who cares. I'm going home."

Chapter 9

Angelina staggered into the house after practice. Kathy's legs weren't the only ones that felt like rubber. She tossed her backpack on the floor. "Hello? Anyone home?" The house was quiet. She went into the kitchen and saw a note hanging on the refrigerator.

Angel,
Your dad and I are going out for dinner. Not sure what time we'll be home. There's plenty of stuff you can heat up if you're hungry.
Love, Mom

If I'm hungry? After the practice I had, I could put Sam to shame. She stuffed a cookie in her mouth and rummaged through the freezer. Looking at her choices, she tossed a bag of frozen chicken breasts aside. *Too much work and takes way too long.* Finding a frozen pizza, she grabbed it. *Ah, that's it. I love nights alone.* She tore open the box and put the pizza in the microwave. *After this, it's off to a long, hot bubble bath then straight to bed.*

Josie popped up in front of her. "I've been meaning to ask you, what exactly is that contraption?"

"What contraption?" She pointed to the microwave. "You mean this?"

"Yes, that." Josie bent down and peered into the door of the microwave. "Whew! That can make a body dizzy." She held on to the counter and watched the plate spin. "What is it?"

"It's a microwave."

"What's it doing?"

"It's cooking."

"Cooking?" She stood and looked at Angelina. "Where's the coal? Or does it use gas? I always worried that having a gas line might blow up the house—" The microwave dinged and Josie jumped back, eyes wide. "What's wrong with it?"

"Nothing's wrong with it." Angelina laughed. "That just means it's done." She took her pizza out of the microwave and walked over to the table.

"Done? Already?"

"Yep. And it's a good thing, too." She tore off a piece, blew on it, and stuffed it in her mouth. "I'm starving. I might have to make another one."

"Another one?" Josie's eyes widened. "How long does it take to make those things?"

She swallowed. "You watched me cook it."

"No." She pointed at the microwave. "I watched that thing cook it. But I never even saw you get it ready."

"I didn't." She took another bite. "It's a frozen pizza. You buy it like this and pop it in the microwave." She wiped her hands on a napkin. "You can put it in the oven, but that takes too long. When you do it this way, it's ready in four minutes."

"Four minutes? Well, land sakes! What's this world coming to? I could've never imagined having dinner on the table in four minutes." Josie clicked her tongue, showing her dissatisfaction. "No wonder you all sleep so much around here. There's nothing left for you to do with all of these fancy, new-fangled contraptions."

"I don't know about that. I usually find plenty of stuff to do. There's school, and homework, and practice, and…"

"Practice." Josie slapped her hand on the table. "I almost forgot. How's the routine coming along?"

"I don't know." Angelina leaned back in her chair.

"Don't worry about it, honey. I'm sure you'll come up with something."

"Well, that's just it—I already have."

"Already?" Her eyes danced. "That was about as quick as using one of those microwaves. How did you come up with it so fast?"

Angelina rubbed the back of her neck. "That's the thing—I really don't know. But I think it has something to do with my dream."

"Your dream? What do you mean?"

"Remember the other day I told you I had a dream and I thought we'd gotten a new cheerleading coach?"

"Yes."

"Well, I keep having that same dream. I'm doing a routine or something, and this coach keeps yelling at me the whole time and calling me Patty and... I don't know. It's weird. But today, I heard this song and this routine just came to me."

Josie rubbed her chin. "Hmm. Interesting."

"Why do you say that? Do you think this could be like my other dreams? Like maybe a ghost is trying to tell me something?"

"No. Most of the time, when a spirit tries to contact you through a dream, it's of the utmost importance."

"Like you did with Tommy? When you were trying to warn me?"

"Precisely. But still... you say in your dream someone keeps calling you Patty?"

That's what I don't get. I don't even know a Patty, except for Mom."

"Hmm."

"And then when Kathy and I were trying to figure out what song to use, we couldn't find the CDs we'd brought. Somehow, both of our CDs had been replaced with these Michael Jackson CDs. Then, to top it off, the stereo kept playing this one song over and over. You know, the same song I knew the routine to."

Josie sighed. "I don't know anything about CDs and those music boxes, but it does sound a bit strange. Are you certain you've never seen this routine before?"

"I'm not sure about anything right now, but I don't remember ever seeing it."

"You probably did, at some point. The mind can do some funny things. Perhaps you've seen it and you're just replaying it in your dream."

"If that's the case, who's Patty?"

"I'll have to think on that one. Are you going to make another one of those things?" She pointed to Angelina's empty plate.

"No, I think I'm done."

Josie's eyes sparkled. "Since we're here alone, why don't we go sit in the parlor and visit like civilized human beings?"

Knowing the bubble bath she longed for had just turned into a quick shower, Angelina nodded. "Sure, but... uh... I have a question." She held up a finger. "Where's the parlor?"

Josie arched her wrinkled brow. "I think you modern folk refer to it as the living room."

"Oh, in that case," Angelina bowed and swept her hand out in front of her, "right this way, Madame."

Josie took a seat on the edge of the couch cushion. Sitting up prim and proper, she folded her hands in her lap. "Now, if we just had someone to serve us tea…"

Angelina plopped down beside her. "I'm thinking that's not gonna happen."

Mustering all the refinement she could, Josie looked down her nose. "I would say not." She sniffed.

Angelina laughed and laid her head back on the cushion. "Even though I didn't have to come up with the routine, it sure wore me out trying to do it." She yawned.

Josie leaned back beside her. "Will Jason be there when you do the routine?"

She rolled her head toward Josie. "Jason? I guess. But why would you bring him up?"

"Isn't that what women do when they get together? Don't they still talk about the men in their lives?"

"Yeah. I mean, I guess. But he's not really in my life anymore."

"Well… you do still like him. Don't you?"

"Yes. Well, sometimes." She traced the flower pattern on the couch with her finger. "Maybe. But he is such a… such a…"

"A boy?"

"Exactly." She hit the arm of the couch. "A boy. And they can be so frustrating."

Josie's laughter rang throughout the "parlor."

"What? What's so funny?"

"It's nice to see not everything has changed. Even with the microwaves, telephones, and televisions, boys are still boys and girls are still trying to figure them out."

"But why, Josie? Why do they have to be so… so boyish?"

"Now if I had the answer to that one, I'd really be the cat's meow, wouldn't I?" Josie shrugged. "You know, I think I could probably hang around this old world for another hundred years and still not have them figured out."

"A hundred? Josie, how long *have* you been here?"

"Oh, honey. Someone in my situation," she vanished then reappeared to make her point, "doesn't pay much attention to time. It has no meaning, anymore. I can tell you I've seen a whole lot of changes, though, except with boys. From way back in my time, all the way to this one, they've basically stayed the same."

"Somehow, that doesn't surprise me." Angelina leaned forward and ran her finger around the edge of the Victorian lampshade, watching the little crystals sway into each other. "Since we're talking about boys, can I ask you a question?"

"If it's about boys, I probably don't know the answer, but I'll try."

"Were you ever married?"

Josie bolted upright, resumed her rigid position on the edge of the cushion, and sat very still.

"Josie? Are you okay? I didn't mean to upset you."

Josie focused on the lamp and sadness filled her eyes.

"Josie, I'm sorry."

Josie gave her a weak smile. "You ask a lot more questions now than you did as a child."

"I'm sorry. You don't have to answer."

"Oh, bother." She wiped at her eyes. "I'm just being a silly old woman. It was a simple question and the answer is yes. I was married, at one time." Her spine relaxed. She let her mind drift to a place Angelina couldn't see. With a voice barely audible, she whispered, "Albert. His name was Albert." She settled back into the couch's plush cushions. "I was with him for only ten short years before he had to go."

"Go? Where did he have to go?"

"It was such a dreary old day. It would rain and then it would stop. Then it would rain some more. By the time the weather had finally cleared, the day was half gone." She put her hand over her heart and tapped her chest. "I tried to convince Albert not to go into work that day." A tear slid down her face. "I had such an awful feeling about it."

Angelina twirled her hair around her finger. "A feeling as in… your gift?"

Josie's eyes met hers. "I hadn't learned to fully trust myself, at that point." She looked down at her hands. "He thought the notion of knowing what was going to happen before it happened was just plain silly and he never paid it any mind." She sighed. "I didn't tell him how strongly I felt about it. I just told him not to go to work. I tried to convince him that he could get a fresh start the next day, but times were hard back then. He insisted he could still put in a few hours before it got too dark. The next thing

I knew, someone was a knocking on the door. As soon as I seen that man standing there with his hat in his hand, I knew. I knew my Albert was gone."

"Oh, Josie! How awful! I'm so sorry. What had happened to him?"

"Albert was a roofer. One of the best, I've been told, and he was putting the roof on one of those big, new buildings going up in town. They'd told him if he done a good job, there'd be plenty more work coming his way." She smoothed away the imaginary wrinkles in her dress. "Oh, he was a dreamer, all right. He thought it was going to be his big break. He knew he shouldn't be up there on the roof after all the rain, but he thought if he could hurry on the first job, he'd be a shoo-in for all the other jobs coming up, and that fit right into his plans of getting us a brand new house." She shook her head. "Turns out he slipped up there on that wet roof and was killed the moment he hit the ground."

Angelina tried to hug Josie. She hated the fact that her arms went right through her. She had to settle for an "I'm sorry." Dropping her arms to her side, she mumbled, "That must have been so hard on you."

"Oh, it was, indeed. But I had to continue. I had a little one that had no one to depend on but me."

"A little one?" She stopped. "Josie, you had a child?"

"Oh, yes." Her eyes gleamed. "A little boy. And like all little boys, he was a handful. But we made it, all right."

"Did you ever marry again?"

"No. In all those years, I could never imagine myself with anyone but Albert. He was my only true love. From then on, it was just me and little Johnny."

"Johnny? Was that your son's name?"

"Indeed, it was." Josie smiled and pointed to the staircase. "How he loved that staircase. I can almost see him now. He'd come sliding down the handrail with a big grin on his little face. Of course, if I got on to him, he would try to convince me he was just trying to help me dust." She laughed. "Oh, I knew I shouldn't let him do it. But he was the cutest little thing. I had a hard time telling him no."

"That staircase?" Angelina pointed. "That very one?"

Josie nodded.

Angelina imagined little Johnny barreling down the stairs and she knew that was what Josie was seeing, as well.

"Josie, you lived here? Of course! That's why you know so much about this house."

"Live here? Oh, heavens no, child. I worked here. After my Albert passed, I had to do something to make ends meet." She clicked her tongue. "Times were so different back then, especially for women. Mr. Clayton hired me to help his wife." Twirling her thumbs around each other, she continued. "Of course, I always suspected he only hired me because Albert was working on one of his buildings when he fell. I think Mr. Clayton felt guilty."

"Mr. Clayton," Angelina repeated. "That name sounds familiar."

"Well, honey, it should. He's the one who had this house built."

"Okay." She nodded. "Now it makes sense. I've heard Mom talk about the Claytons. She learned about them when she was doing research on the house. I remember her saying they were very prominent citizens of the community."

"They were, indeed."

"What were they like? Were they nice?"

"They treated me well. Of course, we were from a different class so as long as I remembered my place and kept Johnny out from under their feet, we didn't have any problems."

"Remembered your place?" Angelina's eyes flashed with anger. "What on earth is that supposed to mean?"

Josie laughed. "For such a sweet girl, you do have a quick temper. You'd do well to keep that in check."

"I'm sorry, Josie. Stuff like that just makes me so mad. I hate it when people act like they're better than others."

"It wasn't like that at all. I was very fortunate to have a job. They treated me well and even let me bring Johnny to work with me when I needed to. If it weren't for the Claytons, I don't know what I would've done. I probably would have ended up starving."

"Yeah, but still… I don't get the whole class thing."

"Times were different, Angel, but classes still exist. The lines are a little more blurry than they once were, but rest assured, they're still there."

"I know, but that still doesn't make it right."

"There are a lot of things that aren't 'right,' but we go on and do the best we can."

"Josie, how long did you work for the Claytons?"

"Well…" Josie cocked her head to the side and smiled. "I'm still here, aren't I?"

"Oh. Oh! Do you mean... are the Claytons still here?"

Josie smiled. "I think you've asked enough questions for one day."

"Okay, but…" She weighed her words carefully. "Can I ask one more, and then I promise I'll leave you alone?"

"What?"

"Do you still see Albert? You know, like… now. I mean, is he… is he…?

"No. I've not seen Albert since that fateful day."

"But why?"

"I guess Albert went on."

"Then why didn't you… go on?"

"Because I still had things to do, I guess, besides I needed to keep an eye on little Johnny."

Confusion streaked across Angelina's face. "You mean… you died when Johnny was still young."

"No. Johnny was a grown man when I passed from this world." Pride danced in her eyes. "John, as he later liked to be called."

"If he was already grown then why did you feel like you needed to stay?"

"He wasn't the only reason I chose to hang around." Josie's hand covered her heart. "He was the main reason to be sure. Just because he was grown didn't mean he no longer needed me, or I him."

"Josie is he… still here?"

"You said *one* more question." Josie wagged her crooked arthritic finger. "But you know my little Johnny as Mr. Eddelson."

Chapter 10

"Sorry. Can't talk, Mom." Angelina rushed past her and headed up the stairs. "I don't suppose you know where the hair ribbon that matches my uniform is, do you?" She called over her shoulder.

Patty laid her book on the end table. "If you'd slow down for a minute, I'd tell you I've already hand-washed the ribbon and it's in the kitchen, ready to go." She picked up her tea glass and took a sip. "But, since you don't have time to talk…"

Angelina spun around and headed back down the stairs. "Have I told you lately what a great mom you are?"

"As a matter of fact, you haven't. I've barely even seen you in the last two weeks."

"I know, Mom, and I'm sorry." She kissed her mother's cheek. "These last two weeks have been kind of crazy. I don't know why Mrs. Cooper thinks we have to perform the routine in front of a crowd so quickly. It's been really tough getting everyone ready in such a short time."

"Oh, you're going to do fine and I simply can't wait to see it." She swirled the ice around in her glass. "Since tonight's the big night, I think it would be okay if you went ahead and told me a little bit about the routine." She peered over the top of her glass. "Don't you?"

Angelina smiled. "You know I can't."

She sat her glass down with a clink. "Even just a little hint?"

"I wish I could, but Mrs. Cooper's insisting we keep it top secret until its 'unveiling'—that's what she calls it. Now, you know how she can be. I think she's gone a little overboard on this but…"

"Oh, I don't know. All this secrecy has caused quite a lot of excitement in town. I bet we'll have a bigger turnout for the game tonight than we've had in a long time. I think she's done her homework on marketing."

"Marketing?"

"Sure. She has the whole town talking about your routine. I think she's trying to rally up some support for when you all go to state. Pretty smart, if you ask me."

"I guess. It *has* been kind of fun keeping it from everyone, though." She looked at her watch. "I really do have to hurry. Did I tell you she even moved our practice into the gym and covered the windows so no one could see in?"

"Oh, how fun!" Patty's eyes sparkled. "I wonder what gave her the idea to keep it so hush-hush?"

"That I don't know. She said this was the best routine she'd ever seen and she wanted it to be a big surprise for everyone."

"Well, it will be that, I'm sure. Not even Marjorie has a clue what you girls are up to." She arched her brows. "Of course, if you were to give me some little tidbit of information—like maybe what song you are using—then, for once in my life, I would know something Marjorie didn't."

Angelina smiled. "Um, no. Nice try, though." She started back up the stairs. "I gotta hurry, but I'll see you at the game."

As soon as the door shut, Patty left her spot on the couch and hurried into the kitchen. Focused on making her "famous" punch recipe, she didn't hear Ken until he poked his head in the door. "Pssst. Is she gone?"

"Barely. Now get in here in case she comes back for something."

He nudged the door the rest of the way open with his foot and made his way into the kitchen. "Is this what you ordered?"

She walked over to the table as he put the cake down. "Oh, it's perfect! She's going to love it."

"Well, I hope so." He stood back with his hands in his front pockets, jingling his change. "Do you know how much that silly thing cost?"

"It'll all be worth it to see the look on her face when she comes in." Patty pulled out a sack that she'd hidden in the pantry. "Here, help me put up these streamers."

"Streamers?" He laughed. "We might be going a little far with all of this, don't you think?"

"Nonsense!" She pulled out several rolls of streamers with matching plates, cups, and a tablecloth. "Angelina has worked very hard on this routine and I wouldn't be a bit surprised if they took first place when they go to state."

"First place?" He watched the decorations pile up on the table. "You haven't even seen the routine yet."

"I don't have to. I know my daughter. If she says it's good, then it's going to be good."

"And you're not the slightest bit biased, are you?" He put his arms around her.

"No." She smiled. "Not in the least."

He shuffled through the pile to see what else she had planned. "So, Angelina's doing okay, right? I mean, no more talking to herself or Josie or whoever?"

"Not even one time since Sam was here." With a bump of her hip, she scooted him out of the way. "Everything's back to normal."

"Speaking of Sam, when's he supposed to get in?"

"Shouldn't be too much longer." She took the colorful plastic tablecloth out of its package. "I hope Angelina doesn't spot him in the stands. I want all of this to be a big surprise, including Sam being here."

"Everything's going to go according to plan. Our only concern, at this point, is going to be finding good seats at the game." He tapped his watch. "Don't you think we should get going?"

"Yikes! I didn't realize it was getting so late." She untied her apron. "But what about the decorating?"

"That can wait." With his hand on her back, he guided her to the door. "We'll make some excuse to leave the game early and we'll get back and have everything done before Angel gets here."

"Okay, but…" She turned back to the kitchen. "We need to get the streamers and the balloons and the…"

"After we get back." He nudged her towards the door.

"Look at this." Daphne held out her hands. "I'm shaking. I don't think I've ever been this nervous in my entire life!"

"You can't get nervous now." Angelina bounced up and down on her toes.

"Want to bet? Have you looked up into the stands? There are hundreds of people here." She tugged at the neckline of her uniform. "I mean, literally hundreds!" She walked around in circles. "Oh, boy." She put her hand to her throat. "Oh boy, oh boy, oh boy. I think I'm going to be sick."

"Oh, no, you don't." Angelina pulled her back in line. "You're going to be fine. And you're going to do great." She swallowed. "We're all going to do great."

"Okay," Daphne muttered, still walking in circles. "You can keep telling yourself that, if it makes you feel better."

"It's true." Angelina put her hand on Daphne's shoulder and turned her around. "All we've done is eat, sleep, and dream this routine for the last two weeks. We know it. Now we just have to get out there and show them what we've got."

"You're right." She stared. "There's just one little problem."

"And what's that?"

With her hand back to her throat, she gulped. "We've only got five minutes until halftime!"

Mrs. Cooper came around the corner of the field house. "Okay, girls. This is it." She walked up and down the line of cheerleaders. "It's almost show time." She took a deep breath. "When the lights go out, you'll have forty-five seconds to get into position. The lights will come back on and the music will start."

Daphne tilted her head toward Angelina "How about now?"

"What?"

"Can I get nervous now?"

The horn blared out across the field, signifying the second quarter was over. Angelina grabbed Daphne's shoulder. "Almost, but wait until after the routine is over."

Coach Hollis—the acting announcer for the night—came over the speaker. "Ladies and gentlemen, may I have your attention, please?" A hush filled the stands. "You're in for a special treat tonight." His voice boomed across the field. "For your pleasure," he paused dramatically as the crowd snickered at his theatrics, "our cheerleaders," he paused again, "are going to perform for you the routine they plan to take to the…" He took a deep breath. "Upcoming. State. Competition!"

A crackling noise came over the microphone followed by a

high-pitched squeal. The crowd moaned and covered their ears. Moving back from the microphone, he regained control. "I am supposed to let you know the lights are about to go off. It's all part of the show, so don't be alarmed." Back to using his booming voice, he bellowed, "Sit back and enjoy!"

The stadium went black. Hidden under the dark sky, the team ran onto the field and took their places. With the lights still off, the intro to the song started. After the sound of the creaking door, a single light lit the field, casting the cheerleaders in shadow. Through the sound of the footsteps and howling, each girl stood anchored to the ground.

In a single burst, the tempo picked up and the rest of the lights flashed back on. Angelina didn't have to see the team to know each girl was executing her part to perfection—she could feel it. They were in-sync. Every flip, every cartwheel, every back handspring was perfect.

When the song neared its end and the creepy voice came across the speakers, the team circled around Daphne. Falling as if she'd fainted into their arms, they handed her up as they formed a three-layer pyramid. Reaching the top, she stood with her arms high above her head and they tossed her into the air. As the sinister laugh echoed across the field, Daphne completed two perfect flips as the pyramid skillfully collapsed. She landed in the outstretched arms of her teammates, precisely when the door slammed, ending the song. The crowd exploded into a thunderous round of applause.

The team stood under the lights of the football field and watched the crowd. "We did it! We did it!" Mrs. Cooper motioned them in as the crowd rushed to the sidelines. Patty ran to Angelina and wrapped her arms around her. "Oh, sweetie! That was magnificent! You were wonderful!" She looked over the team. "You were all just wonderful."

"Thanks, Mom." Angelina bounced up and down with nervous energy. She stopped. "Mom, have you been crying? What's wrong?"

Patty dabbed her eyes. "Nothing's wrong. Everything's so… so right." She hugged her again. "It's a mother's right to get a little weepy every now and then."

"Mom, don't cry." She wiped her own tears. "Now look what you've done."

Ken hugged Patty and Angelina to him. "Women… they cry when they're happy… they cry when they're sad. Sometimes I think they just cry to cry."

Patty laughed. "Oh, my goodness. I must look a mess. We're going to have to leave, but I want you to come home right after the game, okay?"

"Okay, but aren't you going to stay for the rest of the game?"

"Looking like this? I don't think so. We'll see you at home—and hurry up."

"I'll hurry. I love you guys," she called out as they walked away.

Now that it was over, the stresses of the last few weeks came crashing down around her. With more hugs and congratulatory pats on the back, she knew she needed a few minutes to herself. She walked around behind the bleachers and leaned back against an old oak tree. *We did it. We really did it.*

She felt someone staring at her. The hair on the back of her neck stood up as she heard the voice from her dreams say, "Now, you did it right."

"Excuse me?" She turned to see a cheerleader she'd never seen before. A cold chill ran through her as she watched her disappear into… nothingness. It all happened so quickly, she wondered if maybe she'd just imagined the whole thing, right down to the name—Shelly—embroidered on the girl's uniform.

Ken walked Patty to the car and opened her door. By the time he came around the car and got in, Patty had her face buried in her hands and was sobbing. "What in the world's going on here?"

Never looking up, she continued to cry.

He put his hand on her shoulder. "Honey, what's wrong?"

She couldn't answer.

He rubbed her back while she sobbed into her hands. "I understood those prideful tears back there, but this… this is way beyond that. What's the matter?"

She tried to sit up. "Oh, Ken. I'm sorry. It's still just so hard, even after all of these years." She continued to sob.

"What? What's so hard? I'm sorry, honey, but I don't have the foggiest idea what you're talking about."

She dropped her hands and turned her tear-streaked face to him. "No." She took a deep breath. "I guess you wouldn't understand what went on there tonight."

"No, I don't." He laid his hand over hers. "Why don't you fill me in?"

"The routine we saw the girls do tonight…" She tried to swallow the lump in her throat. "It was Shelly's."

"Shelly?" He rubbed the back of her hand. "Who's—" He stopped. "Wait, isn't she… I mean… I thought she was your friend who..."

"Died." She nodded. "Yes. Shelly is the girl who died in that awful car wreck back when I was in high school."

"I remember you talking about her, but what does she have to do with the routine?"

"We were supposed to do that routine as part of our homecoming show, but she died the day before so we never did it. Seeing it performed tonight just brought back so many memories."

"Wait. I don't understand. You mean, you were going to do a routine to the same song and that's what brought back the memories?"

"No, Ken." She rummaged through her purse for a tissue. "We were going to do *that* routine, down to the tiniest little detail."

"I still don't understand. If that was the same routine your team put together, then how does this team know it?"

"Isn't it obvious?" She wiped her face. "Someone had to teach it to them."

"Okay, but who?"

"It had to have been one of my old teammates." She looked across the console. "There are still a few of us around. I'll ask Angel as soon as she gets home so I can personally thank her for such a wonderful tribute."

"Tribute? What do you mean?"

"We all considered that to be Shelly's routine. We all worked on it, of course, but no one worked on it as hard as Shelly did." She smiled. "We would all joke and call her a drill sergeant. See, she was usually the sweetest and mildest-tempered of us all… until it came to that routine. Then, she was something else; she was obsessed with it." Patty laughed at the memories. "Ken, did you ever see the 'Thriller' video?"

"I think so. Wasn't it really weird? Didn't it have, like, zombies or something in it?"

"Yes, that's the one. See, Shelly was a huge Michael Jackson fan and she loved the song 'Thriller,' but she absolutely hated the video. She said our routine was a way to redeem the wrong that had been done to the song. She almost pushed us to the breaking point over that routine." Patty sniffled. "After all of that work, we never got to perform it."

"If it meant so much to her, why didn't you go ahead with it?"

"After Shelly died, we just… couldn't. Of course, all of our homecoming activities were cancelled, but we all thought we'd do the routine one day. But when it came down to it, we just couldn't."

"So, you think one of your old teammates taught it to this bunch of cheerleaders as a tribute to Shelly?"

"That's exactly what I think. And if this group of girls takes it to the state competition, it will just mean that much more."

"So, you're okay with it? I mean, you seemed pretty upset a while ago."

"I'm more than okay with it, Ken. I just let my emotions get the best of me, but I couldn't be happier. Shelly was my best friend and this is the perfect way to honor her."

Chapter 11

Angelina pulled into the drive and shut off the engine. The house was dark. *Why did they want me to come home right after the game if they were just going to go to bed? Whatever. Maybe this will give me some time to figure out who this Shelly is.*

She'd barely unlocked the front door when the lights in the living room came on and she heard a loud "Surprise!"

She stumbled backward. "You guys!" Her eyes widened. "Sam, why are you here?"

"It's good to see you, too, Little Sis."

"Oh, come on. You know what I mean." She pulled her key from the lock and went in. Splashes of blue and gold—the school's colors—filled the room. Streamers wrapped the banister and hung from the ceiling, and at least fifty balloons danced around the room. As her eyes took it all in, she noticed a cake sitting on the table. "Tell me that's chocolate! *Please,* somebody tell me that's chocolate!"

"Is there any other kind?" Patty beamed.

"This is great." Angelina tossed her purse on the couch. "You guys are awesome!" She wiggled her finger toward her dad. "I should have known something was up when you didn't stay for the rest of the game."

Ken pointed at Sam. "That's why he's going to give me a play by play before the night's over."

Angelina turned and poked Sam in the chest. "What? You were there?"

"Of course, I was there. I was slinking around in the shadows so you wouldn't see me, but I wouldn't have missed it."

"Thank you all so much." Angelina looked around the room.

"I don't even know what to say."

"Well, you could always say something like," Sam rubbed his stomach, "'let's cut the cake.'"

"I like how you think." She peeked into the bakery box. "It's so cute. Maybe we shouldn't cut it."

"Good luck with that." Sam pushed her out of the way. "I'm eating it, with or without you."

"In that case, let's cut the cake!"

Patty picked up the bakery box and carried it into the dining room with everyone following behind her. "I can't thank you enough for doing that routine, Angel. You'll never know how much it meant to me." She sliced the cake and motioned for someone to hand her a plate. "Who taught it to you? I've been racking my brain, trying to figure it out."

"Um, taught it to me? I—I guess I don't know what you mean."

"Oh, come on, now. The routine has had its proper unveiling." Patty took the plate Sam handed her. "Which one of my old teammates was behind all of this?"

"Teammates? Mom, I seriously don't know what you're talking about. It was just something that I… uh… I came up with."

Patty sat the empty plate down beside the cake. "Angel, this is a sensitive subject." She stared at her from across the table. "Quit joking around."

Angelina glanced toward Sam for help. He shrugged.

"How can a routine to 'Thriller' be a sensitive subject?"

"I have to say, I don't appreciate your flippant attitude." Patty's chin quivered. "I'm sure whoever taught you the routine filled you in."

Angelina's thoughts raced.

"I'm asking you again, who—exactly—taught you that routine?"

"No one taught it to me."

"How about that cake?" Sam handed another plate to his mom. "It sure looks—"

"Not now, Sam." Patty stood with her hands locked on the table's edge. She stared at Angelina. "You mean to tell me you're going to stand there and look me in the eyes and take credit for Shelly's routine?"

Shelly's routine. Ah, Crap!

Angelina felt as though someone had just punched her in the stomach. She met her mom's icy stare.

"Don't you have anything to say for yourself?" Patty spat. "I've never known you to lie to me, Angelina, but this—this is practically unforgivable."

"Mom, I—I—Who's Shelly?"

"Are you telling me whoever taught you this routine didn't even bother to tell you about Shelly?" Patty walked around the table. "I can't imagine who would do that." She turned to Angelina. "I want a name and I want it right now!"

"Mom, what are you getting so mad about?"

"Let's all try and stay calm here." Ken raised his hands. "Angelina, answer your mother's question. No more kidding around."

Josie materialized next to Angelina. "I have a bad feeling about this. Apparently, that dream of yours was more than just a dream."

"I'm waiting." Patty's tone was cold.

Things were starting to click. Angelina remembered seeing an old picture of her mom wearing a uniform like the one the mystery cheerleader had been wearing. And the name, Shelly, was familiar. And in the dreams about the routine someone kept calling her Patty.

This can't be happening.

"Angelina! I'm talking to you!" Patty's face was red and blotchy.

"I'm sorry. Um, no one taught it to me, Mom." She looked down. "Not like you mean, anyway."

"Careful. You're on very thin ice here." Josie moved close to Angelina, as though trying to protect her.

"I'm going to ask you one more time." Patty drew out the words. "Where did you learn the routine?"

"I don't know. I—I guess I dreamt it." Angelina sat down in a chair at the table. "See, I keep having these weird dreams where someone is calling me Patty and—"

Without warning, Patty reached over and slapped her across the face.

Ken moved between them. "That's enough."

Trying to look around Ken, Patty yelled, "A dream? Do you think that's funny?" Her voice cracked. "Angel, why are you doing this to me? I was so proud of you earlier, and now—"

Ken put his arm around Patty and guided her toward the living room. "I think it's time we all calm down and try to look at this rationally. Surely, there must be a logical explanation."

Sam followed behind. "I wish someone would tell me what's going on around here. A few minutes ago, everyone was happy and now—"

"I'll tell you what is going on. Apparently, your sister has some type of deeply-rooted resentment toward me." Patty dropped into a chair. "And she has come up with a terrible way to hurt me. I would've never imagined she could be this cruel."

"Mom, what are you talking about? How am I being cruel? You know I'd never hurt you on purpose!"

"Angelina, don't raise your voice to your mother." Josie wrung her hands and paced back and forth. "That isn't going to help a thing."

A woman Angelina had never seen before appeared in Josie's path. Her pudgy face twisted in anger. "Josie, you know I'll not tolerate these types of goings-on in my house. You'd better put a stop to it right this instant."

Angelina jabbed the air with her finger. "Who are you and what gives you the right to talk to Josie like that?"

Patty gasped.

"Angelina, you be quiet now," Josie said. "You're in enough hot water as it is."

"Who is she, Josie? Who is this woman?"

Ken, Patty, and Sam all watched Angelina as she talked to no one.

"Oh, for heavens sake!" Josie's shoulders slumped in defeat. "This is Adie. I told you about her. She owns this house… or she did at one time. You ignore her for now and deal with the situation at hand."

"Angelina, I don't know what you're trying to pull here." Patty's face was red and her hands were shaking. "But I've had about all I can take."

"Well, that makes two of us, Missy." Adie folded her arms across her chest. "And Josie, how dare you tell her to ignore me! I have half a mind to go ahead and fire you."

"I don't know who you think you are," Angelina jabbed her finger toward Adie. "Josie does not work for you anymore and even if she did…"

"Angel! Hush now. Be quiet! You know they can't see us. You must look like a raving lunatic to them."

Realizing what she'd done, Angelina scanned the horrified faces of her family. Patty burst into tears and Ken quietly left the room.

Sam walked over and stood beside her. "Angel, who are you talking to?"

"Sam, I—I was talking to—" She threw herself on the couch. "Oh, just forget it."

Ken came back into the room a few minutes later to find Patty and Angelina both crying. "This has gone on long enough." He picked up his jacket. "Let's go."

"Dad, what's going on?" Sam asked.

Ken offered his hand to help Angelina off the couch. "I've been on the phone with Dr. Bowman. Even though it's late, she's agreed to meet us in her office in fifteen minutes."

"Dad, please, no." Angelina pulled her hand back.

"Settle down, Angel." He took hold of her hand again. "Apparently, we can't deal with this in a rational manner, so Dr. Bowman's going to help us sort it out."

"Who's Dr. Bowman?" Sam felt like he was watching a tennis match.

"You should remember her, Sam. Dr. Bowman was Angelina's counselor." Ken nodded to Patty, tipping his head toward the front door.

"Dad, please. Please don't make me go!"

"Angel, this isn't a punishment. I think right now we could all use a little help to get us through this mess."

The trip to Dr. Bowman's was a quiet one. Sam kept glancing over at Angelina as if he expected her to sprout another head or something. No one spoke a word except for Josie cooing into Angelina's ear. "Everything will be okay. We'll get through this, somehow."

They pulled in just as Dr. Bowman was unlocking the office door. As they walked in, she shook hands with each of them and made the expected comments. "It's good to see you," and "My, how you've grown." She went through the office, turning on the lights in the dark waiting room. "As you all know, I've already spoken to Mr. Cartwright on the phone." She turned to them and offered a weak smile. "Given the current circumstance, I feel it would be best if I speak with Angelina alone for a few minutes."

Ken and Patty both nodded while Sam stared at the floor.

"The rest of you go ahead and make yourselves comfortable. Angel, shall we?" Dr. Bowman headed down the hall.

Following her, Angelina swore she was in some type of time capsule. Dr. Bowman was wearing a light yellow, knee-length skirt with matching jacket and shoes. If Angelina remembered right, she also had the identical outfit in pink, in blue, and in lime green.

When they entered the room, all of the memories came rushing back. It all looked and felt the same. As a child, Angelina remembered thinking that a box of crayons must have exploded in the office, splashing bits of color everywhere. The walls were bright yellow and there were several red tables scattered around. Each table had a different-colored wall separating it from the other. There was the green room, the blue room, and the orange room. Each center served a purpose and Angelina remembered them all.

"I guess you've probably outgrown this room by now, but I still have your file in here so we'll make it work for tonight." Dr. Bowman retrieved the file and laid it on her desk.

A file? It looks more like a novel—a very long novel.

"So, would you like to tell me what's going on?" Dr. Bowman opened the file.

Angelina sat silently.

"Well, then, I understand your friend, Josie, has returned. Can you tell me about it?"

Angelina remembered this part, too. Dr. Bowman had asked her a question and now she would wait. Years ago, Angelina would time her. The average time she'd wait for an answer was five minutes. After five minutes, she'd ask the same question again and the clock would start over. This time needed to be different. Angelina had no intentions of spending any more time here than necessary.

"I want to be perfectly honest with you." Angelina took a deep breath. "Yes, Josie's back. I guess, to be fair, I should say she never left. I thought she did, but she didn't."

From the corner of the room, Josie gasped. "Angel! What do you think you're doing?" She looked bewildered. "Tell her—tell her—Oh, fiddlesticks. I don't know what you should tell her."

"Josie, please sit down. You're making me nervous."

Dr. Bowman's eyebrows shot up. "You think Josie's in here with us now?" She sat with her pad and pen in hand, ready to add another chapter to the novel.

"Oh, I know she is." Angelina scooted back in her chair.

"Would you like to tell me about that?"

Angelina listened to the minutes tick by on the clock. After three minutes passed, she said, "I know what you're thinking. I also know what I should say to get out of this mess."

"And what mess would that be?" Dr. Bowman didn't look up as she wrote in her notebook.

"That I'm talking to Josie again." Angelina waited. She wanted to look into Dr. Bowman's eyes before she continued. When Dr. Bowman met her stare, she said, "If I were to tell you that I knew Josie wasn't real, but I sometimes pretended she was to allow myself a way to work out problems on my own, what would you say?"

Dr. Bowman taped her pad with her pen. "I'd say that was a little unusual, but certainly not unheard of." Dr. Bowman looked considerably more relaxed. "So... is that what you're doing? Pretending?"

Josie sat down beside her. "Oooohhh, that's good! We'll be out of here in no time. Keep it up!"

"No, it isn't."

Dr. Bowman stopped tapping her notebook. "If this isn't another form of talking to yourself, what is it?"

Josie shifted in her seat. "Angel, what are you doing?"

"It's okay, Josie. I'm tired of acting as if you don't exist." Angelina was calm as she addressed Josie in front of Dr. Bowman. "Besides, like you said, it's not just you anymore. I can see the others."

"Angel!" Josie tried to grip her hand. "I don't know what you think you're doing, but I want you to stop talking and think this thing through."

Angelina thought Dr. Bowman's paper would burst into flames. She'd never seen anyone write so fast before. Trying to ignore her, she continued talking to Josie. "Don't be mad. It's time to get this out in the open. I've been doing some research and there are other people like me."

The writing stopped. Dr. Bowman looked up. "What kind of research have you done?"

"I've been researching about people like me. And about people like Josie, too."

"And what have you discovered?"

"That we're not alone. There are others like us—like both of us."

"Oh, Angel. Maybe you really are crazy. What in the world do you think you're doing?" Josie started pacing again. "You were so close to getting out of this and now… What have you done?"

Dr. Bowman set her notebook down and leaned forward. "Can you explain what you mean by 'there are others like Josie?'"

"Sure." Angelina helped herself to a piece of candy from the jar. "Josie's a ghost." She unwrapped the mint. "I can see Josie again, and now I can see others, too."

"Others?"

"Yes, others." Angelina paused. "When I was little, it was just Josie. But now, I've met Rosie and Adie, and I think maybe some cheerleader by the name of Shelly."

"And these others are also ghosts?" Dr. Bowman swept her mousy-brown bangs out of her eyes as she reached for the notebook.

"Yes."

"I see."

Angelina shot her a confident look. "Do you? Because during my research I found that many people believe in ghosts. Are you one of them?"

"I believe some people feel they've had an encounter of a paranormal nature."

Josie moved herself in between Angelina and Dr. Bowman, forcing Angelina to look at her. "Angelina, I'm asking you to please be quiet. I don't like this one bit. Just tell her you were joking or… or something. Maybe you could faint. Yes, this would be a good time for you to faint."

"I'm not going to do that, Josie. I'm tired of pretending you don't exist. I'm tired of people thinking I'm crazy. They can either accept it or not. What else can they do to me, I mean, seriously?"

Chapter 12

Angelina drifted in and out of consciousness. She willed herself to wake up. *What's wrong with me?* She attempted to lift her head, but it felt so heavy. Nothing looked familiar—except for Josie. Succumbing to the darkness, she slept.

Josie watched and waited. Hearing a faint "Where am I?" she leaned over the bed. "You're in a hospital," she snorted. "Of sorts."

A hospital? Angelina forced her eyes open. This didn't look like any hospital she'd ever seen. There was a naked light bulb hanging in the center of the room. She rolled to her back and tried to focus. The ceiling tiles above her were water stained. Flicking out her tongue, she tried to moisten her lips. "Why am I here?" Her throat was so dry. It was hard to talk. "Did I get hurt?"

Josie shook her head.

Angelina struggled to sit up. She swung her bare legs over the side of the bed. Holding her head with one hand, she poured a drink of water with the other. "What happened?"

Josie didn't answer.

Realization flashed across Angelina's face and her eyes grew wide with fear. "Oh, Josie!"

"You see?" Josie sighed. "*This* is what they can do to you. What, oh what, have you done, child?"

"Why would my parents do this? Why would they sign those papers to have me put in here?"

"Oh, why, indeed?" Josie arched her sparse eyebrows. "Let me see—maybe it had something to do with you rambling on to that doctor woman about how you could see ghosts." She shook her head. "Angelina, what were you thinking?"

"I don't know. Obviously, I never thought it would come to this." Hoping to relieve the pressure in her head, she pressed her hands on either side and squeezed. It didn't work. She dropped her hands to the bed to keep herself from wobbling off. "Mom was just so mad about the routine and I didn't know what else to do. I thought if I could get everything out in the open… Whatever happened to honesty being the best policy, anyway?"

"Apparently, all honesty does for a body is to get you thrown into the nut house."

Angelina flinched. "Mental health care facility."

"What?"

"They don't call them nut houses anymore, Josie. The correct term is mental health care facility, and given my current circumstances, I think I prefer the latter."

"Call it what you may. All I know is this place is plumb full of crazy people."

Tears filled Angelina's eyes.

Josie came and sat beside her on the bed. "I'm sorry. You know I didn't mean you. You don't belong here." Josie looked around the drab room. "We simply have to get you out of here."

Wiping her eyes, she turned to Josie. "But how are we going to do that?"

"We'll put our heads together and come up with something."

Angelina tried to replay the events of last night in her mind. "Hey, wait a minute. I'm only going to be here for three days, right? Isn't that what they said?"

"Your memory's still a little sketchy, honey. The three days is for your evaluation." She clicked her tongue. "The doctor doesn't even want you having visitors until after then."

"No visitors? What's the point in that?" Putting pressure on her forehead this time, she mumbled, "Why is my head hurting so bad?"

"That probably has something to do with what they called Thorazine."

"Thorazine? What's that?"

"It's something the doctor prescribed. She said it would help 'calm you down.'"

"Calm me down? Render me senseless would be more accurate. I can't even think straight." She squeezed her eyes shut. "I remember going to see Dr. Bowman and… and…" She opened her eyes. "What happened, exactly?"

"Well, after you spilled your guts about being able to see ghosts, the doctor asked your parents to sign some papers so she could give you a 'proper evaluation.' At first, they didn't want to, but then you started in about that cheerleader, and—"

"But still! I can't believe they did this. What about Sam? Didn't he try to stop them?"

"Oh, he tried, all right." A smile tugged at the corner of Josie's mouth. "For a while, I was afraid they were going to give him a shot of that Thorazine, too."

Angelina lay back down on the bed. "So what's up with the three days? What happens after that?"

Josie shrugged. "I guess that's how long you have to convince them you're not crazy."

"And what happens if I can't convince them?"

"I don't know. I guess you'll be staying here for a while."

"I don't want to stay here, Josie." Her voice was shrill. "I want to go home!"

"There, there. Everything will be okay."

"No, it won't! Things will never be okay again."

"Shh, try not to fret. We'll come up with something."

Angelina hugged the lumpy pillow to her and sobbed.

There was a knock on the door and the strangest looking woman Angelina had ever seen stuck her head in. "You'd better cut that out," she snapped as she slipped into the room and plopped down on the only chair.

Angelina sat up holding her tear-soaked pillow to her chest. "Excuse me?"

"Your name's Angelina, isn't it?"

Angelina nodded, noticing that not only was the woman's red hair sticking up in all directions, but she was also wearing an unmatched pair of house shoes. "Do I know you?"

"Nope. But I've been hearing those nurses talk about you." The woman swung her short legs back and forth, making a pink-and-lime-green blur around her feet. "You'd better quit all that crying or it's off to the west wing for you. Doctor's orders."

"What's the west wing?"

"That's where they put the real crazies." She stopped swinging her legs. "Believe you me, you don't want to go there—and I'm speaking from experience."

Angelina hugged her pillow a little tighter. "How can it be any worse than this?"

The woman laughed. "It can. Believe me, it can. This is the Ritz compared to the west wing. At least here you have sheets on your bed." She leaned back in her chair and started swinging her legs again. "On this wing, you're even free to roam around a bit." She lowered her voice. "It's not so bad here, once you get used to it. We've got a TV and game room right down the hall and a lot of nice folk to help pass the time."

"You mean, I can leave my room?"

"Sure, as long as you abide by the rules." She looked toward the door. "And all of this crying you're doing is breaking one of them."

"It's against the rules to cry?"

"Yep. And they call us the crazy ones." She rolled her eyes. "See, in this wing, they like to keep it nice and quiet and your bawling isn't setting too well with the charge nurse. I overheard her say if you didn't stop soon, you'd be going to the west wing."

"I don't care." Angelina's tears started again. "What else can they do to me?"

"An—Ge—Li—Na!" Josie stomped her small foot emphasizing each syllable. "You said those exact words last night. Now just look at you." She wagged her bent finger. "Even after all of this, you haven't learned a thing. I've half a mind to get a bar of soap and scrub your mouth out!"

"You'll care if they put you in the west wing. You've never heard such hollering and carrying on. They keep you locked up in your room all day, too. Sometimes, they even tie you to your bed. If you weren't crazy when they put you in there, you would be in a few days. You'd better listen to me and your friend or I'll go get her that bar of soap she was talking about."

"I said I don't care. They can—*My friend?* You mean you can see her? You can see Josie?"

"Well, of course, I can see her. I may be a little crazy," the woman stuck out her mismatched house shoes in front of her and wiggled her toes, "but I'm not blind—or deaf, for that matter."

"How can you see her? I mean… I thought…"

"You thought you were the only one who could see ghosts?" She laughed. "My, my. You *are* a little full of yourself, aren't you? We're a unique lot; I'll give you that. But there are a few of us around. By the way," she stuck out her hand, "my name's Becca. Rebecca, actually, but my friends just call me Becca, so you can, too."

Angelina tossed her wet pillow aside. "That's it! If you can see Josie, too, maybe we could work together to convince the doctors that neither one of us is crazy."

Rebecca settled back in her chair. "No, that would never work."

"But why?"

"Well, because I *am* crazy." She made a twirling motion with her finger by her temple. Not west wing crazy, but crazy nonetheless."

Angelina sat quietly as she looked at the strange little woman with her wild hair and mismatched shoes. "Because you can see ghosts? Is that why you think you're crazy?"

"Oh, no. I know that part is real. I've always been able to see ghosts." She lowered her voice. "Between you and me, I worry about those who can't." She winked. "But I do have... other issues."

Other issues. As in "I should be scared to be in this room with you" issues?

"Don't look so sad, sweetie. I'm okay with it."

"How can you be okay with everyone thinking you're crazy?"

Rebecca smiled. "Weren't you listening? I already told you—because they're right. At least partially, anyway. Besides, I like it here. I have everything I need and as long as I can stay out of the west wing, they even let my little girl come and visit me."

"You have a daughter?"

"Oh, yes. Sweetest little thing you ever did see. As a matter of fact," Rebecca stood, "she should be getting here soon so I'd better go get my room ready for company."

"Okay. I... uh... hope you enjoy your visit." Angelina stood. "It was nice meeting you."

"We'll be seeing each other again." Rebecca walked to the door and turned around. "Can I give you a little advice before I go?"

Angelina nodded.

"First off," she nodded toward Josie, "your friend needs to make herself scarce. It won't help your case if she's always hanging around. It'll be too tempting for you to talk to her and they frown on that around here."

Josie's arms stiffened at her sides. "I'm not leaving her."

"You will if you care anything about her."

Sorrow filled Josie's eyes as she looked at Angelina.

"Please, Josie, don't go! Don't leave me in here all alone."

Rebecca sighed. "Poor little thing. I guess she does need you. Just be very careful about talking to one another and, at the very least, don't attend her counseling sessions with her."

"But why?"

"Because your doctor will ask you if she's with you. Trust me, it will make things go better. I've been there."

Angelina nodded. "Okay. Anything else?"

"Don't stay holed up in your room all day. They don't like that, either. It's a sign of depression and they tend to get real paranoid about that in this place."

"So no crying and no acting depressed, even though my family has had me committed."

"Now you're getting it." She opened the door and looked down the hall. She smiled. "I don't think anyone's overheard us," she whispered. "Now go wash your face to get rid of those tear stains. A tidy appearance is also important." She slipped back out the door.

"A tidy appearance." Angelina shook her head. "This coming from a woman who has apparently forgotten what a hairbrush is for."

"Maybe we should listen to her, Angel."

Angelina went to the little sink in the corner of the room and turned on the water. "Josie, do you really think we should be taking advice from her? She seems a little paranoid. And she admitted that she was—Wow!" Angelina caught a glimpse of her reflection in the plastic mirror that hung above the sink. Her hair was sticking up as bad as Rebecca's and she had streaks of mascara all over her face. "Josie, you should've told me I looked like this."

Josie came up behind her. "Well, I must admit, I've seen you looking better, but I didn't think it was the right time to point it out to you."

Angelina took the washrag from the lopsided shelf. Not finding any soap, she held the rag under the water. She rubbed her face. "Ouch. I guess they don't believe in fabric softener around here. This washcloth feels more like burlap."

Ten minutes later, Angelina stood at her door with a clean—however raw—face and finger-combed hair. "I don't know about this. Do you really think I should go out there like Becca said?"

"She probably knows what she's talking about." Josie walked toward the door. "Maybe you could just make a quick trip down the hall to let the nurses see that you're not depressed." She stood up a little straighter and squared her shoulders. "Let them know they can't keep you down."

Angelina pushed the door open and peered out into the hall. It looked a lot like her room—dirty, dreary, and depressing. Seeing another patient in the hall, she ducked back in and shut the door. "I can't do it, Josie. I just can't." She took a deep breath. "Will you go with me? Please?"

Josie nodded. "Remember what Becca said, though. Don't talk to me."

Angelina pushed the door open again and stepped out into the hall. She made a right turn, locked her eyes on the far wall, and walked straight ahead. As she walked past the nurse's station, a dark-headed nurse came out from behind the desk. "Here." She thrust some change into Angelina's hand with stubby little fingers that looked more like sausages.

Startled, Angelina looked at the change then back at the nurse.

"The pop machine is around the corner." The nurse turned to leave.

"Excuse me?"

"You're Angelina, right?"

Angelina nodded.

"Your mom left you some money for the vending machine. If you want a pop, you'd better hurry and get it. It's almost time for your session and the doctor doesn't allow beverages in her office."

Tears threatened to spill down Angelina's cheek as she thought of her mother. She saw Josie shaking her head. "No crying, remember?"

Angelina thanked the nurse and continued down the hall. As she went around the corner, she spotted what Becca had called the game room. There were a couple of tattered couches, a TV, and some tables with various games scattered around the room.

"Let's sit for just a minute," Josie whispered, "so you can be seen out and about. Then we'll head back to the room."

Angelina sat on one of the couches, being careful not to acknowledge Josie in any way. Just as she'd decided to go get a Diet Dr. Pepper, a woman with short, black hair—sticking up much like Rebecca's had been—walked up to the pop machine and started talking to it.

Angelina glanced toward Josie and raised her eyebrows.

The woman dug some change out of her pocket. She meticulously stacked it on the table in neat rows as she counted aloud, one nickel at a time. Getting to a dollar, she scooped it up and shoved it all back into her pocket. She moved back to in front of the machine, pulled her money back out, and fed coins into the machine, counting it again. "Five, ten, fifteen, twenty..." Making her selection, she grabbed her drink and, without opening it, promptly threw it into the trashcan.

Angelina bit her lip and looked around. The woman walked over to a table filled with various coffees, teas, and what looked like hot chocolate mixes. She picked up a steaming cup of hot water and downed it.

Josie's eyes widened as she looked at Angelina. "I think that's enough for our first time out. Are you ready to go back to your room now?"

Chapter 13

Angelina lay awake listening to the sounds out in the hall. The clank of the medicine cart and that awful squeaking were worse than fingernails on a chalkboard. *I'm not going to be able to sleep with this going on. I might as well get up.* She didn't move. *But why bother getting up at all? It's just going to be another day of doctors and nurses trying to get into my head.*

A beam of light slashed through the darkness as Rebecca pushed the door open. "Rise and shine. It's time for breakfast."

"Breakfast?" Angelina shielded her eyes as Rebecca snapped the light on. "What time is it?"

"It's almost six o'clock, sleepyhead. You'd better hurry."

"Who eats at six o'clock in the morning?"

"Well, I do." Rebecca opened up the closet. "And you should, too, if you want the good stuff. It's Sunday, you know."

"What's that got to do with anything?"

Rebecca turned from the closet with a robe in her hand. "Here. Put this on. You don't have much to choose from."

Angelina took the robe. "What's the rush?"

"I forget; you're a newbie." Rebecca tugged on her arm. "Sunday morning breakfast is the best meal all week. In case you haven't noticed," she scrunched up her nose, "the food here isn't all that good. But the Sunday breakfast is delicious."

Angelina's stomach grumbled, reminding her she hadn't eaten much the day before. "Oh, believe me, I've noticed." She put on the robe. "What was that stuff they brought me last night, anyway?"

"Brought you?" Rebecca knitted her brow. "Oh, I see." She held up her finger. "That was your first mistake. Don't ever have them bring you your meals. It's always better to eat in the dining room. At least it's hot." She shook her head. "Even though I'm not sure it would've made a difference on last night's meal. All of us in the dining room were debating on what it was. I think we decided it was probably canned dog food."

"Ooh, gross!" Angelina's hand covered her mouth. "You're not serious, are you?"

"Well, not really." Rebecca smiled. "I'm sure that would be against some sort of law. They called it Salisbury steak. But who knows what was in it?"

Angelina shuddered. "You think breakfast will be any better?"

"Oh, I know it will. Do you like pancakes?" She had a blissful look on her face. "They have the lightest, fluffiest pancakes you've ever tasted." She shook her finger. "But you have to eat them while they're hot. Otherwise, they turn all rubbery."

Angelina usually didn't eat breakfast—especially anything sweet—but she was starving this morning. "Is that all they have?"

"Oh, no. That's just my favorite. There will be three breakfast bars set up." Her eyes sparkled. "One has any kind of fresh fruit you can think of. The other has eggs, bacon, sausage, hash browns, biscuits, and gravy. The third one has pancakes, French toast, and waffles with every kind of syrup imaginable."

"Okay. Enough already." Angelina laughed as her stomach growled again. "I'm going to start chewing on my shoe before we get there. But if the food here is usually so awful, why do they go all out for this meal?"

"Oh, that's easy. That's the one meal our families are invited to dine with us."

"Really? You mean my family will be there?"

"No." Sorrow filled her eyes. "Maybe they'll come next week, though, after your evaluation is done."

"Next week!" Angelina hadn't even thought about the possibility of still being hospitalized next week. She plopped back down on her bed as the tears spilled over her cheeks. "I'm not hungry after all, Rebecca. You go ahead."

"Nonsense. You get up and come with me. I'll be your family for the day and if my little girl is able to join us, she'll be your family, too."

"I'm sorry, but I really don't feel like it. I'll have them bring me a tray."

Rebecca tapped her purple-house-shoed foot on the tiled

floor. "And eat rubber pancakes and cold bacon?" She reached for Angelina's arm. "I don't think so. Come on. Let's go."

"Angel, honey, please go with her. You hardly ate anything yesterday and you have to keep up your strength. Come on. I'll go with you. I'm a little hungry myself."

"You?" Angelina's eyebrows shot up. "You're hungry? Josie, I didn't know you could eat."

"Well, I can't, but that doesn't stop me from enjoying all of those wonderful smells, and breakfast *was* my favorite meal." Trying to bring a smile to Angelina's face, Josie sniffed the air. "Mmm, mmm. Just imagine the smell of that bacon as it's cooking."

Angelina's stomach grumbled again.

Josie laughed. "See there?"

"Okay." She patted her stomach. "I guess that makes it three against one. I'll go."

She followed Rebecca down the hall. As they passed a nurse pushing the medicine cart, Rebecca leaned in and whispered, "You just got your first brownie point of the day."

"What?"

"See that chart hanging on the cart?"

"Yeah, I see it. But what did you mean by 'brownie point?'"

"That's the tattletale sheet. They mark down your every move—both good and bad—and give it to the doctor. That nurse just marked down that you were out of your room and socializing with another patient." She smiled. "That makes two brownie points for both of us."

"I guess that's good, but it makes me a little uncomfortable to think I'm being watched so carefully."

"Oh, you'll get used to it. It's just a way of life around here. Somebody's always watching."

A shiver ran down Angelina's spine.

Rebecca clapped her hands like a child. "Follow your nose." She bent at the waist. Walking faster, she sniffed the air.

"What?"

"Can't you smell it? The dining room is right around the corner."

Angelina stopped the moment she entered the door. The food definitely smelled good, but even more surprising was the atmosphere. It was almost… cheerful. The people actually seemed to be having a good time. They were sitting around the tables and visiting like "normal" people. Other than the fact that half of them—like her—were still in their pajamas, you could almost imagine this was a restaurant. Angelina had to admit, this was much better than her dining experience last night, sitting alone in her dingy little room trying to choke down the cold... whatever it was she'd been given.

"See there?" Rebecca's grin spread across her face. "Stick with me, kid. I'll teach you the ropes." She gave Angelina a little push. "Now, go get a plate and fill her on up because it's a long time between Sundays."

After they'd filled their plates, they made their way to the table where Josie was sitting. Angelina sighed as she took her first bite. "I really was hungry and this is so good."

"See? What'd I tell you?"

"Rebecca, I really appreciate how nice you've been to me. I don't think I could survive this place without you and Josie."

"Don't even mention it. I enjoy meeting new people," she said between bites of pancake dripping in syrup. "Besides, you remind me of my own little girl." She grabbed a napkin, wiped her mouth, and waved to someone who was coming up from behind Angelina. "Speaking of, here she comes!"

The way Rebecca talked about her "little girl," Angelina expected to see a child. Instead, a young woman wearing a beautiful pink sweater came to the table, sat her plate down, and kissed Rebecca on the cheek. "Good morning, Mom. How are—*Angelina*?"

Angelina laid her fork down and looked at the young woman. "I'm sorry, but I don't think I know you. Wait a minute. Kobi?"

"Oh, my." Rebecca clasped her hands together. "Do the two of you already know each other?"

"This—this is the sweet little girl you've been talking about?"

"Yes, this is my little Kobi." Rebecca's face lit up. "How do the two of you know each other?"

Angelina noticed the twinkle in Josie's eyes as she leaned back in her chair. She was apparently thrilled over this little turn of events.

"We... uh... go to school together," Angelina said.

"So, the two of you must be good friends, then?" Rebecca smiled. "Kobi, I've never heard you mention Angelina before."

"She's from my new school, Mom. We're just now getting to know each other."

"Well, isn't that nice." Rebecca polished off the last of her pancakes. "Would you look at that? My plate's already empty. I'm going for seconds." She patted the spot next to her. "Kobi, sit down and eat before your breakfast gets cold." She grinned at them. "And I want the two of you to get to know each other so you can become better friends."

With Rebecca out of earshot, Kobi said, "Friends? Yeah, I doubt that. I knew you'd end up in a place like this—the way you go around talking to yourself like some sort of lunatic." Her lip curled into a sneer. "I wonder what your cheerleader friends would think of you now."

Angelina fought back tears—she also had wondered what her friends would think. "I can't believe you're Rebecca's daughter. She's so sweet and you—you're so—"

"Go ahead and whine, Princess, but remember, I'm not the one in a nut house. You are." She leaned back in her chair. "So, tell me. How does it feel to be locked up?"

"I don't think I've ever seen a chip on somebody's shoulder quite that big before," Josie said.

"I don't have a chip on my shoulder and I would appreciate it if you would just mind your own—"

"What?" Angelina screeched. Lowering her voice, she whispered, "You can see Josie? After all of those horrible things you said to me, you could see her all along." She turned to Josie. "She can see you. Did you know that?"

Josie nodded.

"Why didn't you tell me?"

"It wasn't for me to tell. I knew it would come out, eventually."

Kobi glared at the both of them.

When Rebecca returned to the table, Angelina pointed at Kobi. "She can see Josie."

Rebecca smiled. "I told you there were a few of us around."

"Yeah, but... but..."

A nurse walked up to their table and put her hand on Angelina's shoulder. "Is everything okay here?"

Angelina nodded as Rebecca said, "I've just discovered my little girl and Angelina go to school together. They're going to become great friends."

"Oh, I see." The nurse patted Angelina on the back. "Dr. Bowman is in her office and your session is scheduled to start in about ten minutes, okay?"

"Okay." Angelina pushed back from the table. "I was done, anyway."

"Done? You didn't eat enough to keep a bird alive." Rebecca shoveled more pancake into her mouth.

Avoiding Kobi's stare, Angelina said, "I'll see you later, Becca. I don't want to be late for my appointment."

It only took her a few minutes to walk down the hall and into Dr. Bowman's office. As soon as she opened the door, Dr. Bowman said, "I hear you ran into a friend from school in the dining room." Rebecca's words of "somebody's always watching" gave Angelina another chill. She sat down and simply nodded.

She expected the normal and-how-did-that-make-you-feel, but something had changed. Dr. Bowman laid down her notepad and rolled her chair up to where Angelina was sitting. "That must've made you terribly uncomfortable. With your permission, I'd like to ask Kobi to keep this to herself and not spread it around school. I know how cruel teenagers can be."

Angelina shrugged. "It doesn't matter. Everyone will find out, anyway, when I don't show up for school tomorrow."

"I'd like to talk to you about that. I've been visiting with your mother and we feel there's no reason for you to not be in school tomorrow."

It took a few seconds for Dr. Bowman's words to sink in. "You mean… I get to go home?"

Dr. Bowman's face softened. "Let's not get ahead of ourselves. I do have you scheduled for a couple of sessions today and if it's okay with you, I'd like for your mother to join us."

The possibility of going home danced around in her head as she tried to make sense of everything. Her three-day evaluation wasn't even up yet. *Who cares! Home! I might get to go home. Today!*

"Angelina." Dr. Bowman interrupted her thoughts.

"Yes." Angelina made eye contact. "I'm sorry. Did you ask me a question?" She smiled. "All of this has kind of taken me by surprise."

"That's quite all right." Dr. Bowman rolled her chair back to her desk. "I asked if you'd agree to a session with your mother."

"My mother? Yeah. I mean, sure. But what does she have to do with this?"

Dr. Bowman walked over to the window and looked outside. "The relationship between mothers and daughters can sometimes be…" She turned around, leaning against the window sill. "Let's just say it can be difficult. But that's no reason to keep you here. If we did that, this place would be filled to capacity, with people lined up in the streets waiting to get in." She made a steeple with her fingers and tapped her chin as she walked around the room. "So, if everything goes well with your mother, I think you can probably go home this evening."

"That would be great!" Angelina didn't want to rock this boat—the boat that may be getting her out of this place—but still… "I don't have a problem with my mom coming to a session with me, but I don't really understand…"

Dr. Bowman returned to her chair. "That's why I'd like to meet with the two of you together. The night your parents brought you in, I had some concerns—to be sure—but after talking with your mother and getting your test results back, I feel comfortable with treating you as an outpatient."

"My test results? I don't remember taking any tests."

Dr. Bowman laughed. "You always were such a delight. I was referring to your toxicology screen."

"My— You tested me for drugs? You thought I was on drugs?"

"Don't take it personally. It's common procedure in cases such as this. Of course, you know it came back perfectly clean, other than the medication I gave you that night."

"Yeah, but—but did my parents think I was on drugs?"

"No. Actually, they didn't." Dr. Bowman looked at her watch. "I'm expecting another patient in just a few minutes so we have to cut this short, but I need you to come back in two hours."

"Will my mother be here?"

"Yes, dear, she will. Then we'll see about letting you go home."

Home! I'm going home! She had to refrain from skipping down the hall. The nurses would have a field day with that one. She tried to slow her pace as she walked toward her room. *I can't wait to tell Josie.* She saw a nurse coming down the hall with the tattletale sheet in hand. *I can't wait to get out of here!* She pushed the door to her room open. "Josie…" She stopped. "Kobi! What are you doing here?"

"I… uh… Mother's taking a nap and I hoped we could talk."

Angelina walked over to her bed and sat down. "Okay, but… Oh, I get it. I guess one of the nurses told you that you shouldn't go to school tomorrow and tell everyone I'm locked up in a nut house. Just to let you know, I don't expect any favors from you."

"Ouch!" Kobi drew back. "I guess I had that one coming, though. But, actually, I was going to ask you for a favor."

"Me? What could you possibly want from me?"

"Now that I think about it," she raked her teeth across the corner of her lip, "how about a trade? I'll keep my mouth shut at school if you will."

"If I will?" Angelina wrinkled her forehead. "Oh, I see. You don't want me telling people your mother's in here." She sat back down on her bed and looked at Kobi. "Listen, I know you don't know me very well, but I'd never do that. I think your mom's great."

"So do I." Kobi twirled her hair with her fingers. "I wasn't talking about my mom. I was talking about this." She flicked her sweater.

"What?"

"I won't tell anyone you're here if you don't tell them I dress like this when I come and visit my mom."

"What? Are you serious? Kobi, you look great! I didn't even recognize you, at first. I don't understand why you don't dress like this for school."

Kobi snorted. "Not gonna happen, Princess."

"Why not?"

"I only dress like this for my mom's sake. She likes bright colors and pretty things and she sure doesn't get that in here."

Angelina looked around her dreary room. "You can say that again."

Following Angelina's gaze, Kobi asked, "Want me to bring you some house shoes?"

"What?"

Kobi smiled. It was the first genuine smile Angelina had ever seen on her face. "I'm sure you've noticed my mom's house shoes."

"Yeah, but what's that got to do with anything?"

"Color, Angelina." She shook her head. "It's her way of adding some color to this dreadful place." She tugged at her sweater. "That's also why I do this."

"That's so—so sweet! I just…"

"I'm not looking for your approval," she snapped. "Do we have a deal or not?"

"Yeah... I mean, sure. I won't tell anyone you really are pretty and that you might possibly have a heart, and you won't tell anyone I was in here." She smiled at Kobi, hoping that Kobi would understand her sarcasm.

"Fine." Kobi got up to leave then turned around. "So, what do you want me to tell everyone at school—like you're sick or something?"

Angelina smiled. "That won't be necessary. I'm probably going home tonight."

"That was quick." Kobi shrugged. "So, congratulations... I guess."

"Thanks. I'll see you tomorrow."

"Whatever," Kobi said as she walked out the door.

Chapter 14

"Angel, is it true?" Josie appeared as soon as Kobi had shut the door. "You might really be going home today?"

"There you are." Angelina twirled around the room. "It's true! It's really, really true! I may get to go home, Josie."

"Well, my word. What happened to cause this change in events?"

"I don't know and to be honest, I really don't care." Angelina continued to spin. "I'm going home, Josie! Did you hear me? I'm going home!"

"Goodness gracious, child." Josie laughed. "You won't be going anywhere but to the west wing if someone comes in here and sees you acting like this. Now sit down. Just watching you made me dizzy."

Angelina danced over to the corner of the room and flung herself into the chair. "I'm sorry. I'm just so excited." She threw her arms up into the air. "I'm going home!"

"Now, tell me how all of this came about." Josie perched herself on the foot of the bed.

"Well, I went in for my counseling session and Dr. Bowman said she and Mom had been discussing it and there wasn't any sense in me missing school tomorrow."

"Well, land sakes! That's all there was to it? After all of this fuss, they're sending you home out of the blue so you won't miss school?" She repositioned herself on the bed. "Surely they thought about that when they stuck you in here Friday night."

"I don't understand it either, but I'm not going to complain."

"I imagine not!" Josie's eyes danced. "Now, is it a probability or a definite that you're going home?"

"It's a definite probability." Angelina left her chair to spin around the room some more. "Dr. Bowman wants to have a couple of counseling sessions with Mom and me together first. She said I could probably go home after that."

"Counseling..." Josie said the word like it left a bad taste in her mouth. "In my day, folks didn't go in for all of that nonsense. If something was bothering you, you'd just busy yourself with doing something constructive. 'Sweat the poison out;' that's what my poppa would always say." Josie looked off into the distance. "I can't help but wonder though..."

Angelina stopped spinning. "Wonder what?"

"I hope they're not getting your hopes up for nothing. This all seems a bit sudden."

"What do you mean?" Angelina sat back down. "You don't think this is some sort of trick, do you?"

"A trick? No, I don't think so. Even that doctor wouldn't pull a stunt like that. But still, do they think they've cured you from seeing ghosts?"

"I don't know. She never said anything about that." Angelina wrinkled her forehead. "The only thing she really talked about was how they knew I wasn't on drugs and..."

"Drugs!" Josie hopped off the bed. With her hands on her hips, she said, "What in the world would have given them the notion you were on drugs?"

"I don't know. At first, it made me mad, too. But then, I guess I could kind of see their point. I was talking to people they couldn't see."

"Well, yes, but..." Josie waved the thought away with a flick of her hand. "I guess it doesn't matter. If the only thing they're worried about is you talking to ghosts, we won't have any problems because I won't be there." She walked the length of the room and turned around. "What else did the doctor lady have to say?"

"She was talking about how mothers and daughters don't always get along. I don't know what that was all about. I was just so excited about getting to go home."

"Mothers and daughters not getting along? What does that have to do with you seeing ghosts?"

"I don't know, Josie." Angelina slumped back in her chair. "None of it makes any sense. Maybe you're right. Maybe I shouldn't get my hopes up." She chewed her bottom lip.

"Now look at what I've done. You were all happy and now I have you fretting like an old woman. Boy, I must really be a—a fun sucker."

Angelina looked up and smiled.

"Did I say it right that time?"

"You did, you said it right. But you're not a fun sucker. The more I think about it, this does all seem a little too easy."

"Hmm, well I'm sure things will go fine. You march right in and tell them what they want to hear so we can get out of here."

"That's exactly what I plan on doing." Angelina sat up straight and lifted her chin. "I'll do whatever it takes to get out of here."

"That's the spirit." Josie grinned at her. "You'd better get yourself down there so we can go home."

Moments later, Angelina stood outside of Dr. Bowman's office with her hand raised in mid-air, inches from the door. *This is it—my chance to go home.* She dropped her arm to her side and shifted her weight from one foot to the other. *Deep breath in and slowly let it out.* She finally found the courage and knocked on the door.

"Come in."

Angelina opened the door and stopped. When she saw another patient in the chair, she backed toward the hallway. "Oh, I'm sorry. I didn't know you were with someone. I'll come back."

"No, come on in."

When Angelina walked into the room, she realized the other "patient" was her mother. Dr. Bowman motioned her on in. "Come take a seat, Angelina."

She looked sidelong at her mother. She was pale and her hair was matted to the back of her head. Patty *never* left the house with even a hair out of place. "Mom, are you okay?"

"I'm fine, honey." Patty absentmindedly wiped her face.

"Mom, you're not fine. You look… you look—"

"Pitiful, I know." Patty gave her a weak smile.

That's why they're letting me go home. Something awful has happened. "Mom, is Dad okay? Has something happened to him?"

"Your father's fine, Angel."

"How about Sam? Is something wrong with Sam?"

Patty reached over and patted Angelina on the leg. "We're all fine, honey. Just fine."

Shelly shimmered slightly and then became more solid on the couch next to Patty. "No they're not. Everybody's upset and it's my fault."

Oh, no! Not now. Please, not now. Angelina ignored the cheerleader and tried to focus solely on her mother. She watched Patty wad the wet Kleenex into a ball. She then unfolded it and wadded it up again. From the lint all over her pants, Angelina knew she'd been here for a while.

This can't be good. Something's not right.

Dr. Bowman picked up her pen and notepad. "Patty, would you like to start?"

Patty nodded, but didn't say anything.

Angelina waited. Finally, she said, "Mom, what's going on?"

"I'll tell you what's going on," Shelly said. "I messed up. I messed up big time."

Don't look at her. Don't acknowledge her. "Mom, what is it?"

"Give me a minute, honey." Patty drew in a deep breath. "This is a lot harder than I thought it would be. I'm trying to collect my thoughts."

"I know you can see me. Please let me tell you my side of the story because you're the only one who can hear it."

Angelina glanced at Shelly and gave her what she hoped was a discreet nod for her to continue. She had to find out what was going on and at this point, no one else was talking.

"I got confused. See, I have this little head injury." Shelly turned around and showed Angelina the side of her head—or what should have been the side of her head—but most of it was gone. "Anyway," she said, turning back around, "I thought you were Patty. You look so much like her." Shelly looked at Angelina, and then back to Patty. "When did she get so old? I mean, how was I supposed to know she had a daughter? And as if that wasn't weird enough, you're like our age." She glanced back at Patty. "Or at least *my* age."

Angelina remembered what Josie had said about time no longer having any meaning.

By this time, Patty had started talking as well. It was a little confusing trying to listen to both of them, so even though Angelina was looking at her mother, she was trying to focus on what Shelly was saying.

"I kept waiting on her to do my routine. She knew how much it meant to me." A tear slid down Shelly's face. "She should've known I wanted her to do it—I'd waited so long. I got tired of waiting, so I decided to give her—or as it turns out, you—a little encouragement."

Now I get it, sort of.

"I saw you on the field that day and I thought it was her. I followed you home and tried to convince you to do my routine. Now, for some reason, Patty and this bozo doctor both think that either you're crazy, or you cooked up this elaborate scheme to get back at her for something."

Get back at her… Angelina returned her attention to Patty.

"… and when you started in with how you'd learned the routine through your dream, I didn't know what to think. At first, I thought maybe you were unstable. But now I know that was just your way of getting back at me." Patty sniffed.

"Getting back at you? Mom, why would I want to get back at you?"

"I really don't know." Patty continued wadding up the Kleenex then smoothing it back out. "That's why we're here. But I guess it probably has something to do with me making you go to counseling when you were a child."

"No, Mom, it doesn't. It has nothing to do with—"

"Then why, Angelina? Why would you want to hurt me like this?"

"Mom, I would never want to hurt you." *So much for doing whatever it takes to get out of here. That's the one thing I can't do. I won't let her think I'd hurt her on purpose.* As bad as she hated it, she knew she wouldn't be leaving any time soon. "Mom, I need you to look at me. I need to tell you something."

Patty took her hand. "That's why we're here. You can tell me anything."

Here's to staying in here… forever. "For the longest time, I couldn't understand why I would have these dreams and why they'd come true."

"Angel, you told me that was over. You told me—"

"I thought it was, but I was wrong." She squeezed her mother's hand. "I know this is going to sound weird, but I need you to listen to me."

"I'm listening."

"Mom." She took a deep breath "Do you believe in ghosts?"

"Angelina, that's enough." Dr. Bowman tapped her desk with the pen. "These shenanigans aren't going to work anymore."

Patty tried to free her hands from Angelina's, but Angelina held on tight as she looked into Patty's eyes. "I know it sounds crazy, but the truth is, I can see ghosts."

"Angel, if we can't be honest with each other, we'll never get this worked out."

"Mom, I'm being honest. I can see ghosts. Most of the time, I see them as plain as I see you. But sometimes, I can't and... sometimes they come to me in my dreams." She took a deep breath. "Mom, that's how I learned the routine. I didn't realize it at the time, but Shelly came to me in my dream. She's the one who taught it to me."

Patty's head dropped to her chest and she started to sob.

"See what I mean? She hasn't quit crying for days. I really messed things up." Shelly got up and stood behind Patty. She put her hand on her shoulder. "Please, tell her I'm sorry."

"Mom, I know this is going to be hard for you to hear," Angelina choked back a sob, "but Shelly's here with us. She said to tell you she's sorry."

Despite the grip that Angelina had on Patty's hands, Patty jerked them away as if she'd touched a hot iron. "Why, Angel? Why are you doing this?"

Angelina swallowed hard. "I'm not doing anything but telling you the truth, Mom."

Shelly came back around and sat down on the couch next to Patty. "Would you please tell her that nothing has changed? Tell her I still love her like a sis."

Angelina knew she was sealing her fate as she relayed the message. "She says she loves you like a sis."

"Have you been going through my stuff—my mementos?" Patty turned to Dr. Bowman. "That's how Shelly signed our notes in school. 'Love you like a sis.'"

"Mom, I haven't gone through your things. Shelly's here—right now. She told me to tell you."

"Angelina, you may go back to your room." Dr. Bowman's eyes flashed with anger.

Angelina didn't argue. She got up and walked to the door. When she turned to tell her mother good-bye, she watched Shelly lean over and gently kiss Patty's cheek. At that moment, Patty put her hand to her face.

"You felt it, didn't you?"

Uncertainty sparked through Patty's eyes.

"Mom, I know you felt it. You felt something. Shelly just kissed your cheek."

Dr. Bowman stood up. "Angelina!"

"I'm going." Angelina looked at Dr. Bowman, and then her mother. "Before I do, I want to tell you both I would never intentionally hurt anyone. You can go on thinking I'm crazy if you want, but Mom, I never want to hurt you." She walked out the door and gently closed it behind her.

Chapter 15

Dr. Bowman sat down behind her scarred metal desk. Leaning back in her chair, she closed her eyes and rubbed the bridge of her nose. "That didn't go at all as I had hoped it would." She sat back up. "Patty…"

Patty still sat with her hand to her face. "I felt it. I mean… I *did* feel something."

Dr. Bowman sighed. "Patty, you've had a hard day and you're under a tremendous amount of emotional stress. But surely you don't think Shelly is in this room."

"I don't know what to think anymore." Patty dropped her arms down to her side. "Except that Angelina's telling the truth. Or, at least, she thinks she is. I'm absolutely positive about that now."

"I tend to agree with you. She's not doing this on purpose." Dr. Bowman laced her fingers behind her head and leaned back in the chair again. "We've ruled out drug use and she appears to believe what she's saying is true."

"If she's not doing this to hurt me then what does this mean? What's wrong with her?"

Dr. Bowman reached for her notebook. "Let me verify a few things." Her brown eyes scanned the notes. "You said you suspected she was talking to Josie again for about two weeks before you contacted me. Is that right?"

"Yes. As far as I know."

"And you haven't noticed any changes in her diet or sleeping habits?"

"No."

Dr. Bowman picked up her pen. "When I asked you if she'd suffered any major stresses you also said no."

"That's right."

"We may be looking at this all wrong." Dr. Bowman twirled her pen. "As adults, when we think of major stresses, we tend to think of things like maybe a death in the family, an assault, or divorce, but what would Angelina think of?"

Patty sat up a little straighter. "You mean, like breaking up with a boyfriend?"

"Exactly! Has there been a recent breakup?"

"She and her boyfriend did break up a couple of months ago, but she hasn't even mentioned him so I thought she was over it."

"She's a teenage girl; I doubt she's over it. Is there anything else you can think of?"

"No, not really." Patty shrugged. "I mean, normal stuff like school and…" She raked her fingers through her tangled hair. "I'm sure being put in charge of the cheer routine caused her some stress."

"Patty, when you couple these things together, you're looking at some pretty big issues." Dr. Bowman started counting them off on her fingers. "First we have the break up. Then there's the routine. And let's not forget about her brother moving out. I know they're very close."

"I see where you're going with this—I thought the same thing—but when I asked her about it, she told me she wasn't stressed."

"Of course, she did. She wouldn't want you to know she's having troubles. She's at that age of independence. She wants to deal with her problems on her own. No, I think we could be looking at something entirely different than what we were thinking."

"Like what?"

"I think she might be suffering from what we call brief psychotic disorder, also known as brief reactive psychosis."

Patty gasped. "That sounds terrible!"

"No, it isn't. The key word here is 'brief.' This could be a temporary thing. Usually, an episode will last for maybe a month."

"A month?" Patty knitted her brow. "You mean it'll just go away?"

"If it's reactive psychosis, yes, it should. Sometimes when the stresses are relieved, either through time or the mere acceptance of them, the symptoms vanish as quickly as they came."

Patty rearranged her position on the couch. "So… does that mean I can take her home?"

"You can. Of course, you can." Dr. Bowman rolled her chair closer. "But I'm asking you not to—not yet."

Patty's chin quivered. "But why? If all of this is going to just go away, why can't I take her home?"

"Patty, I don't want to alarm you, but sometimes… One thing we worry about with reactive psychosis is the possibility that the patient will try to harm themselves, or even someone else."

Patty's bobbed hair swayed as she sharply shook her head. "No. Angel would never do that."

"Under normal circumstances, I'm sure she wouldn't. But, Patty, these aren't normal circumstances. She thinks she can communicate with the dead."

Patty leaned her head back on the couch. "I'm so confused. I just don't know what to do. What can you do for her here that I can't do for her at home?"

"For starters, she needs to be watched continuously."

"I can do that." Patty sat back up. Determination flashed across her pale face. "She's my child. Of course, I can watch her."

"Patty, I know you would try—you would probably kill yourself trying—but I'm talking about twenty-four-hour care. You have to sleep. Besides, I would also like to try her on some antipsychotic medication and she would need to be monitored."

"This medicine—what's it going to do? Will it stop her from seeing ghosts?"

"It can. It could decrease or eliminate the symptoms all together. As a matter of fact…" Dr. Bowman returned to her notes. A wide grin showing the gap between her front teeth spread across her face.

"What?"

"I can almost assure you the medication will work."

"Why? What makes you so sure?"

"If you remember, when you brought her to my office Friday night, I ended up giving her a shot of Thorazine to help calm her down."

"I remember." Patty's tears flowed down her smooth cheeks. "I'm the one who held her arm."

"Thorazine is an antipsychotic medication." Dr. Bowman leaned back in her chair and put her hands behind her head. "Patty, I can almost guarantee that Angelina has not seen a ghost since she's been in here—until our meeting just now."

"I'm not sure I'm following you."

"Angelina has been watched very carefully since she's been here. There've been no reports of suspicious behavior. None. No hallucinations. No talking to ghosts. That tells me the medication was working. Of course, by now, it's out of her system. That fact, together with the stress over having a counseling session with you, has brought about this latest bout of 'seeing ghosts.'"

"I'm not sure. This just doesn't make sense to me. I can see where stress could bring about some of this but—" Patty reached for another Kleenex. "But how does that explain how she knew the routine?" She dabbed her swollen eyes. "How does it explain how she knew Shelly always said 'love you like a sis?'"

"One thing at a time, Patty. We'll figure this out. You said you had mementos at home—letters and such. I don't suppose you also have a tape of that routine lying around."

"No." Patty pursed her thin lips in thought. "I don't think so. I keep a box in my closet that has old letters and maybe some pictures, but I think that's about it."

"You might want to double check, just to be sure. But even if you don't, I do believe we're on the right track."

Patty stared off as she chewed her nails. "I just don't know... I don't know what to do anymore."

"Patty, look at yourself. You're a nervous wreck. If you take Angelina home, she'll blame herself for your condition. She's in such a fragile state right now. Give me a little more time. I'll get her started on the medication and you can use that time to pull yourself together as well."

"All right. But can we…" Patty cleared her throat. "Can she at least have visitors now?"

"I don't see any harm in that as long as… It's very important she not have any stress. Maybe for the first visit or so, just Sam could come up, if he's still in town. I think he would seem less threatening, right now."

"Okay." Patty continued to chew her nails. "Sam's still here. I'll tell him to keep it light."

"You might also just ask him and Ken when they first had suspicions she was talking to Josie again."

"I don't think they knew anything about it until I told them."

"Just ask to make sure."

Patty got up and paced around the room. "Why is the time frame so important?"

"Angelina told me Josie had never left. I'm sure that's just part of her recent hallucinations. But if Josie has been here all along—which I doubt—it wouldn't be *brief* reactive psychosis."

Patty turned and looked at Dr. Bowman. "If it's been going on for a while, what are we looking at?"

"Let's not borrow trouble. Just ask them so we can be sure."

"If Josie's been here for longer, you'd be thinking more on the lines of schizophrenia, wouldn't you?"

Dr. Bowman cocked a brow at Patty.

Patty turned away and walked to the window. "I have a computer. I know how to Google things."

"Patty, let me be the doctor." She closed her notebook and put it in the drawer. "Go home and get some rest before you end up in the hospital yourself." She smiled. "And stay off the computer."

Angelina walked down the depressing hall from Dr. Bowman's office toward her room. She stopped, turned around, and headed back to the office. She stood outside the door. *I need to see Mom. I need to tell her... what? Please don't worry, Mom. I didn't do this to hurt you. I'm just crazy.* She paced back and forth across the green and gold speckled floor. *Yeah, that should make her feel better.*

She leaned up against the wall next to the office and waited for her mom to come out. She watched a nurse walk past, her white shoes squeaking down the hall. *What's taking them so long?* She thought she could hear the muffled sounds of Patty crying. *Please don't cry, Mom. Everything's going to be okay.*

The same nurse went by again. Of course, she was holding her trusty clipboard—the tattletale sheet as Rebecca called it. *I wonder what she's writing about me now.*

With the next pass, the nurse stopped. "Angelina, is there something I can help you with?" She pronounced each word as though it left a bad taste in her mouth.

"I... uh... no. I'm just going to my room." She started down the hall again. Passing the game room, she saw Josie leaning over a table watching a couple of patients play checkers. Angelina waved and hollered out across the room. "Hey, Josie, you got a minute? I need to talk to you."

Josie's head snapped up. With a disapproving look, she shook her head and disappeared.

Rebecca rushed across the room. "Rebecca, honey. My name's Rebecca." Once she reached Angelina's side, she whispered, "What do you think you're doing? You know better than that!"

"It doesn't matter anymore, Becca. Looks like I'm here to stay."

Rebecca took her by the arm. "Let's go to your room so we can talk."

The minute Angelina stepped into her room, Josie was in her face with her boney little finger wagging. "What's wrong with you? Don't you want to go home? You're so close, Angelina, and you're going to mess it up."

Rebecca looked both ways down the hall before shutting the door. She folded her arms across her chest and tapped the floor with her foot—the foot that was sporting a bright red, fuzzy house shoe. "What's the meaning of this? What do you mean you're here to stay?"

"Here to stay?" Josie gasped. "What in tarnation happened?"

"That's exactly what I'd like to know." Rebecca switched feet and tapped with the blue one.

"Alls I know is she left out of here happy as a lark, saying she was going to go home today, and the next thing I know, she hollers my name halfway across the game room for everyone to hear."

"I know. I heard it, too. I almost choked to death on my potato chip. I tried to cover for her, but there's no telling who all heard her."

Angelina stood quietly, watching Josie and Rebecca discuss her as if she weren't even there. *I wonder if this is what it feels like to be a ghost.*

"Well, what happened?" Rebecca asked as they turned to Angelina.

"I'd be happy to fill you in once you two finish your conversation."

They looked at one another then back to Angelina. They both blinked and said, "Well?" in unison.

"She's going home." Josie's green eyes twinkled. "Look at that smile."

Angelina walked over to her chair and sat down. "No, Josie, I'm not. At least, not today anyway."

"What?" Josie screeched. "Those—those scoundrels!"

"It's okay." Angelina threw her legs over the arm of the chair. "Really, I'm okay with it."

"How can you be okay with it?" Josie paced the floor, wringing her hands. "You were so excited about going home."

"Don't get me wrong; I was upset." She waved her hand in the air. "Who am I kidding? I'm still upset. But seeing the two of you come to my defense makes me realize I'm not alone. I'll get through it and this is better than the alternative."

"What happened, Angel?" Sorrow filled Josie's eyes. "I thought they were going to let you go home so you wouldn't miss any school."

"Yeah, that's what I thought, too, but the price was too high."

"Too high? You mean you have to pay to get out of a place like this?"

"No. The price was letting them think I made this entire 'ghost thing' up to get back at Mom for... something. I couldn't do it. Mom was so hurt."

Josie stomped her foot. "What would ever give them a notion like that?"

"I guess between the two of them, it somehow made sense. They boiled it down to 'I'm either trying to hurt Mom for some reason' or 'I'm crazy.'" Angelina twirled her hair around her finger. "And Shelly helped me convince them I was, indeed, crazy."

Josie's hand flew to her mouth. "Shelly? What was she doing there?"

"I guess she's been hanging around Mom. Of course, Mom can't see her, but Shelly feels really bad about all of this."

"Let me see," Rebecca piped up. "Shelly's the cheerleader ghost, right?"

Josie glanced sideways at Rebecca. "That's right." She turned to Angelina with a sheepish grin. "We talk sometimes. You know, when you're at counseling and stuff."

"That's fine." Angelina swung her legs to the front of the chair and propped her elbows on her knees. "I'm glad you two are friends. That'll make it easier for us to all work together."

"Of course we can work together, but what exactly are we working on?"

"I haven't quite got that part figured out yet." Angelina looked around the room. "My only choice is to convince them I really can see ghosts."

"That's not going to happen." Rebecca peeked out the door. "All you will accomplish is convincing them you need to be here."

"I'm in agreement with Rebecca." Josie clicked her tongue. "That's what got you put in here in the first place."

Chapter 16

Angelina sat on her hard bed swinging her feet, which were clad in the new, brightly colored, mismatched house shoes Rebecca had given to her. She knew they made her look ridiculous, but she didn't care. She liked them anyway.

A knock on her door interrupted the silence. She ignored it. It was probably the nurse wanting to give her more medicine, which she now knew to hide under her tongue and spit out as soon as the coast was clear. Rebecca had taught her that trick, too.

The door opened a little bit and she could see someone trying to peek in through the crack. "Angel? Are you in there?"

She jumped off the bed and threw the door open. "Sam! What are you doing here?" She threw her arms around his thick neck. "I'm so glad to see you. Wait, why aren't you at school?" She dropped her arms and looked over his shoulder. "Where're Mom and Dad? Aren't they coming?"

"Whoa! Slow down, Sis." He laughed. "I can only answer one question at a time. What do you want to know first?"

"What day is it?" She grabbed his hand and led him into the room.

"Uh…" Concern washed over his face. " It's Monday, Angel. Didn't you know that?"

"I thought it was, but if it's Monday, shouldn't you be back at school?"

He shuffled his weight from one foot to the other. "I'm taking a short leave."

"A leave? Sam, you can't do that!" She put her hand on his shoulder. "Sam, please don't do this. Not because of me."

He turned away. "That's not anything for you to worry about."

"But you're going to get so far behind."

"Me? Naw. Besides, I needed a break." He glanced toward the chair. "Mind if I sit down?"

Angelina lowered herself onto the corner of her bed. "Sam, I'm sorry. You really should go back to school."

"They can survive without me for a while." His eyes kept drifting to Angelina's house shoes. "So… how are you? Really?"

"I'm okay." She stuck her feet out in front of her. "Do you like my shoes?" She wiggled her toes.

"Uh, yeah. Sure. They're, uh…"

"Stylish?" She tilted her head and grinned.

"Uh, yeah. I guess."

Angelina laughed. "You're doing it again."

"Doing what?"

"Acting like you're walking on eggshells." She shook her head. "Sam, I know the shoes look ridiculous, so just say it."

"Yeah, okay. They look ridiculous." He relaxed and leaned back in the chair. "So if you know that, why are you wearing them?"

"I'm taking survival lessons from a long-term resident here. The shoes are just our way of adding a little color to this awful place."

"You do know they don't match, right?"

Her hand covered her mouth. "What? What do you mean they don't match?"

He sat in silence.

"I'm kidding." She reached over and shook his leg. "Lighten up, would you? It's me. I'm fine."

He slowly exhaled. "I'm sorry. It's just kind of weird, you know, seeing you here."

"In a nut house? Yeah, I know."

His spine stiffened. "Don't call it that, okay?"

"I tried that for a while myself." She sat up straight and looked down her nose. "'Mental health care facility,' I used to say." She relaxed. "But you know what? No matter what you call it, it's still the same dreary, old place."

He looked around the room. "Yeah, it's kind of depressing." He fidgeted around in the chair. "Is there somewhere else we can go? Maybe, like, for a walk or something?"

"Sure. We could walk down to the game room if you want."

He brightened. "You have a game room?"

"Well, if you can call it that."

"It has to be better than this." He stood. "Let's go check it out."

Angelina led the way. Walking in, she plopped down on the brown, tattered couch. "Want to buy me a Diet Dr. Pepper?"

"Sure." He fished around in his pocket for some change. Handing her the pop, he asked, "So where's the game room?"

"You're in it."

He looked around. "Are you serious? This is it?"

"This is it." She laughed. "Were you expecting an arcade or something?"

"Well, you did say 'game room.'"

"There are games." She opened her pop. "We have checkers. Of course, most of the pieces are missing. We also have decks of cards."

"Wow." Sam nodded. "Okay, so you want to play a hand of rummy or something?"

"We could." She took a sip. "If you don't mind playing with a partial deck." She rolled her eyes at the pun.

"Oh, well. In that case, what else is there to do?"

"We could go outside and play basketball."

"Cool. Let's go." Sam walked toward the door.

Angelina remained sitting. "Or we could take a stroll through our lovely gardens."

Sam returned to the couch and sat down. "There's no basketball court, huh?"

She smiled. "And to think you're in college."

"Funny, Angel." He shook his head. "Okay, you got me. Now what?"

"This is pretty much it, Sam."

"Oh." He leaned back on the couch.

"Where are Mom and Dad?"

"They... uh, they..."

"They're not coming." She took another sip and looked at him. "Right?"

"They will." He propped his elbows on his knees and looked at the floor. "It's just... Dad had to go to the office for a while and Mom's... well... she's at home. She's supposed to be resting."

Angelina sat quietly.

"They'll be here, Angel. This has been really hard on them."

"I know. I saw Mom. She looked really bad. Sam, is she okay?"

"She will be… eventually. The doctor gave her something to help her get some rest. She'll probably be here later."

"Did she say anything to you about our counseling session?"

"Angel, I uh—" He ran his fingers through his hair. "Let's talk about something else."

"Something else?" She arched her brow. "Sam, it was a simple question."

"Listen, this makes me pretty uncomfortable." He dropped his head and stared at his shoes as if they held some kind of answers.

"What makes you uncomfortable?" She put her hand on his shoulder. "Me? Am I making you uncomfortable?"

"No, not you." He took a deep breath, puffed out his cheeks, and slowly blew it out. "I'm not supposed to talk about any of this with you right now. I just wanted to see how you are."

"You're not supposed to talk to me about what?"

He didn't answer.

She slumped down further into the couch. "I get it. You're not supposed to tell me how everyone—including you—thinks I'm a nut case."

"Come on, Angel. Don't. I'm supposed to stay away from topics that might upset you, that's all."

"Oh, okay. Like being in here shouldn't upset me."

The two of them both fell into a lull of silence, not quite knowing what to say next. They watched the other patients in the game room. Most sat around a small television with the sound turned down so low they had to lean in to try to hear.

"Can't they turn it up?" Sam pointed at the TV. "They can barely hear it."

"No, it's preset. They like to keep it quiet in here."

"Oh."

The conversation stopped again as they sat side-by-side on the couch, watching a woman pace back and forth with her hands laced behind her back. When she let out a blood-curdling scream, they both jumped so hard they scooted the couch several inches across the worn linoleum floor.

They sat—wide-eyed—as they watched her slap her hands down on a table where two other patients were playing a card game. "You want to chop my fingers off, don't you?"

Amazingly enough, the two continued playing their game as if nothing had happened. A nurse hurried in. "Lanoe, no one wants to chop your fingers off. Now settle down."

Lanoe laced her fingers behind her back and started pacing again. "Okay," she mumbled. The nurse watched her for a few minutes, and then disappeared around the corner.

Sam stood and offered his hand to Angelina. "Let's go back to your room."

Lanoe rushed up to them and stopped only inches from Sam's face. She stared at him with the most intense blue eyes he'd ever seen. He tried to back away, but she moved in even closer and let out another fierce scream. Then, very calmly, she said, "You want to kill me, don't you?"

Sam's eyes widened further. "No, I, uh… I don't."

The nurse came back in and took hold of Lanoe's arm. "Sorry," she said to Sam. She turned to Lanoe. "No one wants to kill you. Here, take this." She handed her a medicine cup.

Lanoe took the pills. "Is it poison?"

"No, it's not poison." The nurse wrote something on her clipboard.

"I bet it's poison because you want to kill me and chop my fingers off."

"Now why would I want to do that?" the nurse asked as she led her down the hall.

"Poor thing," one of the card players said. "She'd better watch out or she'll be going back to the west wing."

As they neared Angelina's room, Sam asked, "What's the west wing?"

"I've been told it's where they put the real crazies."

"And she doesn't qualify?"

"Guess not."

"Wow." He walked over to the chair and sat down. "Angel, you don't belong in here."

"You think?"

"I'm being serious. I don't think Mom and Dad realize what kind of place this is."

"Sam, it's a mental institution. What did you expect?"

"I—I don't know. Not this. I'm going to tell Mom and Dad they have to get you out of here."

"They think I'm crazy, remember?"

"Yeah, but—but not this kind of crazy."

"I'm not crazy as in I think people want to chop my fingers off. I'm just crazy as in I talk to people no one else can see."

Sam propped his elbows on his knees, put his head in his hands, and stared at the floor. "Angel." He looked up. "I need to talk to you. I mean *really* talk to you."

"Okay, so talk."

"If anyone finds out I'm talking to you about this, they won't let me come back to see you. I was told to keep it light. I guess we're supposed to just talk about the weather or something."

"Who's dictating what we can and can't talk about?"

"Well... they are—Mom, Dad, and that Dr. Bowman."

"I see."

"Don't be mad. They're just trying to help."

"I'm not mad. I'm just..." She shook her head. "It doesn't matter. What did you want to talk to me about?"

He took a breath. "Do you remember Friday night? When everyone was all mad and you started talking to Josie and to—to someone else?"

"I remember. Her name's Adie, by the way."

He hit his fist on his knees. "You have to quit doing that. Sis, come on. You're not crazy. I know you're not."

"You're right, Sam, I'm not. But that doesn't make Josie or Adie or even Shelly any less real."

"Shelly? Angel, are you doing this to get back at Mom for something?"

"*No!* Sam, how could you even think that?"

"I don't know." He dropped his hands to his sides and leaned back in the chair. "You tell me. You tell me what to think."

"Sam, I'm not doing this to hurt anyone. I'm just tired of pretending and I want all of you to believe me."

"Believe what, Angel? Are you talking about our conversation in the park that day? You want me to believe you're psychic? Because I could buy that. I could buy about anything other than you belong in here."

"The psychic thing was your idea. You were just hoping I could help you with your exams. I hate to disappoint you, but you'll have to get your roommate—the burrito guy—to help you on that one. I'm not psychic."

"Okay, if you're not psychic, how did you know about Tommy? How did you know that routine that has Mom so freaked out?"

Angelina kneeled down by Sam's chair. "Sam, have I ever lied to you?"

"No. Not that I know of, anyway." He smiled. "Except for the time you said you didn't break my video game when we both know you did—but you were, like, six."

"Just for the record, I didn't lie to you then, either. Your friend, Chris, broke the game."

"No way! Are you serious? Ah, man. And to think I've been mad at you all of these years."

"Sam, can we be serious? I'm trying to tell you something."

"I know, Angel. I'm sorry. I just don't want to hear you say it. It's like if I don't hear you say it, it won't be true."

"Say what?"

Sam let out a long slow breath. "Mom already told me. You think you can see ghosts."

"Is that really so bad?"

"I don't know, Sis. I don't know what to think."

"Why would you be willing to believe I have psychic abilities, but not be willing to believe I can see ghosts?"

"Because." Sam cleared his throat. "The whole psychic thing was pretty much a joke, but this? It isn't, is it?"

Angelina shook her head. A tear escaped her long lashes and rolled down her cheek. "It's not much harder to believe than your roommate and his Mom being psychic, is it?"

"I don't know. It's different because he's my roommate and you're… you. I don't care what he does but—"

Kobi kicked the door open as she made her way into the room and dumped a stack of schoolbooks on the nightstand. "Hey! What happened? I thought you were getting out of here? Oh! Sorry. I didn't know you had company."

Sam bounced up out of the chair. "No problem. You have any more of those?" He nodded toward the stack of books. "I'd be glad to help."

"Uh, no. That's all. But thanks, anyway."

Wow! Is Kobi actually blushing?

"I need to run anyway, Sis, but I'll be back later." Sam swaggered toward the door. "It was nice meeting you." He flashed Kobi a knock-dead gorgeous grin.

"Uh, yeah. You, too." As soon as the door closed, Kobi fell up against the wall. "Please tell me that's your brother—your *single* brother."

Angelina laughed. "Yes, that's my brother."

"Does he have a girlfriend?"

"Not at the moment. Why?"
"Because he is *so* hot."
"Sam? Oh, gross!"

Chapter 17

Angelina lay across the hard bed with her textbook spread out in front of her. She'd been looking at the same page for the last thirty minutes, but she still didn't know what she'd read.

Josie sat down beside her. "Penny for your thoughts?"

"Hmmm?" Angelina rolled over and stared at the stained ceiling.

"You look as though you're a million miles away."

"Yeah, I guess."

"You want to talk about what's on your mind?"

"I don't know. I just don't get it."

"You don't get what?"

"Kobi." Angelina sat up and tucked her long legs underneath her. "I don't get Kobi."

"Ah, she's a tough one." Josie shrugged. "Or she pretends to be. But I have a feeling she'll come around."

"I kind of doubt that, but I'm not even talking about her bad attitude. That I get—sort of. It's just she comes off like she doesn't want anyone around, but when Sam was here, she, uh… well… she said he was 'hot.'"

"Hot?" Josie scrunched her already wrinkled forehead. "Why would she think that? Is he running a fever?"

"No, Josie." Angelina smiled. "That's just another way of saying you think someone's good-looking."

"Oh! Well, in that case…" Josie wiggled her sparse eyebrows. "I would have to agree with her."

"What?" Angelina laughed. "Did you seriously just say my brother's hot?"

"I did." Josie's green eyes twinkled. "You can't tell me you've never noticed he's a nice-looking young man."

"I—I guess. But… ewww! He's my brother."

"If I were younger," Josie patted her white hair into place, "and not so dead, I would probably have to go after him myself."

"Josie!" Angelina shuddered.

There was a knock on the door and Kobi peeked through the crack. "Mind if I come in?"

Angelina motioned to her to come in as she eyed Josie and shuddered again.

Josie cackled.

Kobi looked from one to the other. "Guess I missed something."

"Nothing that needs repeating. Like, *ever again*!"

Josie winked. "I have some things I need to do so I'll let you two younguns visit." She waved goodbye and disappeared.

"You know, she really shouldn't be in here with you."

"I know, but you have no idea how boring it can get in here."

"Actually, I do. That's why I try to come and visit Mom every day."

Angelina closed the textbook and shoved it into the pile at the head of the bed. "Where is Becca, anyway?"

Kobi lowered her voice. "One of those chatty nurses gave her her medicine and the pill dissolved before she could spit it out." She sighed. "I swear, if they had their way about it, she would sleep her whole life away." Kobi walked over to the chair and sat down. "Since she's sleeping, I thought I'd stop in and see what you were up to."

Angelina noticed Kobi had brushed her hair and touched up her makeup. "Was it me or Sam you wanted to see?"

Kobi's eyes narrowed. "Look, I didn't even know you had a brother until…"

"Okay, okay. You don't need to get your panties in a wad. I was just kidding."

"Well, don't." Kobi flipped her dyed-black hair over her shoulder. After fidgeting around in her seat, she met Angelina's stare. "Listen, I'm sorry. I'm just not used to people being in my business."

"I wasn't trying to get in your business." Angelina paused. "Well, I guess I was. But you're the one who said he was hot and I thought I sensed some chemistry between you and him, that's all."

"Really?" Kobi smiled. "So, why haven't I ever seen him around school before?"

Angelina picked up a book and fanned the bottom of the pages. "He graduated last year. He's in college now."

"Oh. So I guess he's home because… uh, because…"

Angelina tossed the book back into the pile. "Yeah, because his sister's in a nut house."

Kobi lowered her eyes and stared at the floor. "What happened? I thought you were going to go home yesterday."

"Yeah, me, too. But it didn't work out that way. Apparently, the only reason they were even considering letting me go home was they thought I was making all this up so I could get back at my Mom for something."

Kobi's eyebrows shot up. "Wow! How did they come up with that conclusion?"

"I don't know, but Mom was really hurt."

"I bet she was. But why didn't you go for it? I mean, I understand about not wanting to hurt your mom, but it'd be better than being stuck in here."

"I couldn't stand the idea of Mom thinking I'd hurt her on purpose."

"I guess." Kobi twirled her thumbs. "But I still think it'd be better than being in here."

"You wouldn't say that if you'd seen my mom. I'm really worried about her. She looks terrible."

"Yeah, she does. Wait." Kobi put her hand up. "That didn't come out right. What I meant to say was I saw her in the office today and it didn't look like she was handling this too well."

"You saw my mom?"

"Yeah, I was in the school office when she came in to see about getting your homework. That secretary, Mrs. Whatever-her-name-is, kept asking her a bunch of questions. I thought your mom was going to have a nervous breakdown right on the spot."

"What happened?"

"Your mom just came in and asked if she could get your homework and Mrs. Whoever-she-is started grilling her. She wanted to know what was wrong with you, how long you would be out, blah, blah, blah."

"What'd Mom tell her?"

"She told her you were sick and she didn't know how long you'd be out of school. Then she went into this long spiel about how they were running tests on you. When the secretary asked what they thought was wrong with you, your mom started tearing up so I interrupted and told her I'd bring you your homework."

"What'd she say?"

"Nothing, really. She just thanked me and practically ran out the door."

"Thanks for helping her out and for bringing me my work."

"No problem." Kobi nodded toward the stack of books. "I think I got 'em all. If you want, I can bring you the assignments every day so your mom doesn't have to mess with it."

"That'd be great. And who knows? You might run into Sam, once in a while."

"That has nothing to do with it." Kobi laughed. "Well, okay. Maybe a little. But speaking of your brother, can I ask you a question?"

"Sure."

"Does he have the curse, too?"

"What curse?"

"You know," Kobi whispered. "Can he see ghosts?"

"No. But do you really think it's a curse?"

"Uh, *yeah*. Don't you?"

"Not really. Josie calls it a gift."

"She would, wouldn't she?" Kobi shook her head. "You, on the other hand…"

"Me?" She shrugged. "I think it's really pretty cool."

Kobi's mouth fell open. "Cool? You've got to be kidding. You *do* realize where you're at, don't you?"

"Unfortunately." Angelina gestured to the room. "But this is temporary."

"Hello? Have you met my mother?" She slumped back in her chair. "Thanks to her so-called 'gift,' she's got people in three different counties convinced she's crazy—so crazy she'll probably never be on her own again."

"According to your mom…" Angelina stopped, wet her lips, and tried again. "I hope you don't take this wrong but… uh… I don't think her seeing ghosts is the only reason she's in here. She told me she—"

"I know." Kobi rolled her eyes. "She probably told you that she really *is* crazy."

Angelina nodded.

Kobi got up and walked around the room. Keeping her back to Angelina, she wiped her tears. "She tells everybody that, but she's not." She took a deep breath. "At least, she didn't used to be. Places like this made her crazy." Her voice quivered. "You wait until they start tying you down to a bed and stuffing you with all sorts of drugs and see how long *you* last."

Tears filled Angelina's eyes. "They really did that to her?"

Kobi whirled around. "Yeah, they really did that to her." Her voice rose. "This isn't some kind of game, Angelina." She looked at the door to make sure no one was around and lowered her voice. "You have to get out of here before they mess you up, too. My mom wasn't always like she is now."

"Why would they tie her down? Just because she said she could see ghosts?"

Kobi, brushed at her tears. "Because of me." She wiped her wet hands on her jeans. "They tied her down and drugged her because of me."

"I don't understand. What do you mean because of you?"

"As bad as this place is, it isn't as bad as some of them. With the new rules and regulations, they're all better than they used to be but… it still happens."

"What happens?"

"These people—these places—they have too much power over other people's lives." Kobi glanced nervously at the door. "I was only six years old when they took me from my mother." She swallowed hard. "They told her she couldn't see me anymore until she got better. When she got upset about that, they tied her down. They said she was out of control and that's when they stopped letting me see her."

"Oh, Kobi." Angelina closed her eyes as she fought back the tears. "I'm—I'm sorry. I had no idea."

"You still don't." Kobi stared at her. "I'm telling you, you *have* to get out of here. Even if it means letting your mom think you did this to get back at her. It's a way out."

Angelina's head snapped from side to side. "I—I can't!"

"You have no other choice."

"I'll make them believe me somehow."

"And when they don't? You'll get upset. And they'll do to you what they did to my mother—the straightjacket, the pills, and no visitors." She leaned in toward Angelina. "Please," she whispered, her voice thick, "I don't want to see anyone else end up like my mom. I know it's hard to pretend you can't see ghosts, but you have to. Believe me, it's better than this."

"Kobi, don't you see? That's just it; I'm tired of pretending. I don't like lying and when I get caught talking to…"

"Don't!"

Angelina frowned. "Don't what?"

"Don't talk to them. Most of the time, if you ignore them, they'll go away."

"I can't do that. I'm not just going to ignore someone when they're trying to talk to me."

"You don't have a choice if you want to get out of here and have any kind of normal life. It's not that hard to just ignore them. Try to stay to yourself, in case you slip."

"Is that why you—"

"Yes."

"But why? I mean, what kind of life is that?"

"Better than this one." She gestured to their dreary surroundings. "You'll get used to ignoring them. You'll just learn to deal with it. You *need* to."

Angelina's jaw tightened. "I wouldn't want to just deal with it. I don't want to live that way. I'll make them understand."

"You know better than to believe that's possible. You have two choices—stay here forever or learn to keep your mouth shut."

"I'm not talking about broadcasting it to the world—just my family. Surely there's a way to make them believe me."

"You're hopeless!" Kobi flung herself back into the chair and closed her eyes. "Are you sure none of them has the curse? It's usually hereditary."

"I'm sure. I mean, it would have come out by now, with everything that's happened."

An idea softened her frown. "Unless they didn't realize it themselves."

"I sort of think that's something they'd notice."

"Not necessarily. It would depend on their level of sensitivity."

"What do you mean?"

"There are some—like us—who can see and hear ghosts as plain as we see any one. But some people may just notice cold spots or smells or they just get creeped-out feelings." Kobi glanced at the door. "You know, like when the hair stands up on the back of your neck? You know something's not right, but you can't quite figure it out."

Angelina rubbed her forehead. "I don't think…" She jumped off the bed. "Hey! Wait a minute! How about feeling the sensation of someone kissing you?"

"What?"

Angelina snapped her fingers. "In one of our counseling sessions, Mom's friend kissed her on the cheek and she felt it."

"So?" Kobi rolled her eyes. "We were talking about ghosts, not your mom's friend."

"Did I not mention her friend's a ghost?"

"Are you serious?"

"Totally serious! Her name's Shelly. She and Mom were friends back in high school, but she was killed in a car wreck. The other day, in our session, she kissed Mom on the cheek. Right after, Mom put her hand on her face—you know, like she'd felt it."

Understanding sparked in her eyes. "See? I told you. You probably got the curse from her."

"You mean the gift."

"Whatever. Anyway, a lot of people notice things, but they usually write it off as something else." She shrugged. "It still won't help you prove anything."

"No, but…" Angelina whirled around. "I've got it! I can't believe I didn't think of this before. I know how to convince them." She grabbed Kobi by the shoulders. "I need you to help me. I'll get Josie and my parents to all come here. We'll have Josie say something and you and I will both write it down at the same time and let my parents see that you can see Josie, too."

Kobi pushed Angelina's hands off. "Uh, uh. No way are you getting me involved in this."

"Kobi, please! It would work."

"No, it wouldn't. They'd just think you and I got together and decided on what we'd write."

"No. We could tell them to ask Josie whatever they wanted."

"I said no! I'm not going to do it. I've spent my whole life protecting this secret."

"Kobi, please. It would work. I know it would."

"All the begging in the world isn't going to change my mind. You're on your own."

"Kobi—"

"No!" Kobi stood and brushed past her. "I need to go check on Mom."

Angelina paced her room, tapping her forehead. "Think, think, think. There has to be a way to show them!"

"Angel?" She heard her mother's voice from the doorway. When she turned, she saw both of her parents standing there. Her mom looked better than she had last time she'd seen her. She was dressed in a white pantsuit and her hair and make-up were done. She looked almost normal.

"Hey, you guys." Angelina greeted them with a hug. The embrace allowed her to see that her mom's makeup was much heavier than usual and she could still see the dark circles under her eyes. Showing her parents into the room, she picked her books up off the bed. "There's only one chair, but one of you can sit on my bed."

Ken loosened his tie and leaned against the wall. "I've been sitting all day." He nodded toward the bed. "You go ahead."

Patty took the chair. "Angel, who was that girl we just saw leaving your room?"

"That was Kobi. You met her at the school office today."

Patty knitted her plucked brow. "I don't think so. The girl in the office looked… different. I was going to ask you about her. She—she didn't look like the girls you usually run with."

"She dresses a little differently at school."

"If that's the same girl, I'd say that's an understatement." Patty crossed her legs. "How did she even know you were in here?"

"Her mom is a patient here."

"Oh, I see."

Ken cleared his throat. "Is she your friend or Sam's?" He motioned toward the hallway. "When we ran into her, Sam had an uncontrollable urge to go get a pop."

"Sam's here?"

Ken winked. "Well, he was."

Chapter 18

Angelina sat on the couch, waiting on her turn to play the winner of the card game. She had to admit that playing with a deck that was missing cards held a certain challenge. *So this is what it's come down to. I'm not only playing cards, but I'm waiting to play cards. I wonder how bored I could get before I actually die. I'm not talking the typical "I'm so bored I could die" scenario, but for real—where my heart ceases to pump blood through my body, my eyes roll back in my head, and my tongue hangs out of my mouth. That kind of dead.*

"Hey, there you are." Kobi motioned for Angelina to scoot over so she could sit down beside her.

"Do you know there are 560 square tiles on the floor from my room to here?"

Kobi cocked her thick dark brow. "Bored?" She handed over her day's assignments.

"You have no idea." She looked over the assignment sheet and sighed.

"Do you need help with that?"

"No, I already did it." She shrugged and set the sheet down beside her. "I've been working ahead. It gives me something to do."

"You seem pretty down today. Are you okay?"

"I'll be fine."

Kobi shifted around uncomfortably. "Mom's in a counseling session right now. Want me to hang out with you for a while?"

"That'd be great. By the way, I love your t-shirt. Yellow is one of my favorite colors." Angelina smiled. "You know, Becca's right. You really are just like a ray of sunshine in this place."

"Watch it!" Kobi folded her arms over her chest. "And don't get all mushy on me."

"I really don't understand why you don't dress like this for school."

"Yes, you do."

"No, I don't."

"Yes, you do."

"No, I don't."

"Yes! You do!"

"No, I…" Sensing she'd pushed Kobi close to her limit, she cleared her throat and started again. "I know about your policy of keeping everyone at arm's length, but still…"

"Still nothing. That's my policy."

"Does that go for Sam, too?"

"Who?" Kobi innocently stared at the ceiling.

"Whatever. Are you saying you're not interested in my brother?"

"Your brother's totally hot. But I never said I'd change my policy for him… or anyone else."

Angelina pulled on a loose string from the frayed couch. "Okay. But it's not that easy getting to know someone if you don't let them get close enough to know you."

Kobi stared straight ahead. "I never said anything about wanting to get to know him."

"I never said *you* said anything about it." Angelina wrapped the string around her finger and then let it unravel, forming a coil. Once it was loose, she did it again. At least it was something to do.

"Did he say something about trying to get to know me?"

"I don't know. Maybe. But, obviously, you're not interested."

"I never said that, either." The edges of Kobi's mouth twitched. "Speaking of your family, have you come to your senses yet?" An awkward silence hung in the air. "Okay, let's go to your room so we can have a little privacy." She flicked Angelina's hand. "And to keep you from tearing up the couch."

Angelina unwrapped the string from her finger. "Okay." She got up, pulled several bottle caps out of her pocket, and headed down the hall.

Kobi watched with curiosity as Angelina tossed a few of the caps down on the floor. She skipped from one square to the next playing hopscotch, as if the tiles were chalk lines on a sidewalk and her bottle caps were the rocks.

Kobi watched Angelina hop around on one foot. "You *really* need to get out of here."

"You do what you have to do." Angelina bent over—balancing on one foot—picked up the bottle cap, and tossed it a little further down the hall. "It helps pass the time."

"If you say so." Kobi followed along beside her.

They walked into Angelina's room and shut the door. "Now, you were saying?"

"I was asking if you'd come to your senses and just told your family that you made all this up so you can get out of here?"

"I already told you, I won't do that." Angelina sat on her bed, turning her head right and left to get the full effect of her orange and purple house shoes. "I can't." She met Kobi's eyes. "I still think if you were to help me..."

"No!"

"Kobi..."

"Let's not go there again." A deep red crept up Kobi's neck and her look grew icy. "I want you to read my lips: I'm not going to do it. Ever. No matter what."

"Fine!"

"Fine!"

After a few minutes of silence, Angelina said, "Look, Kobi. I'm sorry. I shouldn't ask you to help me like that. I really do understand, but I feel just as strongly about not wanting to hurt my mom by telling her I made it up."

Kobi plopped down in the chair. With elbows on her knees and her head in her hands, her dark hair fell, covering her face. "You don't think this is hurting her?"

"I know it is. That's why I have to make them understand that Josie is real. I just don't know how to go about it. Whenever they come to visit, they have a long list of things Dr. Bowman says we can't discuss unless we're in a session."

"If I can't talk you out of this, then get busy convincing them, because every day you spend here decreases your chance of ever leaving."

"But how?" Angelina sat on the corner of her bed. "I'm not allowed to talk about any of this outside of counseling."

"So don't." Kobi shrugged. "Have Josie come in while they're here and see if she can get them to notice her. You said your mom felt that kiss the other day. Maybe she or someone else in your family will be able to notice Josie."

Angelina raked her fingers through her hair. "If one of them did notice something, what good would that do?"

"I don't know that it would do any good, but it's a place to start. If one of them was sensitive to it, it might eventually gain you an ally."

"This might work."

"Doubtful. But if you do this, you'll have to be *very* careful to not say anything or you'll come off looking worse than before. Just watch them for signs to see if they pick up on anything Josie does. Tell her to take turns focusing in on them—one at a time. You know, really stare them down. Most people are pretty sensitive to that."

"What do you mean?"

"You know, it's like when you're out somewhere and you feel someone staring at you and when you look around, your eyes lock with theirs."

Angelina nodded. "Yeah, I've done that."

"Well, some people get that same sensation when a ghost is looking at them. When they can't find the source, it kind of freaks them out." She cocked her head. "You might also tell Josie to try stimulating all of their senses. I don't remember; does Josie wear perfume?"

"No."

"That's too bad. A lot of people are sensitive to that."

"Josie doesn't wear any, but Rosie does."

"Who's Rosie?"

"She's a ghost I met in a restaurant. I don't suppose you'd be willing to go find her and ask her if she'd help me out, would you?"

"There's no need. You can ask her yourself."

"Hello. I'm not allowed to leave."

"All you have to do is sit quietly and think to yourself, 'Rosie I need you' and she'll come."

"No way!"

"Way."

"Really?"

"Try it."

"Now?"

"Wait until I leave. I don't want any more ghosts hanging around me than necessary."

"Okay. But are you sure it'll work?"

"Pretty sure. When are your parents coming up?"

"Probably around seven."

"That should give you plenty of time to get things set up. Remember, *all* the senses."

"Thanks, Kobi. For everything."

"No mush, remember?" Kobi got up to leave. "Oh, before I go, I was supposed to tell you that Jason says hi."

"Jason?" Angelina grabbed her by the shoulder and spun her around. "Are you serious?"

Kobi pried the grasping fingers from her shirt sleeve. "I guess that answers my question."

"What question?"

"I was going to ask you if there was something going on between the two of you." Kobi laughed. "Obviously, there is."

"There used to be." Angelina's shoulders dropped. "But not anymore."

"You'd never know by the way he was acting."

Angelina's face lit up. "What do you mean?"

"Everyone knows I'm picking up your homework and they've been asking what's wrong with you. I couldn't think of anything else to say so I told them you had mono. It isn't too serious, but it can take a while to get over."

"That's good. But... get to the part about Jason."

"Some of the guys were... well... you know, being guys. They were saying stuff like 'isn't that the kissing disease?' After class, Jason came up to me and asked if you really got mono from kissing."

"What'd you tell him?"

"I told him you could, but when he started acting all mopey, I told him you could also get it from drinking out of a fountain, or sharing a water bottle with someone."

"He acted mopey? Really?"

"You're as bad as he is." Kobi reached for the door. "Try what I said about contacting that other ghost and see if anything happens. I'm going to go see if Mom's awake."

"I'll try. Let me get this straight—I'm supposed to just think about needing help and Rosie will come."

"Always works for me."

"For you? I thought you never wanted them around you."

Kobi smiled and closed the door behind her.

Angelina lay down on her bed and closed her eyes. *This is stupid. I feel ridiculous! Okay, here goes… Rosie, if you can hear me, I need your help. I… uh, I'm trying to convince my family I can see ghosts.* She waited. She reached for her blanket and pulled it up around her. *They must've turned the air conditioner on high. I'm freezing.*

"Is this what she called us here for—to watch her sleep?" Adie complained. "I might be dead, but I still have things to do."

Angelina opened her eyes. Seeing Adie's plump angry face, she quickly shut them. *Rosie. I said Rosie.*

"Angel, sweetie, if you're hungry for Italian, you'll have to come to the restaurant. We don't deliver."

"Rosie!" Angelina sat up and saw not only Rosie, but also Adie, Josie, and Shelly all standing around her bed. "Uh—uh, hi." She pulled her blanket a little tighter around her. "Is anyone else cold?"

"Well, land sakes." Adie stomped her foot and put her hands on her hips. "Did you call us here to talk about the weather?"

"Now, Adie." Josie directed her to the chair. "Be patient. She'll tell us why she called." Josie turned to Angelina. "The temperature dropped because we're all in here together. I like to call it 'ghost conditioning.'"

Angelina's teeth chattered. "That could work to our advantage."

"Our advantage?" Adie scoffed. "What are you talking about? And who are these other ghosts?"

"Oh, I'm sorry." Angelina made the introductions.

Josie watched Rosie with narrowed eyes. "Now that everyone knows who everyone else is, why did you call us, Angel?"

"I need you." Angelina looked around the room. "I need all of you to help me convince my parents that you exist and I can see you."

"Oh, how fun!" Shelly bounced up and down. "Count me in."

"Me, too," Rosie said. "But what are we supposed to do?"

"Kobi said we should try to stimulate all of their senses. If I could get them to notice there is something going on, then maybe they would be more open to at least hearing me out."

"Are you sure you want to do this?" Josie gave a skeptical frown.

Angelina nodded. "It's worth a try."

"I don't know who this Kobi is," Adie scoffed, "but I'm willing to participate if it will help get my house back in order."

"By gum, let's do it!" Josie's eyes twinkled. She turned to Adie. "Kobi is a friend of Angelina's. She's also a seer." She clasped her hands out in front of her. "What would you have us do, Angel?"

Angelina drew the blanket in tight. "Well, this whole cold thing is good. There's no way they can ignore that."

"Check." Josie marched around the room as though she were leading the troops into battle. "What else?"

"I'd hoped we could get one of them to notice Rosie's perfume."

"Check," Josie bellowed. "The sense of smell." She continued to march. "Rosie, it would be best if you were to get in the closet so the fragrance of your lovely perfume will be more concentrated." She pivoted. "Angel, you'll need to take turns sending each of them to your closet to fetch something for you."

"I, uh... don't have much to fetch."

"Put some stuff in there, then." Josie stopped to put her hands on her hips. "Shelly, I'm putting you in charge of the sense of touch, since you've already had some success with that. I want you to take turns touching each of them."

"Gotcha. That includes Sam, right?"

"What? What is it with you people and my brother?"

Josie returned to her marching. "We've already been through this, Angel. He's super delicious."

"He's..." Angelina shuddered. "Let's get back to the plan."

"Adie, I want you to stare at them." Josie was clearly enjoying this.

Adie sat with her hands folded in her lap. "And what are you going to do, Miss High and Mighty?"

"I'm going to try to get them to see me."

"See you?" Adie looked dubious.

"Yes." Josie increased her pace. "You all know that some people can see shadows, or at least detect movement."

"What about the sense of hearing?" Rosie asked.

"I figure we'll all take turns on that one. Different people are sensitive to different pitches. We'll all try talking to them and—" Josie put her hand up. "Shh." She tilted her head to the side and clapped her hands. "Places, everyone. They're coming."

Angelina looked at her watch. "They won't be here for a while."

Josie winked. "They're here."

There was a knock on the door.

Chapter 19

Ken held the door open as Patty and Sam walked in. Angelina noticed Ken and Sam were both carrying metal folding chairs. She pointed. "What's that?"

Sam patted her on top of the head. "It's called a chair, Little Sister. Look, it's a pretty cool invention." He opened it up and sat down. "See? You can sit on it."

"Very funny, you jerk." She punched him in the arm. "I know what it is. I meant where did you get it and why are you carrying it around the hospital?"

"Come on, you two, don't make me separate you." Ken grinned. "To answer your question, one of the nurses was nice enough to loan them to us so we'd all have places to sit while we're here visiting."

"Oh, that was nice." Angelina turned to Sam and stuck out her tongue.

Patty laughed. "I'll pretend I didn't see that since he deserved it." She hugged Angelina then sat down in the only chair that was already in the room—which happened to be where Adie was sitting.

"Well, I never!" Adie exclaimed as she got up and came through Patty.

Freaky! Angelina watched her mother. If she "felt" anything, she wasn't showing it. "Mom, you look better. How are you feeling?"

"Oh, I'm fine, honey." She waved a dismissive hand in the air. "Don't worry about me."

"She does look better." Shelly leaned over and placed another kiss on Patty's cheek. "Maybe not quite so old."

There was no reaction. Patty sat with her hands folded in her lap.

Josie walked back and forth in front of each of them.

Nothing.

She flapped her arms as though she were trying to fly.

Still nothing.

"Hello? Can you see me? Can you hear me?" She cupped her hands around her mouth. "Yoo-hoo!" she called. "There's a ghost in the room. Run for your lives!" Josie bent over and slapped her knees. "Woo! This is fun."

"Well, my word." Adie walked around the room. "Can we please do this with some form of dignity?"

"We could," Shelly replied. "But where's the fun in that?" She fell in behind Josie, putting her hands on Josie's hips and forming a mini conga line. They weaved in and out as they sang, "Ya-ta-ta-ta, da-DA!"

None of the family acted as though they noticed anything at all. *This is hopeless. Funny, but hopeless.*

Adie leaned in close to Sam. With her face only a few inches from his, she stared at him. "Can you see me, young man? Don't you know it's considered rude behavior to ignore someone?"

Sam scooted to the back of his chair. *Was that a coincidence or did he feel something?*

Adie looked at Angelina and winked. "I think we might've found one." She moved in closer.

After a few minutes, Sam rubbed his chin, stood up, and actually walked around Adie. He stood in the center of the room with his arms folded across his chest.

"Bingo!" Adie shouted. "Ask him why he got up."

"Sam, where are you going?"

"Nowhere. You know me; I can't sit still for too long." He stretched his arms above his head. "I just need to move around a little."

"Look at your dad," Josie called. Every time the conga line would pass on Ken's right, he would turn his head. After three or four times of this Ken swatted at the air.

"Dad? What are you doing?"

"I keep thinking I see something out of the corner of my eye. Is there a fly in here?"

"I don't see one."

He swatted at the air again, this time barely missing Josie.

"There's something buzzing around in here. Patty, do you see it?"

"I don't see anything." Patty rubbed her arms. "I don't think a fly could survive these temperatures, though? Why is it so cold in here?"

"Hello!" Rosie yelled from the closet. "Did you forget about me? Send her to the closet to get a blanket."

Angelina *had* forgotten about Rosie. It was much harder than she thought it would be to watch for everyone's reactions and try to carry on a normal conversation. "Mom, there's an extra blanket in my closet, if you want one."

"Oh, thank you, honey." Patty walked to the closet. "I don't remember it being this cold in here on our other visits. I'll talk to them about it before I leave so you don't end up with pneumonia."

Great. It's usually so hot in here you can hardly breathe. "That's okay, Mom, I'm sure they'll get it regulated."

When Patty reached for a blanket, Rosie jumped up in front of her and shouted, "Boo!"

Patty never flinched.

"Shoot." Rosie pouted. "I thought it would be more fun than that."

Still standing at the closet, Patty wrapped the blanket around her. "Did they change the policy about allowing you to have perfume in here?"

"No. Why?" *We may be getting somewhere after all.*

"I could've sworn I just got a whiff of perfume." Patty pulled a corner of the blanket up to her nose. "Hmm… it must be the laundry soap."

"Laundry soap! I'll have you know that perfume cost me a small fortune!"

Angelina tried to hide her smirk.

Patty closed the closet door. With the blanket wrapped tight around her, she waddled over to the chair. "I can't believe you guys aren't cold."

"It's a little cool, but not too bad." Ken swatted the air again.

"I'm actually kind of warm." Sam fanned his face with a notebook.

"Warm?" Angelina turned to look at Sam. *Oh, I see.* Shelly had left the conga line and had her arms wrapped around him.

Shelly laughed at the disgust on Angelina's face. "Okay." She dropped her arms. "Maybe it's a little weird to have a crush on your best friend's son, even if we're close to the same age."

Kobi walked in, holding two bottles of Diet Dr. Pepper. "Sorry to interrupt." She handed one to Angelina. "I owed you this from yesterday and wanted to get it to you before I left."

Angelina took the bottle. "Thanks." *What's she up to? She didn't owe me a Dr. Pepper.*

Sam rushed over and held his chair out for Kobi. "Here, you can have my seat."

Ah, now I get it.

Kobi smiled. "That's okay. I'm not staying. I don't want to intrude."

"Nonsense." Ken motioned to the chair Sam had offered. "Have a seat and let us get to know you."

"Well, okay. I can't stay long, though. Mom is waiting on me."

Angelina had to hand it to Kobi. If she didn't know better, she'd never suspect that Kobi could see the ghosts. Despite everything going on around her, she kept the conversation flowing. She talked about school and her plans after she graduated. She never faltered, not even when Shelly accused her of trying to steal her man.

This will work out perfectly. With Kobi here, I can keep a closer watch on everyone's reactions.

Josie circled Ken again. "So, you think I'm a fly, do you? What would a fly do? Maybe this?" She touched the end of Ken's nose with her fingertips.

Ken rubbed his nose.

Josie picked a new spot for the "fly" to land each time she made her way around Ken's chair. She gently touched his forehead, his cheek, the tip of his earlobes then back to his nose. Wherever she touched, Ken rubbed.

Shelly stood in front of Patty and did some ridiculous cheer about peanut butter.

You have to be kidding me. Peanut butter? Please don't tell me you guys used to do that.

"Angel, have you ever heard the peanut butter cheer?" Patty asked.

"The—the what?" *Did she hear Shelly?*

Patty's melodic laughter seemed out of place in the depressing room. "We used to do this cheer about peanut butter. I don't think we ever did it at a game, but we would play around with it at school and on the buses."

"Uh, no. I don't think so. What would make you think of that, Mom?"

Patty shrugged as a wave of sadness washed across her face. "I have no idea. I haven't thought about it in years. Sometimes your mind just takes you back, I guess."

"Yeah, I guess."

Angelina watched Shelly mimic eating a sandwich as she danced around saying, "Peanut, peanut butter. First you bite it, bite it, bite it, and then you chew it, chew it, chew it…"

"Are you going to drink that pop Kobi brought you or are you just going to hold it all day?" Ken asked.

"Hmm?" Angelina returned her attention to Ken. "Yeah, I'm going to drink it. Why—do you want one?"

"Just a sip."

"Oh, goody!" Rosie's excited voice came from the closet. "Let's try this again. Send him to the closet. There are extra cups in here."

"Dad, my throat's a little sore. Maybe you shouldn't drink after me. If you look in my closet, I think the nurse put some disposable cups in there." Angelina rubbed her throat. "If you'll get one, I'll pour some pop in it before I drink out of the bottle, just in case I'm coming down with something."

"All right." Ken strolled to the closet, oblivious of the test to come.

Rosie tried again. As soon as the door opened, she jumped up and yelled, "Boo!" just as Kobi was taking a drink of her Dr. Pepper. Kobi jumped, gasped, and shot Dr. Pepper through her nose.

Angelina burst out laughing.

"Angel! That's not funny," Sam said with a grin tugging at the corners of his mouth. "Are you okay, Kobi?" He handed her some paper towels.

"I'm fine."

The room grew quiet as Kobi dabbed at her face and t-shirt. She looked up. "Actually," she snorted and more Dr. Pepper trickled out of her nose, "it was pretty funny."

"Oh, Kobi." Patty laughed. "You *are* a treasure."

A nurse pushed open the door. "May I remind you this is a hospital?" She looked at her watch. "Visiting hours were over ten minutes ago."

Ken stood up and folded his chair. "We apologize."

"Let's wrap this up." The nurse scanned the room. "You can come back tomorrow."

Still dabbing her face with paper towels, Kobi walked to the door. "It was nice visiting with you all, but I need to run by Mom's room and tell her good night."

When the door closed, Patty said, "She seems like such a sweet girl." She furrowed her brow. "Angel, are you sure she's the girl I met in the office?"

Angelina nodded. "I'm sure."

"Speaking of friends…" Ken propped his folded chair against the wall. "Patty, didn't you bring a little something for Angelina?"

"Oh, I almost forgot." Patty picked her purse up off the floor and started looking through it. "Here." She handed her a picture.

"What's this?" Angelina looked at a picture of a huge bouquet of balloons.

"Daphne brought them by after school. They're from the cheerleading squad."

"Okay," Angelina frowned, "I'm confused. Why would Daphne bring a picture of a balloon bouquet?"

"She didn't bring the picture. She brought the bouquet. I took the picture so you could see it."

"Oh. I wish you would've brought the bouquet. It would've helped brighten the room."

"I…" Patty glanced over at Ken. "It isn't allowed, honey. I tried but…"

"Not allowed? Are you serious?" She spoke in quick sharp jabs as if each word was causing her physical pain. "What could possibly be wrong with having a bouquet of balloons?" She stomped around the room. "They said I couldn't have a mirror because I could cut myself or use it as a weapon." She shook her head. "Not that I'd ever do something like that, but I could at least understand their reasoning. I even understand that I can't have perfume because I might drink it. Gag. But balloons? Seriously?"

"There's no sense in getting so upset, Angel. They have their rules and we have to abide by them."

A hush fell over the room.

Angelina took in a deep breath. "I'm sorry, Mom. I overreacted. It's just hard getting used to all of this."

"Quite understandable." Ken wrapped his arms around her. "We'll be back tomorrow." His voice cracked. "Visiting hours are over and we have to abide by those rules, too."

Angelina grabbed his shirtsleeve. "Dad, please, can't I just come home?"

A tear slid down Ken's cheek. "There's nothing in this world that would make me happier than for you to come home."

In all of Angelina's seventeen years, she could not remember seeing her dad cry. She let go of his sleeve and her arm fell limply to her side. "Dad, I'm sorry. I just…"

He hugged her tight to his chest. "I know. Soon, Angel. You'll get to come home soon." He picked up his chair and Patty and Sam followed him out the door.

"Soon…" Angelina threw her arms up in the air. "Who does he think he's kidding? I'm never getting out of here."

Shelly walked up beside her. "Don't say that. You'll get out."

Angelina's eyes scanned the room. "What good did any of this do? I'm still here." She threw herself on the bed. "It's hopeless. I'm always going to be here."

"Drat it!" Josie's hand flew to her mouth. "I'm—I'm sorry. Just look at me cussing like a sailor when I know it isn't going to help our situation one bit." She shook her head in despair. "But neither is having a pity party."

Rosie sat down on the bed beside Angelina. "This isn't the time to give up. I know it didn't turn out as you'd hoped, but it was a start. At least they noticed. They all noticed something."

"Yeah, they noticed." Angelina sniffed. "They thought I had a fly in my room and that my room was too cold. What good was any of it?"

Adie reclaimed her chair. "It was a start. The question is where do we go from here?"

Josie resumed marching. "It's time to take it up a notch."

Chapter 20

Angelina sat with Rosalie on the bed. They watched Josie march from one wall to the other. Occasionally, Josie would stop and say, "Maybe we could…" She'd then shake her head. "No, that would never work." She'd resume her marching while Shelly dodged out of her way.

Adie sat on the edge of the chair with her hands properly folded in her lap as she stared straight ahead. She jumped and snapped her head around when the door opened. Rebecca walked in and took a step back. Looking down the hall, she closed the door and leaned up against it. "It's a good thing visiting hours don't apply to ghosts."

"They don't?" Shelly asked. "I was thinking we should leave, but… Ah, wait. I get it; they can't see me so I can stay as long as I want. That's pretty cool."

Rebecca made her way across the room. "So, who's your blonde friend?"

"I'm not blonde. I'm a… hey! That's not very nice." Shelly turned to show Rebecca the side of her head. "See, I have this little head injury and sometimes…" She whirled back around. "Wait a minute! Can you see me?"

Rebecca met Shelly's stare. "Nope. It's just me and Angel in here." She pointed her finger. "And of course her, and her, and her, and you."

"You can see me!" Shelly clapped her hands. "You can see all of us!"

Rebecca shook her head.

"You don't need to act like I'm stupid." Shelly rolled her eyes. "Most people can't see us, you know."

"I'm not most people."

Rosalie leaned in toward Angelina. "I spent years with no one being able to see me, but since I met you, it seems as though everyone can."

"Not everyone. Just a few of us."

Rosalie crossed her legs. "I think that young girl who was in here earlier could see us, too. Is she the seer Josie was talking about?"

"Yeah." Angelina laughed as she recalled Kobi shooting Dr. Pepper out her nose. "This is her mother, Rebecca. Becca, this is Rosie of Rosalie's Italian restaurant; this is Shelly, my mom's friend from high school; this is Adie, she—"

Rebecca's eyes widened. "Did you say Rosie of Rosalie's Italian restaurant?"

"One and the same."

Rebecca offered her hand to Rosalie. "It would be an honor to shake your hand. Rosalie's is my all-time favorite place to eat."

Rosie shook her hand. "Well, thank you, Rebecca."

"No, thank you!" Rebecca licked her lips. "The best meals I've ever had came from that restaurant. I've tried every single item on the menu." She smiled. "Some of them I had to try more than once."

"The secret's in the sauce. I came up with it on my own. See, my mother always told me that to make a really great sauce you need to—"

"Oh, for heaven's sake! Are we going to stand around trading recipes or are we going to discuss how to get Angelina out of this dreadful place?" Adie tapped her black boot.

Josie turned to Angelina. "If I didn't know better, I'd think she missed us being at the house."

"I think you're right."

"Don't be getting all full of yourselves. I'm just ready to get things back to normal. You know I don't like things off kilter in my house and that place has gone topsy-turvy since Angelina's been gone." Adie folded her arms across her chest. "I think Mrs. Patty has forgotten what a dust rag is for. I, for one, can't imagine the lady of the house doing such menial things, but if she's not going to hire someone to get it done, then she needs to get back to it."

"I thought Mom was doing better."

"She is... to a degree." Adie picked imaginary lint from her dress. "At least she's stopped most of that bawling. But she still just wanders around the house, not accomplishing a thing. That place is a mess. She used to do such a nice job in keeping it up, but not since this fiasco. You need to get yourself home so we can return to some type of routine."

"Believe me, I'm trying. But where do we go from here?"

"I have an idea," Shelly said. "What if I were to tell you some things that no one else ever knew about your mom and me?" She laughed. "I have to admit, we had some wild times. I could tell you stories that you could relay back to her so she'd know I was really here and that you can see me."

"I don't know..." Angelina chewed on her fingernail. "I'm almost scared to try. Any time your name comes up, she gets very emotional."

Josie swatted at Angelina's hand. "Quit biting your nails," she scolded. Turning her attention to Shelly, she said, "I have to agree with Angel on this one. You think she would have caught on when Angel knew that routine of yours, but she lets her emotions get the best of her where you're concerned, and then she just doesn't think straight."

"But if I told you enough stuff, she'd have to accept it. I could tell you about the time she was grounded and I wanted her to go to the movies with me. See, I had a date, but my date had a friend that we needed to find a date for, so..."

Josie held her hand up. "Hold on a minute. You've given me an idea. I don't think we can use your stories because it would be too emotional for her to deal with. But," Josie's eyes sparkled, "what if we told her some things that weren't so emotional?"

"Like what?"

Josie looked at Adie. "We'll tell her things about the house. You know how she loves all of that stuff. She's always going on about little tidbits of information she's discovered." Josie clasped her hands together. "Who better to tell her than the home's original owner?"

"Indeed!" Adie exclaimed. "I think you may be on to something, here. I could relay some things through Angel about the house that no one knows."

"This really could work," Angelina said.

"Are you serious? She's into house history? B.O.R.I.N.G. What happened to Patty? She used to be such fun." Shelly's full lips turned into a pout.

"She grew up." Adie's full bust heaved with a sigh. "Out of all the owners I've seen come and go over the years, she's always been my favorite. She loves the house almost as much as I do."

"Yeah, but what am *I* supposed to do? I don't know anything about that house."

"You could always come to my room and share some of those juicy stories with me," Rebecca winked.

Adie waved them away. "This is what we're going to do. When they get here tomorrow night for their visit, we'll…"

"Tomorrow!" Rosie interrupted. "I can't possibly make it tomorrow. We're hosting a big to-do at the restaurant and I simply have to be there."

Angelina's shoulders slumped. "I guess we could put it off for a day, if we have to."

"No. We. Can't!" Adie's plump finger jabbed at the air. "I need the two of you to come home."

A mischievous spark lit Josie's eyes. "See, she does miss us."

"Humph," Adie snorted. "We can still make this work. Shelly, you can spend the evening with Rebecca, telling her your sordid stories." She shuddered. "But the two of you stay close by, just in case we need you to come in for back-up."

"Back-up. I like the sound of that! We'll be like Charlie's Angels and come rushing in if they get into trouble."

Adie shrugged. "Rosie, you go ahead and do whatever it is you need to do at the restaurant. Josie, you, Angelina, and I will have the task of convincing the family that, just because they can't see us, it doesn't mean we don't exist."

"What kind of things are we going to tell them? I mean, Mom already knows a lot about the house and we're going to have to be able to prove it to her."

"You let me worry about that." Adie stood to leave. "There are a couple of things I need to check on to refresh my memory. Josie, we'd better go. It's almost time for evening tea."

"Tea?" Shelly cocked her perfectly waxed brow. "You still get to drink tea?"

"No, I don't drink tea! I'm a ghost!" She ran her hands over her dress to smooth out the wrinkles. "That's no excuse to lose one's refinement, though. I still observe teatime." With that, she disappeared.

"She's a bit bossy, isn't she?" Rebecca said.

"That," Josie laughed, "was nothing. You should've seen her *before* she died."

Adie didn't reappear, but her voice boomed throughout the room. "Josie, am I to get ready for tea by myself? Again?"

"It's good to be needed." Josie waved and vanished.

"I wish I could do that," Rebecca said.

"Do what?" Angelina stared at the spot where Josie had stood.

"Just poof and disappear."

"You mean like this?" Shelly snapped her fingers and vanished.

"And this?" Rosie followed suit.

Rebecca smiled. "And that, my dear, is how you clear a room of ghosts. If you brag on one, the others will follow." She took the vacated seat. "Now, tell me how you feel about this plan. Do you really think it'll work?"

"I'm not sure. But at this point, I'm willing to give it a try."

Rebecca settled back into the chair. "You inspire me, Angel." She moved her brightly-clad feet back and forth. "I've been here for far too long and it's time for me to go home."

"Home?" Angelina sat up a little straighter. "What do you mean?"

"Home. You know, a place of my own. A place where I can paint the walls any color I want. I could even plant some flowers outside." Rebecca closed her eyes. With her arm out in front of her, she said, "Oh, look, Angel. Can you see my garden? It has flowers of every color." She pointed. "And there's me and Kobi sitting on the porch sipping lemonade."

"I—I'm not sure I'm following you. I thought you liked it here. I thought this *was* your home."

Rebecca opened her eyes. "I've fooled myself into thinking that—I had to to survive. But you've shown me there's more to life than just existing." A tear slid down her cheek. "I want to live again, Angel."

"I don't know what to say, Becca. I mean, that's great, but how?"

"Oh, it's not going to be easy, but I've taken the easy way for far too long." Rebecca leaned in, intensity flashing in her eyes. "What's that saying—where there's a will, there's a way?"

"If that's really what you want, I'm happy for you." Angelina twirled her hair around her fingers. "I just thought you were content being here."

"I've tried to be because I didn't think I had a choice. When they took my Kobi from me, it broke my will. I tried to do as they said so I could at least see her." Rebecca squared her shoulders. "But not anymore."

"What do you mean?"

"As hard as it is for me to believe, Kobi's not a little girl anymore. She's almost eighteen. Once she's of age, they can't keep her from me. Don't you see? I can make a home for both of us. We can be together again. I know Kobi's practically grown and will probably be going off to college soon, but at least this way, she'll have a home to come home to."

"Becca, this is wonderful!" Angelina's eyes danced. "Kobi's going to be blown away. When are you going to tell her?"

"I'm not." Rebecca shifted around in her seat. "And I don't want you to, either."

"Are you serious? Why?"

"I've always been a disappointment to her, Angel. I know she doesn't think I can take care of myself on the outside, so I'm just going to have to show her." She settled back in her chair. "I'm going to have to make a lot of changes."

"Is there anything I can do to help?"

"You bet there will be. But for now, let's concentrate on getting you out of here. I'm going to need an ally on the outside."

Chapter 21

Angelina circled her room like a caged animal. The worn spots on the tiled floor indicated she wasn't the first. *Where are you, Josie? My family will be here any minute and you're supposed to help me.*

Josie appeared along with a cloud of dust. "Not to worry." She coughed. "I'm here." She coughed again.

Angelina noticed the film of dust covering Josie from head to toe. "What happened to you? You're a mess."

"This—" Josie tried to shake the dust from her dress. "This is what happens to that little space between walls after a hundred-plus years." She picked the cobwebs from her hair. "So, are you ready to get out of here?"

"I've been ready since the day I got here." Concern dotted Angelina's brow as she heard Josie cough again. "Why were you in the space between the walls?"

"Adie wanted to do a little sleuthing to help our cause."

"Sleuthing? What do you mean? Why would you—"

"There's no time for that." Adie appeared, looking as prim and proper as ever. "Your family's coming. Once they get here, let's start with getting their attention. Be a fly, Josie. Irritate them. The good Lord knows you're capable of that."

Angelina whirled around. "I'm getting a little tired of how you always—"

There was a knock on the door and Patty, Ken, and Sam walked in.

"Hello, honey." Patty hugged her. "How was your day?"

"Okay." Angelina glared at Adie and sat down.

Josie started "buzzing" around the room.

Patty looked through the stack of books. "Are you keeping up with your homework?"

"Yeah. Actually, I'm working ahead."

"That's nice, honey." Patty sat in the chair at the end of the bed.

Josie held out her arms and soared around the room like a plane. She stopped now and then to touch one of them on the nose. "Whew! This can wear a body out."

Adie watched with a glint of humor in her eyes. "Keep it up. You're doing just fine."

Angelina was too busy gauging everyone's reaction to notice the awkward silence that had fallen over the room.

Patty cleared her throat. "I might as well get this over with so we can get on with our visit."

"Get what over with?" Angelina noticed her Dad and brother hadn't unfolded the chairs they'd brought in.

"Sam, would you please close the door?" Patty lowered her voice. "This is a little over the line for what we're supposed to talk about outside of counseling."

"What's going on?" Angelina looked at each of them. "Is there something wrong?"

Patty clasped her hands together and leaned forward in her chair. "Angel, I just want you to know there's no shame in being here." She spoke as if she were talking to a five-year-old. "A lot of people need help sometimes."

"Okaaaay. So what brought that up?"

"I can't continue to explain your absence without letting people know where you are. I've already had to tell the school to get them to continue sending you your homework. They assured me it would be held in the strictest of confidence."

Angelina sat quietly as she thought of the school and the faculty. She knew how those "strict confidences" worked at South West High. First, it would go around the office then to the teachers, and finally to the students. Soon, everyone would know she was in a nut house. They probably already did.

"Angel, honey, I'm sorry. I couldn't continue to lie."

"Mom, I never asked you to lie." Angelina wiped her tears.

"The superintendent guaranteed me the information will go no further than him."

Yeah, whatever.

"The problem is... Mrs. Cooper keeps calling. She wants reassurance that you'll be there for the state competition." Patty leaned back in her chair and sighed. "And Daphne's about to drive me crazy. She calls the house continuously." Patty picked at her fingernail. "Then there's Sarah. I've lost count how many times she's called, wanting you to watch Tommy."

"You're the one who said there was no shame in being here." Angelina pulled her pillow to her and squeezed it tight. "So, tell them—tell them all. I don't care."

"Oh, honey. I know you care! I just don't know what else to do."

"Tell them." Angelina threw her pillow back onto the bed. "I'd rather that they know I was here than what they're probably already thinking."

"What do you mean?"

"C'mon, Mom. You know how teenagers are. Everyone's probably speculating that I'm pregnant, or something."

Patty hissed as she drew in a sharp breath. "I never even thought of that. Oh, surely not—they wouldn't think that. Not about you." She waved her hand in the air as if that would make the thought go away. "It doesn't matter. You'll be back in school long before nine months and then they will see—"

"Will I? At first, you thought I'd be here for three days. We're going on two weeks here, Mom."

"Well, yes... but nine months!" Patty's pinched expression softened. "Honey, you'll be out of here way before then."

"Try telling that to Becca. Twelve years, Mom. That's how long she's been here."

"Twelve years! My goodness. But—but Rebecca's..."

"Crazy? No, Mom. She's not. She's exactly like me—or at least she was at one time—but they're doing their best to make her crazy."

"Now, Angel. That's not true."

"You don't know, Mom." Angelina looked around the room. "None of you do. They poke all sorts of drugs down us. If we don't 'toe the line,' as they say, then it's off to the west wing where they tie you to your bed and do who knows what else."

Silence fell over the room as everyone let the image Angelina painted fill their minds.

"Buzz, Josie, buzz." Adie wiped the tears from her eyes.

Ken broke the silence as he swatted the air. "That darned fly!"

"Now's your chance, Angelina." Adie sniffed. "Tell them. Tell them we're here."

Angelina took a breath. "Mom, Dad… I want to come home. I'm not crazy and I don't belong here."

Ken removed his glasses and rubbed the bridge of his nose. "You're going to come home, sweetheart. You just need a little more time and counseling, and then…"

"No, I don't! Josie's not imaginary." Angelina tried to calm her voice. "Please," she whispered. "Just listen to me. Josie and Adie are both here right now. I know you can't see them, but I can."

"Oh, Angel." Patty dug in her purse for a Kleenex. "Every time you're faced with a stressful situation, you revert back to this. Honey, there are no such things as ghosts. You have to know that."

"We are clearly stepping over the bounds that Dr. Bowman set," Ken said.

"You're right." Patty stood. "Maybe we should go and take this up during our next family counseling session."

"No!" Sam spoke for the first time since coming into the room.

"What?" Ken looked at him as though he'd forgotten he was even there.

"Everyone's okay with Mom breaking the 'rules' and talking about taboo topics, but as soon as Angelina tries to talk, you shut her down."

"Son, your mother and I…"

"Yeah, yeah I know. You know what's best."

"Sam!" Ken glared at him. "I don't like your tone, Son."

"Dad, I'm sorry, but come on! You and Mom have always told us there's nothing we can't discuss with you. Angel's trying to talk to you, but you're going to let some doctor dictate what we can and can't say." Sam shook his head. "This isn't right. She's your daughter. *We*," he drew a circle with his finger, "are family, and *we* should be able to say whatever's on our minds."

Ken and Patty sat in stunned silence.

"Thank you, Sam." Angelina tried to swallow the lump in her throat.

Sam nodded. "I, for one, would like to hear what she has to say. If you two want to leave, then go ahead. But I'm staying." He made a big show of opening his chair and sitting down.

Ken put his hands in his pockets and paced the room. "If we

can all stay calm," he looked at Sam, "I don't think it would hurt anything to hear what's on Angelina's mind."

"Ken..."

"She is our daughter, Patty. Let's hear what she has to say." He unfolded his chair and sat down, completing the little circle.

Angelina took a deep breath. "Thank you." She looked into each of their eyes. "Before I begin, I'm asking that you keep an open mind and listen to me." She paused. "I mean *really* listen."

"That's exactly what we're going to do." Ken rubbed the end of his nose where the "fly" had landed once again.

"Some of this is going to be hard to believe, but hear me out. As I said earlier, Josie and Adie are both in here with us—right now."

Ken, Patty, and Sam all sat in silence.

"Dad, that fly you've been complaining about? Isn't a fly at all; it's Josie. She's been trying to get your attention. She keeps touching you on the end of your nose."

"Can you have her to do it again?"

"Ken..." Patty tapped the arm of the chair.

"Josie, please touch Dad on the nose again."

Josie appeared next to Ken then faded away.

"Josie?"

A faint image of Josie flickered a few times then she was gone again.

"Josie!" She turned to Adie. "What's wrong with her?"

"Oh, dear. I'm afraid we've worn her out. She doesn't seem to have enough energy to manifest."

"I don't understand. What do you mean she doesn't have enough energy to manifest?"

"I had her doing some investigative work for me before we left the house. Then, she's been buzzing around constantly, trying to be noticed. We've apparently zapped her energy."

"Is she going to be all right?"

"She'll be fine. She just needs time to recoup."

After listening to the one sided conversation, Patty stood. "I think it's best if we leave now and let you rest."

Angelina jumped up. "I don't need rest! I'm not the one who's tired; it's Josie."

Ken stood up. "Calm down, sweetheart. Maybe we'll try this another time when your friend isn't so tired."

"You better stop them now. All we've done thus far is convince them you're worse off than they thought. If you let them walk out the door, the doctor will persuade them to throw away the key."

"Mom, Dad, don't go... Sam, please don't let them go—not yet. Josie will be back. She's just tired." Angelina turned to Adie. "You do it, then. You touch them."

The lights in the room flickered. "I would, but there's no need." The lights flickered again. "That's our girl." Adie smiled. "I knew she'd find a way. She's getting energy from the light source. She'll be here any minute."

Ken watched the lights dim as electric buzzing filled the room. "What in the world? I'm beginning to think this place has some serious safety issues."

"It's Josie. She's trying to regain her strength. Please don't leave—not yet. Adie says she'll be back very soon."

"Who's Adie?" Sam asked.

"Adie's the original owner of our home. Mom, you know her. Or, at least, you know about her. The Claytons are the people who had the house built."

Patty sat back down. "I know there was a couple by the name of Clayton, but still..."

"She's here, Mom. Adie Clayton is right here. Go ahead. Ask her anything you'd like to know about the house."

"Honey, surely you don't think she's here! She was an older woman when the house was built, and that was in 1908. That would put her at... what?"

"Mom, I'm not saying she's still alive. Adie's a ghost. She died a long time ago, but she's still here."

"Oh, Angel. You know that just isn't possible, honey."

"You can tell Mrs. High And Mighty I wasn't that old when the house was built. I had just turned sixty; I was in the prime of my life. I wasn't much older than she is right now."

Angelina grimaced—her mom was only in her forties. "Adie said she was sixty when the house was built."

"Yes, I believe it was something like that. I always have wondered why they had such a magnificent house built at such an old age."

"I wasn't old!" Adie spat. She reminded Angelina of a hen who had gotten her feathers riled up. She shivered as if she were putting her feathers back in place. "We built it because we could. We had always done well, Cecil and I. But he made the big money after the development downtown."

"She says they built it then because that's when they could afford to do it right. Cecil was a developer."

"Cecil… Was that his name? All the documentation I could find called him C.L. Clayton."

"That's right. C.L. Clayton. That was my Cecil." Adie squared her shoulders and sat up a little straighter. "Most of the important men of the town went by their initials." She laughed. "Poor Cecil was terrified people would find out his middle initial stood for Louise."

"Louise?" Angelina arched her brow.

"Yes, poor thing. His grandmother wanted a child named after her so badly. She thought Cecil was her last chance so she made her daughter promise she would name the baby after her. Little did they know, less than a year later a granddaughter would be born." Adie shrugged. "But it was too late by then."

"Who's Louise?" Ken asked. "You said the name Louise then you quit talking."

"Adie was just telling me the story of how her husband got his name; C.L. stood for Cecil Louise."

"Louise?" Ken said. "How'd he get stuck with a name like that?"

"Ken!" Patty snapped. "I don't think it's a good idea to encourage this."

Ken put his hands up in the air. "I was just asking."

"This is a delusion. There is no Cecil Louise." Patty grabbed her purse and stood up. "I think it's best if we go now."

"What happened to hearing Angelina out?" Sam's eyes hardened.

The lights flickered once again. Ken took Patty's hand and gently pulled her back down to her seat. He watched the lights. "We're listening."

"Ken…"

Ken squeezed Patty's hand. "Continue, Angel. What else does Adie have to say?"

Chapter 22

Angelina couldn't be sure if her dad was starting to believe her or not, but she wasn't going to let this chance go by without giving it her best shot. "Okay, Adie. What else can I tell them to make them believe you're here?"

Patty leaned her head against the back of the chair. "I'm telling you, Ken, I don't think we should be doing this."

"Humph." Adie squared her shoulders. "Well, let's see. They already know when the house was built, but do they know I picked the house out from the National Builders Supplement catalog?"

"What's that?"

"It was a catalog put out by Sears and Roebuck. Cecil brought it home and told me to pick out any house I wanted." Adie lifted her head high. "He said to not even worry about the price."

Angelina tucked her legs under her. "You ordered it from a catalog? Seriously?"

"What?" Sam leaned in. "What's she saying?"

Patty's eyes narrowed and she shook her head.

"She said…" Angelina paused, looked at her mother, and then continued. "She said she picked our house out of a Sears's catalog."

"A catalog! Whoa." Sam sat back. "And I thought you could only buy clothes from a catalog."

Patty tapped her foot. "I've already told you all that our house came from a catalog."

Adie repositioned herself so she could look at Patty. "Well, does she know the Victorian Queen Anne style home you now live in was the most expensive one? Poor Cecil. He never should have told me not to worry about the cost." She smiled. "He should have known better."

"Perhaps, Mom. But did you know it was the most luxurious one at the time?"

"This is ridiculous! Honey, I'm sorry, but all you're doing is repeating the same things I've already told you about the house."

"I don't remember you ever telling me this stuff."

"Well, I have—many times."

Sam turned to his mom. "I'm not trying to be rude, Mom, but the rest of us never really cared about all of that, so we just kind of tuned you out."

Ken stifled a laugh.

"So, she wants something more personal, does she?" Adie turned back to Angelina. "Okay, then. I bet she didn't know my house was the first one in town to have a water closet."

"A what?"

Josie flickered as she reappeared. "They call it a toilet, nowadays." She faded back out.

"Oh." Angelina arched her brow.

"What?" Sam asked.

"Did you know our house was the first one in town to have an indoor toilet? Or as Adie called it, a water closet?"

Patty leaned forward. "I doubt it was the very first, but I know it was one of the earliest. According to the library, most homes around here didn't have any type of indoor plumbing until around 1912."

"I never said we had indoor plumbing. We didn't get that for several years after our house was built. She needs to clean the wax out of her ears. What I said was we had the very first water closet in town."

"If you didn't have indoor plumbing, how did you have a toilet?"

"There was a cistern on the roof to catch the rainwater, which was used to flush the toilet. It only took one hour to refill the tank and bowl once the toilet was flushed. It was top of the line."

"Are you serious? It took a whole hour?"

"What took an hour?" Patty asked then placed her hand over her mouth.

"Apparently they had a cistern on the roof that caught the rainwater. You see, they had a toilet before they actually had running water but it took an hour to refill the tank after it was flushed."

"It may not have been quite as fast as what you have today, but back then it was really something to behold. Let me tell you, it caused quite a stir, too. Especially with that Mrs. Maddox. She always had to be the first at everything—but not this time. No, siree. I beat her on that one. I had the first water closet."

"Who was Mrs. Maddox?"

"Who was Mrs. Maddox?" Adie laughed. "Oh, boy! That serves her right. Everyone knew who she was."

"Maddox..." Patty wagged her finger. "Doesn't the Maddox home sit on the end of our block?"

"One and the same. She thought she was the only high society woman around here. She couldn't stand it that someone might be getting ahead of her in any way."

"What did she do?"

"She had her lips around the ears of half of this town while my home was being put up. She started talking about how we must be dirty people to even consider having a water closet put in our home."

"I don't get it. Why would she say that?"

"Pure and simple jealously, that's why! She went on and on about what kind of people we must be to relieve ourselves right in the house."

"That's too funny." Angelina laughed.

"What? What's funny?" Ken asked.

"Adie stuck it to Mrs. Maddox by being the first to have a bathroom so Mrs. Maddox tried to bad-mouth them around town by saying they were unsophisticated to use the bathroom inside their own house."

Even Patty smiled at that one.

"Turns out, Mrs. Maddox wasn't quite as sophisticated as she thought. She claimed she couldn't fathom having one of those nasty things in her house. She could understand the need for a chamber pot on the coldest of nights, but she'd never have a water closet in her home."

Angelina giggled. "So what did the rest of the town think?"

Adie shrugged her shoulders. "Some claimed to agree with her—mainly those who couldn't afford to modernize their homes and bring them up to snuff." She waved her hand through the air. "But, boy, let me tell you, we sure had a rash of remodeling going on in town that next year." She cocked her head to the side. "Including Mrs. Maddox, I might add."

"For real?"

"Oh, yes! Of course, she claimed she would've never done it, had it not been for her arthritis getting so bad and making it hard for her to get to the outhouse." Adie laughed. "Arthritis, my foot. Everyone knew she was blowing smoke. She sure had to eat a lot of crow that year."

Josie reappeared looking refreshed and as strong as ever. "Sorry about that, but I'm ready now."

"It's about time," Adie said. "Now try touching them while we talk."

"I'm on it." Josie buzzed around the room, once again trying to make herself known.

"Angel, ask them if they know the house was also the first one in town to have electricity."

"It was? Wow! It really was top of the line, wasn't it?" Angelina turned her attention back to the family. "Did you guys know our house was also the first one in town to have electricity?"

Ken cleared his throat and glanced over at Patty. "I'm afraid you're wrong about that one, honey. The house was built with gas lighting. We found the old gas pipes when we were doing some remodeling."

"You can tell Mr. Know-It-All I would know what my house did and didn't have," Adie scoffed. "You can also tell him the house had both."

"Why would it have both?" Angelina asked.

"As I've already said, no one else around here had electricity in their homes at the time and Cecil, bless his heart, didn't quite trust it. He said we could put it in and give it a try, but he wanted gas lighting just in case."

"Did it work?"

"Oh, yes. It worked just fine. But truth be known, Cecil was a little scared of it. He was afraid when he touched the light switch, it would shock him. For the longest time he wouldn't allow me to turn it on." Adie smiled at the memory. "He had a long, rubber-coated pole he would use to reach halfway across the room to turn the switch on. The whole time the electric lights were burning, Cecil wouldn't allow the rest of us anywhere near them."

"Sorry, Dad, you're only half right. Adie says the house was both gas and electric. Thought you caught me, didn't you?"

Ken knitted his brow and slowly shook his finger. "Patty, remember the contractor who was helping us with the remodel? He said the original lights could have been there as long as the house, but since we knew it had gas lighting, we just assumed the electricity had been added."

The room grew quiet as each of them contemplated the conversation.

Josie continued around the room, touching each of them on the nose.

Ken swatted the air.

"You felt it, didn't you, Dad? That was Josie."

Ken shook his head. "No, I don't think so. I just had an itch."

Josie touched him again and he once again twitched his nose.

"Dad, that's her! Concentrate. You did feel it."

"Wait a minute." He sat up straight. "Have her do it on the count of three. One, two…"

"Ken, please." Patty put her hand on his knee. "Can't you see? This is just encouraging her."

"Mom, you said you would listen and give me a chance."

"Honey, I have listened, but you haven't told me anything I didn't already know."

"That's not true. You didn't know our house was the first one in town to have a toilet, or that it was the first one to have electricity."

"And I still don't." Patty stood up. "Ken, I think it's time we go."

He nodded. "Maybe your mom's right—we should probably go."

"No, please!"

"Now blast it all," Adie said. "I'm not finished."

"Quick, Adie, what is it?"

"Ask your mother if she's ever heard of a Lou Rickter."

"Wait, Mom. Before you go, have you ever heard of Lou Rickter?"

"Yes, and so have you. Lou bought the house right after Mrs. Clayton passed away. Mr. Rickter was the mayor at the time." Patty sighed and picked up her purse. "Like everything else, I already told you that."

"Humph. Did your mother tell you that Mayor Rickter was the biggest bootlegger in the county? Did she tell you he made his sin juice right in my home?"

"Mom, did you know he was a bootlegger?"

"Oh, for goodness sake, Angel. He was not! He was a good and decent man. He was a very prominent citizen in this town."

"Good and decent?" Adie's hand flew to her chest. "Well, she's right about one thing." She cocked her brow. "He was prominent with a certain ilk of people. And he had the lowest of them all traipsing around my house at all hours of the night. Go ahead and ask her what happened to good old Mr. Rickter."

"What else do you know about him, Mom?"

"Not much. I guess he moved off or something. I know he didn't run for mayor again."

"I'll tell you what happened to him. He's probably in the bottom of the lake somewhere. When you keep those cohorts, that's generally what happens. All I know is late one night, the house was filled with those scoundrels. They went right up to the attic, walled off his whiskey still, and took off out of there like they'd been shot. I never saw Mr. Rickter again."

"Really? Do you think someone killed him?"

"I wouldn't be a bit surprised. 'Course, I don't think anyone cared much. There *was* an investigation of sorts—he was the mayor, after all. A few police officers came around, from time to time, but I think they were more interested in finding the alleged whiskey still than in finding him."

"Did they ever find it?"

"Well, no. They never found it. It's still right there in the attic where they walled it off."

"It's still there?" Angelina's eyes glistened. "Are you sure?"

"Of course, I'm sure. Josie went and had a look at it today. Now, if you could get one of them to..."

"Mom, Dad, please. I'm going to ask you to do one thing for me. Adie said the whiskey still Mr. Rickter used is walled up in the attic. If you'd just go home and look, you'd see…"

"Angel, honey, I've been over every inch of that house, including the attic. I assure you, there isn't a whiskey still anywhere in the house."

"Mom, please, just…"

"We have to go now, Angel." Patty pulled on Ken's hand. "We can talk more about this later."

"No, we won't. If you're not going to listen to me now, you never will. I'll be just like Rebecca and be stuck in here forever."

Rebecca walked in. "Did someone mention my name?"

Angelina blinked. "Becca?" She almost didn't recognize her. Rebecca's hair was combed and she was wearing a matching pair of house shoes.

"Hello, dear. How are you, Mr. and Mrs. Cartwright?" She nodded. "Sam, Adie, Josie—how are you?"

"You can see them?" Sam asked. "You can see Adie and Josie?"

"Of course, I can." Rebecca smiled.

Patty walked toward the door. "It's time to go. Nice seeing you again, Rebecca."

"But, Mom—"

Patty opened the door. "It's time to go, Sam."

Chapter 23

As they headed across the parking lot, Sam lagged behind. The parents were at it again. He kicked a rock into one of the potholes. This wasn't going to be a pleasant ride home.

"I told you, Ken. I told you we shouldn't let her talk about those things outside of counseling. We've probably set her therapy back by several weeks, and I can assure you Dr. Bowman's not going to be happy about this." The click-click-click of Patty's heels grew louder and quicker across the pavement. "I don't know. We may have even caused irreparable damage."

"Don't you think you're overreacting a little bit?" Ken had to lengthen his stride to keep up. "We didn't hurt her." He unlocked the doors to the car. "We just let her talk. And you have to admit, some of what she said kind of makes you wonder."

Sam slid into the back seat and leaned his head back on the headrest.

"Wonder about what, Ken?" She got into the car. "Do you really think she's talking to ghosts?" She threw her purse into the back seat, barely missing Sam's leg. "Come on! You can't seriously believe that." Each word burned her mouth like acid.

Ken got in and slammed the door.

Patty glared at him across the console.

"Sorry," he muttered. "I didn't mean to shut the door so hard." He took a deep breath. "And no, I don't actually think she was talking to ghosts." He put the keys into the ignition and started the car. "But it appeared something was going on."

"I'll tell you what was going on." She scowled. "The longer we allowed the conversation to continue, the more delusional she became. That is exactly what Dr. Bowman said would happen."

"I don't know, Patty." He gripped the steering wheel tight, making his knuckles turn white. "A lot of what she said somehow made sense. How'd she know all of that stuff about the house?"

"I've already told you—she was just repeating things she'd heard from me."

"Not all of it." He rubbed his hands across his face. "What about that guy—Lou Rickter? You said yourself you didn't know what had become of him."

"Ken, listen to me. *She. Doesn't. Either.* Don't you see? It's all in her mind." She leaned her head up against the window and closed her eyes. "None of it's true."

"So you think she's making all this up? You think she's—she's what? Lying to us?"

She sat back up and looked over at him. "No, I don't think she's intentionally lying. I think she believes what she's saying. But it's all in her head."

"Maybe you're right." Ken paused. "I mean, of course you're right. It's not as though she has a direct line to communicate with the dead." He reached over and put his hand on Patty's leg. "Listen, I'm sorry. From now on, I'll try to play by Dr. Bowman's rules."

She laid her hand over his and nodded. "I only wish you'd decided that before this visit." She attempted to smile. "But thank you. I just hope we haven't already messed everything up."

Sam went straight to his room and slammed the door. He stormed around, opening and closing his fist. He yanked his suitcase from the closet, threw it on the bed, and started packing. Mindlessly throwing things in, he heard a knock on the door. He swiped at the tears that streaked down his tan face. "Come in!"

Ken eyed the suitcase lying on the bed. "Going somewhere?" He shut the door behind him.

"It's time for me to get back to school."

"I thought you'd been approved to take a leave of absence."

"I was, but why bother? What's the point in me sticking around? I can't do anything to help." He yanked a drawer out of the dresser and dumped its contents into the suitcase. "You guys put Angel in that place and she's obviously not coming home anytime soon." He put the drawer back in its slot and turned to his dad. "I'm not accomplishing anything here, and if I stay around, I'm going to explode." He slammed his suitcase closed. "I can't take this anymore. Call me crazy, but I believe her." He ran his fingers through his hair. "I guess if I don't watch out, you and Mom will put me right in there with her."

"Sam, that's not fair. You make it sound as though we wanted to put Angel in there. Son, we're trying to help her." Ken turned his head and brushed the tears from his eyes. He slumped down on the edge of the bed with his back to Sam.

Sam opened his duffle bag and, with a swipe of his hand, cleared the top of his dresser into the bag.

Ken cleared his throat. "I'm going to take your Mom out to dinner. You know, try to relax her a little. I hope you'll reconsider leaving and will still be here when we get back."

"Dad, please don't ask that of me. I need to get out of here. Surely, you can understand." His voice cracked. "She's my sister—my little sister. It's my job to protect her, but you and Mom have tied my hands."

Ken rose to his feet and stood quietly for a minute. "I guess we all have to do what we feel is right. As I said, I'm going to take your Mom out to dinner. If you're gone when we get back, I'll understand." Ken glanced toward the door to make sure they were still alone. "If you choose to stay, remember—there's a hammer in the kitchen drawer."

"What…?" His eyebrows shot up. "A hammer?"

Ken nodded and lowered his voice. "Am I really the only one that's curious about the whiskey still?"

Sam took a few steps back. "Dad, what are you saying?"

Ken wagged his head from side to side. "I really don't know, Son. But if there was a still hidden somewhere, we'd have to take what she's saying a little more seriously."

"Dad, do you believe her? I mean… do you think there's something to all of this?"

"I don't know what to think anymore. I'm—I'm just not sure." He patted Sam on the back. "I hope you're still here when we get home."

Angelina stared at the cold, colorless door as her family walked out. Her hope for any kind of future was gone. The sound of the latch closing somehow felt final—hopeless. "Did they leave because of me?" Rebecca asked. "Did I come on too strong?" She paced the room. "I didn't know what to do. I was standing outside the door and it sounded like they were leaving. I thought if I told them I could see Josie and Adie, they would at least consider—"

"It wasn't you. They'd already made up their minds to go." Angelina walked to her bed. "Becca, sit down. You, too, Josie." She plopped down on the bed. "I'm sorry. I just can't take this pacing."

"It's no wonder." Josie walked to the bed. "I'm surprised we haven't rubbed a hole completely through this floor." She put her hand on Angelina's shoulder. "Don't you fret. We'll come up with something."

Adie spoke up. "When they get here tomorrow, we could—"

"Don't you see? Don't any of you see? It's not working!" Hot tears spilled down her face. "They left me! They left me *again*!"

Rebecca looked at the door. "Angel," she whispered. "Please calm down. It isn't over. We'll work until we get you out of here. I promise."

Angelina pulled her pillow up to her chest and squeezed it tight. "I'm sorry." She looked around the room. "I appreciate all of you, but I…" She wiped her tears. "I can't do this right now. I just really want to be left alone."

"If that's what you want." Josie reached out to pat her arm. "But if you need anything…"

"She knows how to contact us." Adie stood to leave.

Rebecca walked to the door. "I'm right down the hall if you need me."

With the room to herself, she curled up in a ball and closed her eyes. She couldn't go on pretending she was okay. She wasn't. She buried her head into the pillow and grieved her loss—the loss of her freedom, the lost security of family, and the loss of her life as she had once known it.

With her mind and body depleted, exhaustion took over and she fell into a fitful sleep, only to wake and start the crying process all over again. Lying in the dark with her back to the door, she heard someone come in. The frightening thought that one of the nurses had heard her crying and had come to take her to the west wing was a very real possibility.

She pulled the pillow tighter and silently begged her body not to betray her with more tears. She listened. The sounds she heard made no sense to her overwrought brain. She thought she heard a sob, and then another. She waited.

"Angel, sweetie? Are you awake?"

She rolled over. The effort made her head feel like a thousand needles were pricking her brain. She opened her swollen eyes and saw the silhouettes of several people huddled together in the doorway. *They've come to take me to the west wing.* "Please don't," she whimpered. "I'll be quiet."

"Angel." The voice sounded like her mother's, but she knew it wasn't. *It can't be.* Her mother was gone. Everything she cared about was gone.

Another figure appeared in the shadows behind them. "Excuse me." She recognized the voice of the nurse. "Visiting hours are long over."

"Excuse me!" Patty reached in and snapped on the light. "This is our daughter and we don't need visiting hours to see her."

Angelina bolted upright, shielding her eyes from the burning light. Her family walked in and Ken shut the door in the face of the gawking nurse.

In three strides, Patty had her arms around her. "I'm so sorry. Can you ever forgive me?"

The room spun and it was hard to focus. Angelina pushed the sides of her head, trying to relieve the pressure. "Forgive you?"

Patty held her at arm's length and gasped. "Ken!" Tears filled her eyes. "Look at her. Look at what I've done!"

Sam went to the sink to get a cold rag to put on Angelina's swollen eyes.

Ken threw open the closet door. "There isn't time for that right now. The nurse is probably getting security. Let's go."

"Go?" None of this made any sense. Her head hurt so badly. Patty pulled her to her feet as Ken put the robe around her shoulders.

"Are we ready?" Sam opened the door.

Two nurses met them in the hall. Ken pushed between them. The fat one with sausage fingers called out, "Mr. and Mrs. Cartwright, you can't leave. Not like this."

Patty whirled and jabbed her finger at the nurse. "It was my signature that put her in here and it's my choice to take her out."

Chapter 24

Angelina looked through the rear window of the car, watching the hospital fade into the night's darkness. She couldn't take her eyes off the place until it was completely gone. She turned to Sam. "Am I really going home?"

He took her hand. "We're all going home."

She laid her pounding head against the back of the seat. "But why?"

"Because, you never should've been there in the first place."

She closed her swollen eyes. She knew she must be dreaming, but she didn't want to wake up. Listening to the hum of the car's engine, she gave into the fantasy and let the feeling of going home seep into her tired body. It all seemed so real...

Sam nudged her shoulder. "Don't you want to get out?"

She sat up and stared out the window.

Home.

Their house loomed in front of them, even more beautiful than she remembered. With lights burning in every window, she could see the old tire swing sway gently in the breeze. As children, she and Sam had spent countless hours playing on it.

She closed her eyes again, hoping that, if this were a dream, she'd never wake up. She didn't want to see the colorless walls of the hospital. She didn't want to smell the dank, putrid odor that seemed to permeate everything. She didn't want to hear the squeaking wheels of the medicine cart going down the hall. She just wanted to stay here—in the dream.

Patty opened the car door and offered her hand. "Angel, do you need help?"

She took her mother's hand. It felt soft and warm. Stepping out of the car, the cool night air felt good on her tear-chapped face. She stood looking at the house. She breathed in the fresh, cedar-tinged air.

Home.

Walking around the car, Sam pulled on her arm. "Come on. I want to show you something." He took her hand and led her up the cobblestone path to the front door.

She stood in the living room and wrapped her arms around herself. "Sam, is this for real? Am I really here?"

"Its for real, little sister. You're home." He tugged her arm. "Come on. I need to show you something."

She followed him up the stairs with Ken and Patty trailing behind. Passing her room, she stopped. "Can I—?"

"In a minute." He pushed her forward.

As they turned the corner, she gasped. The staircase that led to the attic was covered in a thick layer of dust, and splintered wood dotted the stairs. Tears sprang to her eyes. "What happened?" She scanned the destruction. "Was there an explosion?"

"Of sorts." Ken reached down and picked up a hammer from beneath the debris. "This and your brother exploded our attic."

She dabbed at her burning eyes and turned to Sam. "You did this?"

He flexed his biceps. "Sure did."

"But why?" Bewilderment flashed across her face. "Why would you do this?"

They all stood quietly and waited…

Angelina's eyes met Patty's. "You're okay with this—this awful mess?"

Patty nodded, tears glistening on her cheek. "It's the most beautiful thing I've ever seen."

Angelina looked around. "What's wrong with you people? Why would you do this?"

"You really don't get it, do you?" Sam asked.

She shook her head.

"Come on then, I'll show you." He pulled her toward the stairs.

She pulled back. "Are you kidding? I'm not going up there. It doesn't look safe."

Ken put his hand on her back and gave her a nudge. "Go on, we'll be right behind you. Trust us."

She stumbled through the wreckage as Sam dragged her up the stairs. When he pulled her into the attic, she stopped. She blinked, trying to make it all make sense. Everything was different…

"Don't you get it?" Sam pointed. "Adie was right! That's Mr. Rickter's whiskey still!"

The dim light in the attic made it hard to see. "But—but—"

"There it is! Right where you said it would be."

He pulled her over the piles of rubble to the far corner. There was… something—a vat of some sort, with tubes and pipes sticking out of it. She'd never seen anything like it before. "Is this a whiskey still?"

"Well," Sam scratched his head, "I'm no expert, but given the circumstances, I'd say that's exactly what it is."

She threw her arms around his neck. "You believed me! You must've believed me to do this."

"Actually," he gestured toward their dad, "it was his idea."

"What?" Patty poked Ken in the ribs. "Oh it was, was it? In that case, I know who gets to clean up this mess."

Angelina rolled over and looked at her alarm clock. It was four in the morning and she still hadn't fallen asleep. But who cared? She was home.

My clock, my bed, and my room. The next time she looked at her clock it read 4:37. She tossed her blanket aside. *Who even wants to sleep? I'm home!*

She tiptoed out into the hall. The house was quiet. She wrapped her hand around the banister and relished the familiar feel of it as she went down the stairs. It was the same—but better. She walked around the living room, wondering if the carpet had always felt this soft on her bare feet. She sniffed the air. *Is that coffee?* She went into the kitchen and saw her mom sitting alone at the table. She slid into the chair next to her. "I guess you couldn't sleep, either."

"No. But that's okay—you're home." She put her hand on top of Angelina's. "I know I have no right to ask for your forgiveness but—"

"Mom, it's okay." She looked her mother in the eyes. "Really, I understand. I mean… ghosts?" She grinned. "Come on."

"But it's true… and it's always been true."

Angelina shifted in her seat and nodded.

"Angel, I don't mean to make you uncomfortable. I'm just trying to wrap my mind around all of this. Is it okay if we talk about it?"

"Sure. I mean, as long as you're okay with it."

Patty took a sip of her coffee and leaned back in her chair. "I have so many questions. I'm not sure where to start." Her chest rose with a deep sigh. "Have you always been able to see them?"

"No. Of course, when I was little, I could see Josie, but after the counseling…" She shrugged. "I couldn't for a long time."

"I wonder why?"

"Josie said it was because I didn't want to." She looked down at the table. "See, that's where the dreams came in. I guess when Josie," she cleared her throat, "and others wanted me to know something, they would come to me in my dreams."

"And now? You just talk to them—like you and I are talking now?"

"Yes."

She leaned over her cup. "Can you actually see them, or do you just hear them?"

"I can see them."

Patty got up to refill her coffee. "Want some?"

"Sure."

Patty put the cups on the table. "Angel, I want you to know, I believe you." She sat down. "How could I not after seeing the still? I just don't understand how this is possible."

Josie slid in beside Angelina at the table. "Tell her there are a lot of things in this old world that are hard to understand. Sometimes we just have to take them for what they're worth and go on."

Angelina traced the pattern on her coffee cup with her finger. "There are a lot of things in this old world that are hard to understand. Sometimes we just have to take them for what they're worth and go on."

"That doesn't sound like something you'd say." She laughed. "That sounded more like something an old woman… Oh! Oh, my! Does that mean she's here? Is she here right now?"

Angelina smiled. "I never thought I'd be able to do this, but Mom, this is Josie, and Josie, this is my mom."

Patty got up and walked around the kitchen. "Um, I'm not sure what to say. I'm not sure what to do."

"It's okay, Mom. You could… I don't know… start with saying 'hello.'"

"Yes—yes of course. Where are my manners? Hello, Josie. Can I get you anything? Would you like a cup of coffee?"

Angelina laughed. "Uh, Mom? She's a ghost. She doesn't drink."

"Actually, if she's got an extra, I'd enjoy wrapping my hands around the warm mug." Josie sighed. "This is one of the things I miss the most. I used to love sitting around the table and having coffee with friends."

"I guess I was mistaken, Mom. Josie would like to join us for coffee."

"Could you make that two?" Adie asked as she joined the group. "Since we're all getting to know one another, I have a little favor I'd like to ask of your mother."

"Um, Mom, could you make that two more cups? And uh, Adie has a favor she wants to ask."

Patty put the steaming cups on the table and Angelina slid one to each of their guests. Wide-eyed Patty stared at the empty chairs. "What kind of favor?"

Adie wrapped her hands around her coffee cup. "If you'll look behind that vile man's whiskey still in the attic, you'll find a matching chair to the one in Angelina's room."

"Really? You mean, Josie's chair?" Angelina asked.

"Josie's!" Adie screeched.

"Well, I sure polished them enough to consider them mine."

Adie smiled. "Indeed, you did."

"What? What are they saying?"

"Oh, sorry, Mom. They were just discussing ownership of some chairs."

"Now, back to what I was trying to say," Adie continued. "If you can imagine, that man took my," she glanced at Josie, "took *our* chair up there to sit in while he made his poison." She tsk-tsked with her tongue. "I'd… *we'd* like it to be brought down, cleaned up, and placed with the other one in front of the living room window."

"Mom, there's a chair that matches the one in my room. Adie thinks it's up there by the still and she wants you to get it and put both of them in the living room by the bay window."

"Of course, I will." Patty's eyes danced. "I never knew there were two chairs. I bet they would look beautiful sitting together in front of the window."

"They always did," Adie said. "That's where they sat from the day I moved here to the day I died. Cecil bought them for me as an anniversary gift long before we had this house."

"This is exciting! I've always wanted to restore this house as close as possible to how it was originally."

"In that case," Adie's spine stiffened. "What were you thinking when you painted my bedroom that color? It looked much better—"

"If she's handing out favors, I've got something to ask from her, too." Rosie sat down. "Angel, be a dear and get me a cup as well, would you?"

Angelina poured another cup and sat it down.

"Angel, what are you doing?" Patty asked.

"Mom, we have another guest. I believe you met Rosie a long time ago. She was the manager of—"

"Hey! Are we having a party?" Shelly strutted into the kitchen. "Oh, yum! Is that hot Dr. Pepper? I want one."

"No." Angelina shuddered. "It's coffee. Who ever heard of hot Dr. Pepper?"

"Hot Dr. Pepper? My goodness! I haven't heard of that in ages. Shelly and I used to—" Patty put her hand up to her mouth.

Ken walked into the kitchen. He yawned. "Doesn't anybody sleep around here?" He sat down and looked at the line of coffee cups. "Are we expecting company?"

Patty's eyes glistened with unshed tears. "You never know, Ken. You just never know."

Epilogue

Angelina walked down the sidewalk, reveling in the warmth of the sun on her skin. It had already been three months since she'd left the hospital, but everything still seemed so... perfect. She knew it was corny, but the air really did smell cleaner, the colors were more vibrant, and she knew the birds had never sung this beautifully before. Her mom told her things would go back to normal. She hoped her mom was wrong.

As wonderful as everything was, nothing quite compared to how good Jason's hand felt in hers. She looked up at him and smiled. "C'mon. You promised!" She still couldn't believe how gorgeous he was. Of course, she'd known that even before she was put in the hospital. "Today's the day. I'm waiting."

"Do I have to?"

She looked down and watched their feet move in unison. She knew if she looked him in the eyes, he'd give in. "You promised."

"Okay." He stopped and turned her to face him. "But you have to promise me two things first."

"Two? That's not fair." She stretched up and placed a soft kiss on his perfectly sexy lips.

He smiled. "Nice try, but it's two—that's the deal."

"Okay, fine. Wait. What two things?"

"Too late. You promised." He rubbed his hands together and grinned. His eyes roamed over her. "Now, what should I ask for?"

"Jason!" She laughed. "Can't you ever be serious?"

"Who says I wasn't being serious?"

This was turning into dangerous territory. She knew if she didn't break eye contact, she might agree to do just about anything. She turned back to his side, gripped his hand, and started walking. "Within reason, what two things do you want from me?"

"Okay, if it has to be within reason," he squeezed her hand, "number one is for you not to laugh, and number two is for you to tell me the truth about how you contracted mono."

"Seriously?"

"Seriously."

"Okay, but you go first."

"All right, but I feel like an idiot." He took a breath, and then talked really fast. "I broke up with you because I felt you were too good for me."

Never letting go of his hand, she shoved him with her arm. "I'm being serious. I want to know the real reason you broke up with me."

"That *is* the real reason. Think about it, Angel. You're so perfect. I mean, look at you—you're sweet, beautiful, and smart. You come from a great family. You're just… you're so *together.* You're already applying to different colleges and me…" He shrugged. "I can't even decide what to have for breakfast most mornings."

"If you're being serious, you're an idiot." She stopped walking and pulled on his arm. She kissed him again. "See? I'm not so perfect." She looked into his eyes. "I mean, how perfect could I be? I'm in love with an idiot."

"Get a room, you two." Kobi walked up to the fence with mud all over her hands.

"Hey, Kobi! Wow, I didn't realize we'd already walked this far."

"Of course, you didn't. You were too busy staring into lover boy's eyes." She wiped a streak of mud across Jason's cheek. "There. Maybe that will help you to resist him." She wiped the rest of the mud on her jeans. "You guys want a drink before Mom figures out you're here and puts you to work?"

Jason saluted. "I wouldn't dream of drinking Captain Becca's lemonade before putting in my time." They followed her to the porch.

Sam opened the door. "Glad to hear you say that. It's time to paint the ceiling and I could sure use you in here." He kissed the top of Kobi's head as she walked in under his arm.

Angelina looked around the house. "Wow! I can't believe the changes you guys have made since last weekend." Walking into the kitchen, she squealed. "Red! A red kitchen!" She hugged Becca. "It looks wonderful."

Becca handed each of them a glass of lemonade. She winked at Jason. "I'll go ahead and pay you in advance, but I've got my eye on you."

"Yes, ma'am. Rest assured, I'll work extra hard today."

"This is all so exciting," Angelina said. "What else needs painting? I suddenly have an overwhelming urge to paint."

"Not today, Princess." Kobi shook her muddy hands at her. "Today we work in the garden. Mom insists she have flowers of every color planted." She sighed. "Do you have any idea how many colors of flowers are available?"

Rebecca smiled. "My dreams are coming true. Kobi, dear, I want to show Angel my writing room. I need her opinion on something. You go ahead with the planting. We'll be along in a little bit."

"Of course." Kobi tried to scowl, but it came out more of a smile. "We couldn't have Angel getting dirty, now could we?"

Rebecca took Angelina's hand and led her down the hall. They stood in front of a closed door. "Ready?"

Angelina nodded.

"May I present…" Rebecca flung open the door, "my writing room!"

Angelina walked in. The room was painted the same shade of yellow as the t-shirt Kobi used to wear to the hospital. A border of bright sunflowers ringed the room and a matching bouquet sat on the desk next to the computer. "Becca, it's beautiful." She ran her finger along the spines of a row of books in the cherry bookshelves that lined the wall. "Did you say writing room?"

Rebecca smiled. "My own little sanctuary."

"What do you write?"

"I dabbled in several things before…" She shrugged. "You know. Anyway, I used to write for garden magazines and various other things." She took a book from the shelf. "This is my only book, so far." She handed it to Angelina.

Wide-eyed Angelina read the cover. The book was titled, *Our Paranormal World*. Angelina smiled when she read the author's name, Rebecca Farland. "Becca, I don't know what to say. I had no idea you were an author."

Rebecca shrugged. "Was. But who knows? Maybe, I will be again one day."

Angelina read the back cover. "Rebecca, is this a true book? Is it about you and—and— "

"Ghosts." Rebecca nodded. "Not everyone thinks it's crazy. It actually sold a lot of copies."

"Rebecca, this is awesome."

"I'm so glad you feel that way. That's why I brought you back here. I've been working on something I want you to read. It's purely fictional," she winked, "but I want your approval, just in case I try to get it published." She turned the computer on. "I'll take over your gardening chores." She pointed to the chair. "Just for today, you read." Rebecca walked out and closed the door.

Angelina scrolled down the page. She read the title, *Allison's Secret*, by Rebecca Farland. Her breath caught as she read:

The premonitions always made her feel this way—weak, disoriented, scared. Allison clutched a nearby branch to keep from falling as she watched the water shimmer under the morning sun. She closed her eyes, hoping the sound of the ripples would calm her. She jolted. Something wasn't right. A sense of dread washed over her as her eyes shot open and darted around the park. Nothing had changed.

But still...

This edition of *Angelina's Secret* also includes a bonus short story:

Angelina's Friend

A Prequel Story
to Angelina's Secret by

Lisa Rogers

Chapter 1

Josie sat in her favorite chair, the one that faced out the window of the old Victorian home. She put her hand on the cool glass as she admired the gardens below. This family had been good for the house. It was sometimes hard to believe it was now over a hundred years old.

And to think, she could remember this land back before anything had been built on it.

A smile tugged at the corners of her mouth as the grandfather clock downstairs chimed three times. The children would be home from school soon. She thought Sam still could see her sometimes, but she couldn't be sure. He was such a typical boy—couldn't be still long enough to focus on much of anything except for that silly contraption he spent hours in front of. All she knew about the thing was it must be some sort of game. He held something in his hands and pushed buttons as he looked at an ever-changing screen. Sometimes it was almost as if he was driving one of those car machines right through the parlor. Things sure had changed over the years.

At least Angelina paid no never mind to those kinds of games. She played with things Josie understood—her crib and baby dolls. Of course, her dolls did things that sometimes made a body wonder if they were real babies after all. She clicked her tongue thinking about the doll Angelina had gotten for Christmas last year. It drank a bottle and actually wet its diaper of all things. Why someone would want a doll to do *that* was beyond her. Dolls were supposed to be fun, not yell out in the middle of the night, "Feed me! Feed me!" Remembering how Angelina's daddy had run into the room late one night and taken something out of the back of the doll to make it be quiet made a smile creep across her wrinkled face.

Josie stood and straightened her dark green apron when the bell called her to tea. Little Angelina had gotten things ready for them quickly today. She was such a sweet, sweet child, and there was something special about her.

She might even have the gift. If that were true, considering her own gift, she and Angelina could make quite a team some day. Given her condition, that was a rare and special thing indeed.

Patty watched her five-year-old daughter sitting at the little table having a tea party with her imaginary friend. She held up a cookie to the empty seat for a moment, and then burst out laughing.

"No, Josie," she giggled. "You have to take a real bite."

Patty bit her lip as a sick ache of worry filled her. This imaginary friend business was getting out of control. It hadn't been cute for a long time. Patty had hoped that once Angelina started school and made some real friends she would forget about "Josie." If anything, it had only gotten worse. Angelina would come in from school and immediately set her table for tea with Josie. She wanted to show Josie her papers from school, to tell Josie about her friends and her teacher.

Knowing it was ridiculous Patty still couldn't help but be a little jealous. She'd chosen to be a stay-at-home mom so she could share these moments in her daughter's life. Instead, Angelina wanted to share everything with Josie.

Patty walked over to the table. "Let's go outside and swing."

"Okay, Mommy." Angelina brushed the crumbs from the table onto her napkin and looked at the empty chair. "See? I remembered to clean up after myself like you said."

Patty took her daughter's hand. "I'll race you to the swing."

Angelina put her little index finger in the air and shook it. "Proper young ladies don't run in the house."

Where does she get this stuff? Patty laughed. "Oh, I didn't realize we were being so proper today, Miss Angelina." She bowed and waved her arms out in front of her. "After you, my dear."

Angelina's eyes danced as she watched her mother's theatrics.

She bowed, imitating her movements. "After you, Josie." She gave a wave of her hand.

Patty sighed and got down on her knees and looked into her daughter's crystal blue eyes, so much like her own. "I was hoping just you, Sam, and I could go swing today. Okay?"

Angelina looked past her mother. "Is that okay?" she asked the empty chair. She nodded and smiled. "Josie said okay. She said it was special Mommy time."

Patty stood and straightened Angelina's blonde pigtails. "Good. I like special Mommy time. Sam!" she yelled up the stairs. "Let's go outside."

Swinging the kids and rolling around in the yard made Patty remember all the things she loved about being a mother. Days like this made it so easy to forget the unpleasant side of things. Falling into a lawn chair, laughing, and picking grass from her hair she noticed her husband watching them from the back door, a glass of iced tea in his hands. She motioned him outside. "I could sure use one of those. These kids have shown me exactly how old I am."

Handing her a glass of tea, he joined her in the adjacent chair. "Looks like you were having the time of your life."

"Mommy!" Angelina called. "Push me!"

Taking a much-needed drink of her tea, Patty shook her head. "Mommy's tired, honey. Sam, would you push your sister?"

"Aw, Mom, can't I play my game now?"

Patty looked at her watch. "I guess, but only for a little while."

Ken and Patty watched Angelina kick a ball around the yard. She stopped, looked up at her bedroom window, and waved. "Can I go play with Josie now?"

"Sure, punkin." Ken held out his arms. "After you give Daddy a hug."

She wrapped her arms around his neck, and then squealed and squirmed to get away when he started tickling her. "Stop it, Daddy! Josie's waiting on me."

"Well in that case, you better hurry."

With the back yard now quiet, Patty said, "Ken can I ask a favor of you?"

"Sure." He smiled. "Let me guess, now you want me to push you on the swing, right?"

She placed her hand over his. "No. What I want is for you to be serious for a minute."

"Ooooh, serious." He sat up straight. "Am I in trouble?"

"Ken," she laughed. "Come on."

"Okay." The teasing light left his eyes. "Let me save you the trouble. I know I messed up by telling Angel she could play with Josie." He sighed. "I just don't understand what the big deal is. A lot of kids have imaginary friends. It's perfectly normal."

"I know it's normal. I just don't think we should encourage it. It isn't like it used to be when she talked about Josie once in a while. It's all the time now." Patty's voice quivered. "She rushes in from school and can't wait to see Josie. It's as if I'm not even important to her anymore."

"Now I know you're overreacting. Haven't you seen how she looks at you? You're her whole world. You have nothing to worry about. No one is going to take your place, especially not some imaginary friend."

Patty looked over at her husband and smiled. "Thanks, I needed to hear that. I must sound like a jealous buffoon. It's just that now with both of them in school, I feel so… so useless."

"Useless? Never! Who else could I get to do my laundry, polish my shoes, and," his eyes gleamed with mischievousness, "…draw my bath."

"Oh, now I'm supposed to even 'draw' your bath, am I? Sure, no problem. I'll boil you like a lobster."

He stood and reached for her hand. "Speaking of lobsters, what's for dinner?" Seeing "the look," he cleared his throat. "I thought I'd help you cook tonight."

She laughed as she allowed him to pull her up from the lawn chair. "Oh, you'll do better than that. Tonight, you're in charge of dinner."

He shrugged. "So... you want me to call in for a pizza, huh?"

Chapter 2

Patty rushed to answer the ringing phone. As she turned the corner, she smacked her hip into the table. Rubbing the spot with one hand, she grabbed the phone with the other. "Hello."

"Mrs. Cartwright, I hope I haven't called at a bad time. This is Mrs. Foust, Angelina's teacher, and I was hoping to have a few minutes of your time."

"Oh, yes of course. What can I do for you?"

"I saw you'd signed up to volunteer for extracurricular activities at the school and I was hoping I could get you to help Angelina's class with a craft project."

Giving up on soothing her hip, Patty took her calendar from the drawer and sat down at the table. "I'd love to. What are you working on?"

"We're going to do a little finger painting project," she laughed. "As you can imagine trying to finger paint with two dozen five-year-olds is quite an undertaking. I can use all the help I can get."

"Oh, that sounds like fun—and a mess. When do you want me there?"

"If you could be here Friday morning, say, 10 o'clock that would be great."

Patty flipped open her calendar and her heart sank. "This Friday?"

"Yes, at ten. I was thinking we could…"

"I am so sorry. But I've already volunteered to go on a class trip with Sam on Friday."

"Oh pooh! There just don't seem to be enough moms to go around. I've almost exhausted my list."

"I'm terribly sorry. Maybe you could reschedule the project."

"I'd hate to do that. I've already gotten a couple of moms scheduled to come in, but I just don't think it will be quite enough." She paused. "I don't suppose you could ask Josie to do it, could you?"

Patty gripped the edge of the table with white-knuckled fingers. "Excuse me? What did you say?"

"I asked if you could perhaps ask Josie to do it. She's not on our list of volunteers but the way Angelina carries on about her I'm sure she'd be great."

"I'm afraid there's been some kind of mistake." Patty brushed at the tear that rolled down her cheek. "Josie is… um, well, she isn't real. She's, um, Angelina's imaginary friend."

"Oh!" Mrs. Foust laughed. "I see. I must look foolish. I just assumed she was Angelina's grandma or your housekeeper from the way she talks about her. It's always 'Josie this' and 'Josie that.'"

"Yes, I know what you mean."

"Well okay, then. I guess I better continue on down my list. Next time we have a project I'll call on you."

"Please do." Patty hung up the phone. She poured herself a cup of coffee and sat back down at the table. Turning her computer on she thought, *this has definitely gone on long enough.*

She'd hoped browsing the internet would give her some answers. Instead, it scared her half to death.

Ken took his glasses off and tossed them on the kitchen table. "Patty," He paused as he rubbed the bridge of his nose. "Honey, I think you're just borrowing trouble. A lot of kids have imaginary friends." He looked out the window at the children playing in the backyard. "I mean look at them. They're perfectly normal kids. Both of them."

"Ken, you didn't read those articles. Do you want me to pull them up for you?" Patty picked up the rag and started wiping down the already clean counters. "Sometimes it's normal to have imaginary friends, sometimes it can be a sign of a severe problem. It could mean she's not developing socially." She sniffed. "Every article mentioned warning signs to look for and… and she *has* them." She threw the rag into the sink. "What do you want me to do, just ignore them?"

He racked his fingers through his thick dark hair and loudly exhaled. "I just don't think it's anything to get so worked up about."

"I'm not worked up, Ken! Every one of those articles said if parents had any concerns they should seek help. That's all I'm asking to do. I just want to have her checked out to make sure she's okay."

Ken shook his head. "I wouldn't even know where to take her for something like this. I mean, it's not like she's sick or anything."

"There's a child psychologist right here in town who specializes in this sort of thing. We could just take her in for—"

"Ah Patty, come on! A shrink? You know I don't believe in all of that psychobabble nonsense. Just leave her alone. There's nothing wrong with her."

"Fine, Ken, but when she marries an imaginary man and gives us imaginary grandchildren I'll remind you of this conversation."

"Ah honey, don't be like that."

Patty glared at him for a moment. "I'm going upstairs to take a bubble bath. You can watch the children this evening because apparently I'm just their mother and I don't know what's best for them." She stomped up the narrow Victorian staircase and slammed the door.

Sinking into the hot bath, she let the water ease her tension. *Maybe I'm overreacting.* A lot of children had imaginary friends, and she knew that. She sank deeper into the tub and closed her eyes. Almost fully relaxed, she remembered a time when she'd been a little girl and woken up to find Band-Aids stuck all over her bedroom window. Come to find out her sister had gotten up in the night because her imaginary friend, the elephant, had gotten hurt and had come to her for help. She smiled at the memory. She'd have to ask her sister about it the next time she talked to her, but for now she needed to get the kids ready for bed and possibly apologize to her husband.

She had to hand it to Ken. He made a pretty good stand-in when she needed him to. After her bath, she found Sam already tucked into bed and Angelina in the middle of her bedtime routine of one more drink and one more trip to the bathroom and one more anything else she could possibly think of. She smiled at Ken's patience. "I'll take over from here." She placed a kiss on his cheek.

"You sure? Because I can—"

"I'm sure. You've done enough and I—I appreciate it."

"Wow, that must have been some bubble bath."

She took Angelina's hand. "Come on, let's get you into bed." Walking into the bedroom, Patty went to the little white bookshelf. "What story would you like to hear tonight?"

"Josie's going to read me *Snow White*."

Patty took the book from the shelf and sighed. "No, Mommy's going to read to you." She opened the book and looked into her daughter's defiant little face. "Are you ready?"

Angelina crossed her arms over her chest and pouted. "I like the way Josie reads it better."

Just as Patty bent to sit down, Angelina screamed. Patty bolted from the chair. Angelina flung herself at her mother. "Don't sit on Josie! You'll hurt her."

Patty hoped her heart rate would return to normal before her own bedtime. "That's enough, Angelina. Get into bed and let me read you the story." She sat down in the chair.

Angelina burst into tears. "Mommy, you're mean! You sat on Josie on purpose!"

Ken opened the door. "Whoa, what's all the yelling about?"

Angelina flew off the bed and into his arms. She buried her face in his shoulder. "Mommy's mean. She's hurting Josie."

Chapter 3

Ken's bouncing foot jiggled the couch, and Patty fought the urge to snap at him. A pastel rainbow framed the sun-shaped clock on the wall, but the cheery décor felt forced and artificial. Angelina had only been in Dr. Bowman's office for ten minutes, but it already seemed like an eternity.

Angelina sat in the brightly painted room coloring in the book the doctor had given her.

"I bet you know all of your colors, don't you?" Dr. Bowman asked.

Angelina bobbed her head up and down.

"Can you hand me the red one?"

Angelina did. They went through all of the colors with Angelina handing them to her one at a time. "You're a very smart girl." Dr. Bowman's warm smile spread across her face. She took a bag of numbered wooden blocks and dumped them on the table. "I bet you even know your numbers, don't you?"

"Yes."

"Can you put the numbers in order?"

Angelina's pudgy little hands maneuvered the blocks into a line ordered one through ten.

Dr. Bowman clapped. "Angelina, you're so smart. I'm glad you agreed to play with me today. Are you having fun?"

Angelina nodded.

"Good. Let's play another game then we'll go see your mom and dad."

"Can Josie play too?"

"I don't see Josie. Is she in here?"

"Yes."

Dr. Bowman looked under her notepad. "She's not under here." She looked into the bag of blocks. "She's not in there either. I think you're just pretending."

Angelina's rosy cheeks shook with laughter as she pointed to a chair in the corner. "She's over there."

Dr. Bowman picked up her notepad and pen. "Angelina do you know the difference between lying and pretending?"

She nodded.

"Pretending is fun but lying can get you into trouble. Have you ever told a lie before?"

Angelina lowered her head and peered at Dr. Bowman through her lashes.

"You're not in trouble." Dr. Bowman kept her voice soft. "We're just talking. Can you tell me about a lie you told?"

Looking down at the table, her eyes welled up with tears. "One time I ate Sam's cookie and said I didn't."

"I bet that made you feel bad, didn't it?"

Angelina sniffed and nodded.

"That's why we don't lie. It makes us feel bad." Dr. Bowman brightened. "But we can pretend because that's fun. When you said Josie was over there, were you pretending?"

"I'm not pretending." She pointed to the corner. "She's right there."

Dr. Bowman walked to the chair. "Is she in this chair?"

"Yes."

Dr. Bowman looked disappointed. "Angelina, no one is in this chair. So are you pretending, or are you lying?"

Angelina looked at Josie and shrugged. "I want my mom now."

"First I want you to tell me the truth. Is someone sitting in this chair?"

Josie wiped the tears from her eyes. "I'll see you at home." She blew a kiss, waved goodbye, and disappeared.

Dr. Bowman asked the question again. "Is someone sitting in this chair?"

"No."

"Good. Now let's play one more game. We're going to pretend. Okay?"

"Okay."

Dr. Bowman joined Angelina at the table. "Can you pretend that you're a dog?"

Angelina got down on the floor and started barking.

"Oh my, you make a good dog! What about a cat? Can you pretend to be a cat?"

Angelina meowed and hissed as she pawed at the air.

"Oh my goodness. You're pretending to be a mean cat, aren't you?"

Angelina giggled.

"Okay come back to the table. It's my turn to pretend. What do you want me to be?"

"A lion." Angelina spread her arms wide. "A big lion."

Dr. Bowman leaned her head back and roared. "Oh, it's fun to pretend to be animals, isn't it?"

Angelina watched as Dr. Bowman got up and walked over to an empty chair. "Now I'm going to pretend that your mom is sitting here." She stuck out her arm as if she were shaking hands with someone. "Well hello, Patty. How are you today?" She cupped her hand around her ear. "What? Oh, you want to see Angelina pretend. Okay then. Angelina can you come and pretend that someone is sitting in this chair?"

Angelina stood in front of the empty chair. "Hello, Josie. Would you like some tea?"

"Do you like to have pretend tea parties?"

Angelina nodded.

"I do too. Playing pretend is fun. Is Josie really in that chair or are you just pretending?"

Angelina looked down at her light-up tennis shoes. "I'm just pretending."

Dr. Bowman sat behind her desk looking at two very concerned parents. "I honestly don't think we have anything to worry about. Angelina appears to be a happy, well-adjusted child."

Ken slowly let out the breath he'd been holding and took a hold of his wife's hand. "Whew, that's good."

"But…" Patty bit down on her trembling lip. "What about Josie? I mean is *that* normal?"

"Yes." Dr. Bowman formed a steeple with her fingers and tapped her chin. "It's true that most children outgrow their imaginary friends by now… but that doesn't mean there's anything wrong with her."

Patty snaked her fingers under her long thick hair and attempted to rub the tension from her neck. "If most children outgrow it by now…" She swallowed hard trying to get rid of the lump in her throat. "Why hasn't she?"

"Just like anything else, children develop at different rates. Some walk much earlier than others, but that doesn't necessarily mean there is anything to worry about."

"You said doesn't *necessarily* mean that there is something wrong." Patty licked her dry lips. "Does that mean there could be something wrong?"

Ken threw his arms into the air. "Oh for crying out loud, Patty! She said she's *fine.* Can't you just leave it at that?"

"I need answers, Ken!" she snapped. "I have a right to ask questions."

"I only agreed to this to try and get some peace but look at you… you're still going."

Dr. Bowman leaned in with her arms casually across the desk. "I don't need a degree in psychology to see that this is causing some tension between the two of you."

"He always accuses me of overreacting."

Ken folded his arms across his chest, leaned back in the chair, and sighed.

Dr. Bowman pushed her brown bangs back from her eyes. "Typically it is the mothers who are willing to seek counseling if they feel something is wrong with their children." She gave Ken a weak smile. "And dads are more willing to see how things 'play out.' The important thing is that you not let this cause trouble between the two of you."

Her words hung in the air as Ken and Patty silently looked at one another.

Patty brushed at a tear that threatened to roll down her cheek. "Ken… I'm sorry." She took a deep breath. "She said she was okay… I just need to make sure."

He placed his hand on her shoulder. "No apology necessary. You're a great mom and you sometimes worry…that's what mothers do."

A smile lit up Dr. Bowman's eyes showing flecks of gold amidst the brown hue. "I think the both of you are doing a great job with Angelina." She wagged her index finger into the air. "As they say, it's always better to be safe than sorry. If you ever have any concerns please feel free to call me."

Ken stood to leave. He stuck out his hand to shake Dr. Bowman's.

"How long do children generally keep their imaginary friends?" Patty asked.

"Generally," Dr. Bowman tapped her desk with a pencil, "until about age four."

Patty hissed as she took a sharp intake of breath. "But... but Angelina's five."

"Generally means most of the time." Dr. Bowman smiled. "I've seen children hold onto them until age seven."

A look of dread flashed through Patty's blue eyes. "Seven!"

"It happens, but in those cases there are usually extenuating circumstances." Dr. Bowman walked toward the door. "I think you will see Josie disappear much sooner."

Patty relaxed her shoulders.

"Angelina is still working on the concept of 'pretend.' *If* Josie is around much longer I'd like to evaluate her again."

Chapter 4

Josie sat on the edge of Angelina's pink canopy bed. She ran her fingers over the lace cover and waited for her to come home. She'd tried to make herself scarce since that fiasco years ago when Angelina's parents had taken her to that doctor woman to see if there was something wrong with her.

Pooh, there isn't anything wrong with her. She has the gift.

Josie knew that for sure now. Today Angelina was turning eight years old—way past the time when most children stopped seeing her. She'd always had "the feeling" that Angelina was special, and she'd been right.

Angelina was still too young to start her training as a seer but Josie wanted to keep the lines of communication open until the time came. The tricky part lay between letting Angelina see her and not causing the family any alarm. It was proving to be a difficult task.

Angelina ran up the stairs and threw her bedroom door open is such haste she caused a picture to fall from the wall. She stopped in mid-stoop as she was going to retrieve the picture. "Josie! You're here! Are you coming to my birthday party? Because today is my birthday."

Josie's face lit up with pride and happiness. She patted the spot next to her on the bed. "Close the door, honey, and come sit down for a minute."

Angelina skipped over to the bed and plopped down. "Are you coming to my party?" Her blue eyes glistened with excitement. "Ann's going to be there and Emily and Daphne and Kathy and—"

"No, honey. I can't come to your party. I wanted to come by

and wish you a happy birthday, though."

"Please Josie! Please, please, please. We're going to have cake and ice cream and I'm going to get presents."

Josie hated telling the child no—but she just simply couldn't allow herself to go. "You go to the party and when it's over you can come and tell me all about it. Okay?"

Angelina crossed her arms over her chest and pouted. "I don't like it when you're just my bedroom friend." She looked at Josie with pleading eyes. "You used to play with me in the living room and outside and in the kitchen." She stuck out her bottom lip even further. "Now we only play in my room."

Josie fought back her tears. "That's our new game. Don't you remember? We're secret friends."

Angelina turned her back as the tears spilled down her cheeks. "I don't like you anymore, Josie!"

Patty pushed the door to her daughter's room open. "Angel, sweetie! Why are you crying?"

Angelina threw her arms around her mother's neck. "Because Josie's mean. She won't come to my party!"

Patty's spine stiffened. Things had gotten better over the years, but Josie's name did come up from time to time. She peeled Angelina's arms from her neck and looked at her tear-streaked face. "Angel, Josie is your pretend friend. Remember? Now I want you to quit crying and be a big girl because your *real* friends will be here in a little while."

"Josie is my real friend." Angelina pointed to the corner of her bed and sniffled. "Josie, please come to my party."

"Angel, that's enough. Now go get cleaned up for your party."

Patty made her way to the kitchen to make last minute preparations. *I don't care what Ken says I'm calling that doctor back and there will be no talking me out of it this time around.*

Keep reading for a sample of...

Half-Blood

A Covenant Novel by

Jennifer L. Armentrout

SPENCER HILL PRESS

CHAPTER 1

MY EYES SNAPPED OPEN AS THE FREAKISH SIXTH sense kicked my fight or flight response into overdrive. The Georgia humidity and the dust covering the floor made it hard to breathe. Since I'd fled Miami, no place had been safe. This abandoned factory had proved no different.

The daimons were here.

I could hear them on the lower level, searching each room systematically, throwing open doors, slamming them shut. The sound threw me back to a few days ago, when I'd pushed open the door to Mom's bedroom. She'd been in the arms of one of those monsters, beside a broken pot of hibiscus flowers. Purple petals had spilled across the floor, mixing with the blood. The memory twisted my gut into a raw ache, but I couldn't think about her right now.

I jumped to my feet, halting in the narrow hallway, straining to hear how many daimons were here. Three? More? My fingers jerked around the slim handle of the garden spade. I held it up, running my fingers over the sharp edges plated in titanium. The act reminded me of what needed to be done. Daimons loathed titanium. Besides decapitation—which was *way* too gross—titanium was the only thing that would kill them. Named after the Titans, the precious metal was poisonous to those addicted to aether.

Somewhere in the building, a floorboard groaned and gave way. A deep howl broke the silence, starting as a low whine before hitting an intense shrill pitch. The scream sounded inhuman, sick and horrifying.

Nothing in this world sounded like a daimon—a hungry daimon.

And it was close.

I darted down the hallway, my tattered sneakers pounding against the worn-out boards. Speed was in my blood, and strands of long, dirty hair streamed behind me. I rounded the corner, knowing I had only seconds—

A whoosh of stale air whirled around me as the daimon grabbed a handful of my shirt, slamming me into the wall. Dust and plaster floated through the air. Black starbursts dotted my vision as I scrambled to my feet. Those soulless, pitch black holes where eyes should have been seemed to stare at me like I was his next meal ticket.

The daimon grasped my shoulder, and I let instinct take over. I twisted around, catching the surprise flickering across his pale face a split second before I kicked. My foot connected with the side of his head. The impact sent him staggering into the opposite wall. I spun around, slamming my hand into him. Surprise turned to horror as the daimon looked down at the garden spade buried deep in his stomach. It didn't matter where we aimed. Titanium always killed a daimon.

A guttural sound escaped his gaping mouth before he exploded into a shimmery blue dust.

With the spade still in hand, I whirled around and took the steps two at a time. I ignored the ache in my hips as I sprinted across the floor. I was going to make it—I had to make it. I'd be super-pissed in the afterlife if I died a virgin in this craphole.

"Little half-blood, where are you running to?"

I stumbled to the side, falling into a large steel press. Twisting around, my heart slammed against my ribs. The daimon appeared a few feet behind me. Like the one upstairs, he looked like a freak. His mouth hung open, exposing sharp, serrated teeth and those all-black holes sent chills over my skin. They reflected no light or life, only signifying death. His cheeks were sunken, skin unearthly pale. Veins popped out, etching over his face like inky snakes. He truly looked like something out of my worst nightmare—something demonic. Only a half-blood could see through the glamour for a few moments. Then the elemental magic took over, revealing what he used to look like. Adonis came to mind—a blond, stunning man.

"What are you doing all alone?" he asked, voice deep and alluring.

I took a step back, my eyes searching the room for an exit. Wannabe Adonis blocked my way out, and I knew I couldn't stand still for long. Daimons could still wield control over the elements. If he hit me with air or fire, I was a goner.

He laughed, the sound lacking humor and life. "Maybe if you beg—and I mean, really beg—I'll let your death be a fast one. Frankly, half-bloods don't really do it for me. Pure-bloods on the other hand," he let out a sound of pleasure, "they're like fine dining. Half-bloods? You're more like fast food."

"Come one step closer, and you'll end up like your buddy upstairs." I hoped I sounded threatening enough. Not likely. "Try me."

His brows rose. "Now you're starting to upset me. That's two of us you've killed."

"You keeping a tally or something?" My heart stopped when the floor behind me creaked. I whirled around, spotting a female daimon. She inched closer, forcing me toward the other daimon.

They were caging me in, giving no opportunity to escape. Another one shrieked somewhere in the pile of crap. Panic and fear choked me. My stomach rolled violently as my fingers trembled around the garden spade. Gods, I wanted to puke.

The ringleader advanced on me. "Do you know what I'm going to do to you?"

I swallowed and fixed a smirk on my face. "Blah. Blah. You're gonna kill me. Blah. I know."

The female's ravenous shriek cut off his response. Obviously, she was very hungry. She circled me like a vulture, ready to rip into me. My eyes narrowed on her. The hungry ones were always the stupidest—the weakest of the bunch. Legend said it was the first taste of aether—the very life force running through our blood—that possessed a pure-blood. A single taste turned one into a daimon and resulted in a lifetime of addiction. There was a good chance I could get past her. The other one… well, he was a different story.

I feinted toward the female. Like a druggie going after her fix she came right at me. The male yelled at her to stop, but it was too late. I took off in the opposite direction like an Olympic sprinter, rushing for the door I'd kicked in earlier in the night. Once outside, the odds would be back in my favor. A small window of hope sparked alive and propelled me forward.

The worst possible thing happened. A wall of flames flew up in front of me, burning through benches and shooting at least eight feet into the air. It was real. No illusion. The heat blew back at me and the fire crackled, eating through the walls.

In front of me, *he* walked right through the flames, looking every bit like a daimon hunter should. The fire did not singe his pants nor dirty his shirt. Not a single dark hair was touched by the blaze. Those cool, storm-cloud-colored eyes fixed on me.

It was him—Aiden St. Delphi.

I'd never forget his name or face. The first time I'd caught a glimpse of him standing in front of the training arena, a ridiculous crush had sprung alive. I'd been fourteen and he seventeen. The fact he was a pure-blood hadn't mattered whenever I'd spotted him around campus.

Aiden's presence could mean one thing only: the Sentinels had arrived.

Our eyes met, and then he looked over my shoulder. "Get down."

I didn't need to be told twice. Like a pro, I hit the floor. The pulse of heat shot above me, crashing into the intended target. The floor shook with the daimon's wild thrashing and her wounded screams filled the air. Only titanium would kill a daimon, but I felt confident that being burnt alive didn't feel too good.

Rising up on my elbows, I peered through my dirty hair as Aiden lowered his hand. A popping sound followed the movement, and the flames vanished as fast as they appeared. Within seconds, only the smells of burnt wood, flesh, and smoke remained.

Two more Sentinels rushed the room. I recognized one of them. Kain Poros: a half-blood a year or so older than me. Once upon a time we had trained together. Kain moved with a grace he'd never had before. He went for the female, and with one quick swoop, he thrust a long, slender dagger into the burnt flesh of her skin. She too became nothing but dust.

The other Sentinel had the air of a pure-blood to him, but I'd never seen him before. He was big—steroids big—and he zeroed in on the daimon I knew was somewhere in this factory but hadn't seen yet. Watching how he moved such a large body around so gracefully made me feel sorely inadequate, especially considering I was still lying sprawled on the floor. I dragged myself to my feet, feeling the terror-fueled adrenaline rush fade.

Without warning, my head exploded in pain as the side of my face hit the floor *hard*. Stunned and confused, it took me a moment to realize the Wannabe Adonis had gotten ahold of my legs. I twisted, but the creep sank his hands deep into my hair and yanked my head back. I dug my fingers into his skin, but it did nothing to alleviate the pressure bearing down on my neck. For a startled moment, I thought he intended to rip my head right off, but he sank razor sharp teeth into my shoulder, tearing through fabric and flesh. I screamed—*really* screamed.

I was on fire—I had to be. The draining burned through my skin; sharp pricks radiated out through every cell in my body. And even though I was only a half-blood, not chock-full of aether like a pure-blood, the daimon continued to drink my essence as though I were. It wasn't my blood he was after; he'd swallow pints of it just to get at the aether. My very spirit shifted as he dragged it into him. Pain became everything.

Suddenly, the daimon lifted his mouth. "What are you?" His whispered voice slurred the words.

There was no time to even think about that question. He was ripped off me and my body slumped forward. I rolled into a messy, bloody ball, sounding more like a wounded animal than anything remotely human. It was the first time I'd ever gotten tagged—drained by a daimon.

Over the small sounds I made, I heard a sickening crunch, and then wild shrieks, but the pain had taken over my senses. It started to pull back from my fingers, sliding its way back to my core where it still blazed. I tried to breathe through it, but *damn*...

Gentle hands rolled me onto my back, prying my fingers away from my shoulder. I stared up at Aiden.

"Are you okay? Alexandria? Please say something."

"Alex," I choked out. "Everyone calls me Alex."

He gave a short, relieved laugh. "Okay. Good. Alex, can you stand?"

I think I nodded. Every few seconds a stabbing flash of heat rocked through me, but the hurt had faded into a dull ache. "That really… sucked something bad."

Aiden managed to get one arm around me, lifting me to my feet. I swayed as he brushed back my hair and took a look at the damage. "Give it a few minutes. The pain will wear off."

Lifting my head, I looked around. Kain and the other Sentinel were frowning at nearly identical piles of blue dust. The pure-blood faced us. "That should be all of them."

Aiden nodded. "Alex, we need to go. Now. Back to the Covenant."

The Covenant? Not entirely in control of my emotions, I turned to Aiden. He wore all black—the uniform Sentinels wore. For a hot second, that girly crush resurfaced from three years ago. Aiden looked sublime, but fury stomped down that stupid crush.

The Covenant was involved in this—coming to my rescue? Where the hell had they been when one of the daimons had snuck into our house?

He took a step forward, but I didn't see him—I saw my mother's lifeless body again. The last thing she ever saw on this earth was some god-awful daimon's face and the last thing she'd ever felt… I shuddered, remembering the body-ripping pain of the daimon's tag.

Aiden took another step toward me. I reacted, a response born out of anger and pain. I launched myself at him, using moves I hadn't practiced in years. Simple things like kicks and punches were one thing, but an offensive attack was something I'd barely learned.

He caught my hand and swung me around so I faced the other direction. In a matter of seconds, he had my arms pinned, but all the pain and the sorrow rose in me, overriding any common sense. I bent forward, intent on getting enough space between us to deliver a vicious back kick.

"Don't," Aiden warned, his voice deceptively soft. "I don't want to hurt you."

My breath came out harsh and ragged. I could feel the warm blood trickling down my neck, mixing with sweat. I kept fighting even though my head swam, and the fact that Aiden held me off so easily only made my world turn red with rage.

"Whoa!" Kain yelled from the sidelines, "Alex, you know us! Don't you remember me? We aren't going to hurt you."

"Shut up!" I broke free of Aiden's grasp, dodging Kain and Mister Steroids. None of them expected me to run from them, but that's what I did.

I made it to the door leading out of the factory, dodged the broken wood and rushed outside. My feet carried me toward the field across the street. My thoughts were a complete mess. Why was I running? Hadn't I been trying to get back to the Covenant since the daimon attack in Miami?

My body didn't want to do this, but I kept running through the tall weeds and prickly bushes. Heavy footsteps sounded behind me, growing closer and closer. My vision blurred a bit, my heart thundered in my chest. I was so confused, so—

A hard body crashed into me, knocking the air right out of my lungs. I went down in a spiraling mess of legs and arms. Somehow, Aiden twisted around and took the brunt of the fall. I landed on top of him, and I stayed there for a moment before he rolled me over, pinning me down into the itchy field grass.

Panic and rage burst through me. "Now? Where were you a week ago? Where was the Covenant when my mother was being killed? Where were you?"

Aiden jerked back, eyes wide. "I'm sorry. We didn't—"

His apology only angered me further. I wanted to hurt him. I wanted to make him let me go. I wanted… I wanted… I didn't know what the hell I wanted, but I couldn't stop myself from screaming, clawing, and kicking him. Only when Aiden pressed his long, lean body against mine did I stop. His weight, the close proximity, held me immobile.

There wasn't an inch of space between us. I could feel the hard ripple of his abdominal muscles pressing against my stomach, could feel his lips only inches from mine. Suddenly I entertained a wild idea. I wondered if his lips felt as good as they looked… because they looked awesome.

That was a wrong thought to have. I had to be crazy—the only plausible excuse for what I was doing and thinking. The way I stared at his lips or the fact I desperately wanted to be kissed—all wrong for a multitude of reasons. Besides the fact I'd just tried to knock his head off, I looked like a mess. Grime dirtied my face beyond recognition; I hadn't showered in a week and I was pretty sure I smelled. I was *that* gross.

But the way he lowered his head, I really thought he was going to kiss me. My entire body tensed in anticipation, like waiting to be kissed for the first time, and this was definitely not the first time I'd been kissed. I'd kissed lots of boys, but not him.

Not a *pure-blood.*

Aiden shifted, pressing down further. I inhaled sharply and my mind raced a million miles a second, spewing out nothing helpful. He moved his right hand to my forehead. Warning bells went off.

He murmured a compulsion, fast and low, too quick for me to make out the words.

Son of a—

A sudden darkness rushed me, void of thought and meaning. There was no fighting something that powerful, and without getting out so much as a word of protest, I sank into its murky depths.

Pure

The Second Covenant Novel

SOME RULES ARE
MADE TO BE BROKEN...
BUT BREAKING
THE ULTIMATE RULE
CAN CHANGE
EVERYTHING.

Jennifer L. Armentrout

APRIL 2012

Also from Spencer Hill Press:

Minder

A Ganzfield Novel By

Kate Kaynak

Spencer Hill Press

MINDER

CHAPTER 1

I felt the eyes on the back of my head, like a too-warm itch within my skull. Someone was watching me.

Hunting me.

Cold dread splashed through my chest and my pace quickened. I'd gotten flashes like this before—I knew to trust them. I needed to find other people. More than a block away, cars whooshed along the main road.

Hurry.

I pulled my bag in close and started to run, cutting across the suburban lawns in the fading late-afternoon light. Perhaps I could flag someone down or even step out into traffic and cause a scene.

I didn't make it.

I glanced back at the rumble of the approaching engine and a white van thunked over the curb behind me, screeching to a stop halfway on the sidewalk. The side door rolled back with a metallic scrape. Quick footsteps slapped the sidewalk and thudded in the grass behind me. Rough hands grabbed my arm and closed over my mouth, stifling my scream.

The driver pulled out so fast the tires squealed. Someone tried several times to close the side door of the lurching vehicle before the latch finally caught. The large hand of my attacker remained clamped over my mouth and my breath ripped through my nose.

Oh my God…oh my God…oh my God.

His weight crushed my chest and my hammering heart pounded against the pressure. The smells of stale cigarettes, cheap beer, and a slightly rancid locker room overwhelmed the small space. I nearly threw up.

The driver laughed. I knew that laugh—I'd heard it in the lunchroom and halls at school. Delbarton Evans was a junior—like me—although we weren't in any classes together. His friends called him Del, and I wasn't one of them. The other two in the van also looked familiar.

Mike. Carl.

Mike was the one holding me down. He joined Del in his laughter. Carl stared at me, paling to an even more sickly green when he realized I was staring back at him.

The van pulled into a garage and the door motor hummed overhead as the last of the daylight slid away.

Oh, no, no, no, No. No. NO. NO!

That closing door was my last chance. I shifted and bit down hard on Mike's hand. He yelped in pain, and then growled—actually growled—and punched me in the jaw. Pain speared through my head and I tasted blood. Del jumped from the driver's seat and grabbed the arm that Mike couldn't hold. The alcohol smell hit me again as his face came close to mine. He looked me straight in the eye. Then, with his free hand, he grabbed the front of my shirt and ripped it straight down to my waist.

Oh, God. No.

"Shut up and lie still," he said, as his eyes slid down my body. Mike laughed and grabbed at the button of my jeans. I tried to kick him away but he crushed my legs with his knees. Carl, still looking sick, hung back and silently watched.

How could this be happening? Panic threatened to overwhelm me again.

No!

I felt a surge of energy start low in my gut—growing taller and stronger—burning like an icy flame up into my mind. I squeezed my eyes shut. "No!" I shouted. It sounded as if I was in chorus with many other versions of myself as an unseen fire exploded from my forehead. The hands gripping me momentarily tightened, and then fell slack.

I opened my eyes. All three of my attackers had fallen to the floor. Del lay face down only inches from me. His eyes were open and empty without the colored ring of an iris.

What the hell?

I shoved myself out from under Mike. I felt as if an electrically charged spike had driven itself through my forehead. I was shaking so violently I could barely get to my knees. Mike was also shaking, but it looked like he was having a seizure. As I watched, he went still. He wasn't breathing. I glanced at Carl. He'd slumped against the side of the van and his face hung slack from his skull as though he'd started to melt. The only sound in the van was my own ragged breathing.

Dead—they were all dead.

And I knew—somehow—I had killed them.

I've got to get out of here. I stumbled from the van, tripping over Mike's sprawled leg. I couldn't make my mind work—couldn't figure out how to open the garage door. I pulled on it, hearing my own desperate sobs echo in the cold space. The single bare bulb suddenly clicked out, plunging me into darkness. My scream came out as a whimper. *Oh, God. Help me. I'm trapped. I'm trapped in the dark and they're dead, dead, dead. Oh, God!*

My hands slid along the side of the van until I felt the handle.

Trapped in the dark.

I finally opened the driver's door and the dome light flashed on. My fingers groped for the button on the driver's visor. I tried not to look in the back.

All dead.

Light worked its way across the garage as the outside world reappeared under the rolling door. I couldn't stop myself; I looked at my three dead attackers. *Oh, God. What happened—what did I do?*

WHAT AM I?

The Ganzfield Books

Minder ◆ Adversary ◆ Legacy ◆ Accused

by Kate Kaynak

Sixteen-year-old Maddie Dunn needs to figure out how to use her new abilities before somebody else gets hurt. Ganzfield is a secret training facility full of people like her, but it's not exactly a nurturing place.

Every social interaction carries the threat of mind-control.

A stray thought can burn a building to the ground.

And people's nightmares don't always stay in their own heads.

But it's still better than New Jersey, especially once she meets the man of her dreams...

"Absolutely flawless!"
◆ *Reading Teen*

"Dynamic, original, thoughtful, and entrancing... nothing short of brilliant."
◆ *Book Crazy*

"If I were asked 'What Young Adult series would I recommend?' The Ganzfield Novels would be it."
◆ *Escape Between the Pages*

Masters of the Veil

Book One of the Veil Trilogy

Daniel A. Cohen

COMING IN MARCH 2012 FROM SPENCER HILL PRESS:

Life can't get much better for Sam Lock. Popular, good-looking, and with a future as a professional football player… every guy at Stanton High School wishes he were Sam. That is, until his championship football game, when Sam accidentally links with an ancient source of energy known as the Veil and reveals his potential to become a powerful sorcerer.

Sam's dreams are crushed as he is whisked off to Atlas Crown, a community of sorcerers who utilize the Veil as a part of everyday life. Once there, he trains beside a mute boy who speaks through music, an eternal sage who is the eyes and ears of the Veil, and a beautiful girl who's pretty sure Sam's an idiot.

As it becomes clear that Sam is meant for power magic—the most feared and misunderstood form of sorcery—people beyond Atlas Crown learn of his dangerous potential. An exiled group of power sorcerers are eager to recruit Sam, believing that he is destined to help them achieve their long-held goal. If they succeed, they could bring about the downfall of not only Atlas Crown… but all of humankind.

978-1-937053-02-4

Acknowledgements

I've always wanted to be an author and when I finally had the time to sit down and write, I remember thinking, "How hard can it be?" You simply write a book and get it published. Right? Well... not exactly, at least it wasn't that way for me. Now, many drafts later I find myself with a whole lot of people to thank. My first shout out goes to Query Tracker, this is an awesome website for aspiring authors. I've gotten so much information and support here I couldn't begin to name all the members who've helped me, but they know who they are and they have my undying gratitude.

In a roundabout way, Query Tracker—thanks Jennifer Armentrout!—helped me find my publisher Spencer Hill, which leads me to my next BIG thank you. The people at Spencer Hill have been wonderful to work with. My first contact at Spencer Hill was with Kate Kaynak. She not only designed the cover for *Angelina's Secret,* but also held my hand through the entire process of seeing my first book published. In a word, she is awesome.

Spencer Hill is full of wonderful people and each of them has had a part in bringing *Angelina's Secret* to the bookshelves. My heartfelt thanks goes out to my editor, Deborah Britt-Hay, and to Rich Storrs, Keshia Swaim, and Marie Romero.

Before there was a need for Query Tracker, agents, editors, or publishers, I needed someone to kick a few ideas around with and that's where my husband and best friend, Wes, came into the picture. *Angelina's Secret* started coming to life one night when Wes and I were out having dinner at our favorite restaurant. I'm pretty sure if he'd known exactly what he was getting into, he would've done a whole lot more eating and a whole lot less talking. Little did he know that was to be his last good meal for a while because the deeper I got into writing, the less I cooked. He never complained, well, not too much at least, and on occasion, he even recognized my need for sustenance and brought me something to eat as well. So I say thank you to him, not only for helping me with ideas but for also being so proficient in ordering pizza.

With the idea for the book planted firmly in my head, I was finally ready to write. I was so excited and needed nothing more from anyone. That fantasy lasted about as long as it took me to type the words: "Chapter 1." It was at that time, I realized I had forgotten all of those little grammar rules I supposedly learned from school so I turned to my daughter, Keshia. She not only re-taught me things I'm not sure I ever knew but she was also a great critique partner. So I want to say thank you Keshia for tirelessly answering all of my questions, and for reading the manuscript over and over and over and...

I would also like to thank my son, Troy, for sharing his college stories with me and keeping me young at heart. He has always been, and I suspect will always be, a constant source of entertainment for me and for anyone who has the pleasure of knowing him. I'd also like to thank his wife, Meagan, for taking my profile pictures.

Without my family, my dream of becoming an author would've remained only a dream. I thank them all for their support and give an additional thank you to Wanda, Tammy, Kim, and Cathy for serving as Beta readers.

Photo by Meagan Rogers

Lisa Rogers worked in the medical field until she hung up her stethoscope to help her husband pursue the dream of owning his own business. After opening the business while also raising their two (she insists) wonderful children, the time has come for her to fulfill a dream of her own—which is, was, and will always be, writing.

With her children now grown, she dedicates her time to writing and learning about paranormal phenomena. When she's not strapped to her computer at their rural Oklahoma home, she can generally be found poking around a dilapidated old building or visiting some historical place, perhaps searching for her next "out of body" character.

Find out more about *Angelina's Secret* at:

www.SpencerHillPress.com